VENUS EQUILATERAL
Volume One

Also by George O Smith

VENUS EQUILATERAL
Volume Two

George O Smith

Venus Equilateral

VOLUME ONE

Futura Publications Limited
An Orbit Book

An Orbit Book

First published in Great Britain in 1975
by Futura Publications Limited
Warner Road, London SE5

To James Clerk Maxwell, whose Electromagnetic Equations
founded the art of electronics and thus made Venus
Equilateral possible ...
And to my son, George O Smith (Jr), who may some day
work there.

ISBN 0 8600 78612
Printed in Great Britain by
Hazell Watson & Viney Ltd
Aylesbury, Bucks

Futura Publications Limited
Warner Road, London SE5

CONTENTS

5

INTRODUCTION

Sometimes it's a little hard to get people to realize that not only has the world changed in the past, but that it is changing now, and will change in the future. In fact, it takes something of the order of an atomic bomb to blast them out of their congenital complacency.

And it took the literally shocking violence of the atomic bomb to make the general public understand the fact that science-fiction is *not* 'pseudo-science' (that's what you find in Sunday Supplements – fiction, pretending to be science) but an entirely different breed of thing – fiction stories based on science, and attempting to extrapolate the curves of past development into future years. On August 6, 1945, people suddenly discovered that that fool fantasy stuff about atomic bombs hadn't been quite so fantastic as they had – well, to be brutally frank, *hoped*.

Their immediate reactions were that a good guess or two, a chance, coincidental correspondence between fiction-fantasy and fact, didn't mean much. Still, relatively few people have learned to understand how science-fiction originates – why it does successfully predict.

The answer is, actually, that science-fiction's prophecy is to a large extent phony. It isn't prophecy at all, not in the true sense. It's more like the astronomer's prophecy that there will be an eclipse of the sun visible for many seconds, on such and such a day, at a specified point. The astronomer's prediction is based on information he has that is not generally recognized – though anyone who wants to get it can go dig it out of the text books.

The science-fiction author predicts in the same general way.

With the knowledge of what has been accomplished in the laboratories, and a general understanding of what people have wanted in the past, want today, and will probably want in the future, it's not hard to guess how those laboratory facts will be applied.

By 1915 it was generally known among scientists that there was an enormous store of energy locked in every pound of matter. Men have, sadly, wanted more deadly killing instruments for all human history – and will pay much more for a means of killing an enemy than they will to save a friend's life. From these facts it's a simple prediction that atomic energy will some day be released – and probably first in the form of a bomb.

Science-fiction made such predictions. When the laboratories found U-235 was probably capable of a chain reaction, the science-fictioneer began saying U-235 bombs instead of the more generalized 'atomic' bomb.

The essentials for good prophetic fiction – and hence good science-fiction – are fairly easily stated.

It takes a technically inclined mind.

That mind must be intimately acquainted with one or more technologies – and by that I mean both the branch of theoretical science and that branch's engineering applications as of today.

Imagination is a third requirement; if imagination is put first, fantasy, not science-fiction, results.

An understanding of how political and social set-ups react to technological changes must be added, for the best types of science-fiction.

George O. Smith's 'Venus Equilateral' series represents an excellent progressive development of a single line of extrapolation.

George O. Smith is a radio engineer; at the time the Venus Equilateral series started, he was working on radar equipment and Army communications radio units. It was only natural that

8

he should pick the field of communications engineering as his line for development – he was intimately acquainted with the problems and possibilities of that field and with the past history of the art.

'QRM Interplanetary,' the first of the stories, appeared in Astounding Science-Fiction to start the series; typically, it serves merely to introduce the concept of the equilateral relay station as a necessary link in interplanetary communications. But the story has been so constructed that the working out of its plot gives a good concept of the general nature of the station, and of its functioning. Still, the story is essentially simply a suggestion that interplanetary communications will require the construction of a station in space to relay messages.

The immediately following stories of the series introduce successive problems of the purely technical art; only gradually are the associated social and political reactions of the rest of that civilization of the future brought in. From the start, the author's problem has been simplified by picking a small, almost wholly isolated segment of the culture, so that only the technology itself need be discussed.

As the series develops, however, more and more the social and political effects of the developments are brought into the picture, until, in the end, practically nothing but the social-political effects remain. The story 'Pandora's Millions' appeared in Astounding Science-Fiction and was devoted entirely to the cultural, rather than technical, problems of the matter transmitter.

In essence, Venus Equilateral represents the basic pattern of science-fiction – which is, equally, the basic pattern of technology. First starting from the isolated instance, the effects spread outward through the culture. Scientific methodology involves the proposition that a well-constructed theory will not only explain every known phenomenon, but will also predict new and still undiscovered phenomena. Science-fiction tries to do much the same – and write up, in story form, what the results look like when applied not only to machines, but to human society as well.

The science-fiction writer can be extremely accurate in the guesses he makes of future progress – and yet there are factors that may make a complete failure of his prediction.

George O. Smith is a radio engineer; radio is his field of technology. As such, his predictions tend to be based on the extrapolation of a single line of activity. But it may be that all his predictions may come to nothing due to a development in an entirely separate field of technical progress. It might be, for instance, that Dr. Rhine's work on extra-sensory perception developed into a science, that equipment was developed capable of recording, receiving, amplifying and broadcasting whatever strange energy form is involved – and that telepathy completely displaced radio engineering. The atomic pile is the only form of nuclear energy machine we have available; because war-time engineering was operating under forced draft, and war-time basic science was in abeyance, we have no basic science from which to predict more advanced forms of energy-harnessing devices. But it is quite conceivable that, long before we reach Mars and Venus to establish colonies, we will achieve the ultimate in energy-harnesses for atomic energy – a small, sealed box with two projecting terminals from which unlimited electric power can be drawn directly.

Also, any extrapolation whatsoever is, necessarily, based on the implied, but unstated proposition, 'If things go on as they have been . . .' The proposition is, right now, open to serious question. For one thing, whenever science becomes engineering, it meets legislation made by men. Now the laws of Nature are predictable, understandable, and absolute. They don't depend on the viewpoint of the individual, or the social theory popular at the time, or the Majority Leader's severe chronic indigestion. The patent law very definitely does. At the moment, as a matter of fact, an extrapolation of the trend of patent law suggests that half the Venus Equilateral series will be rendered plotless; there won't be any patents.

The science-fiction writer is, therefore, faced with a simply stated problem: Taking off from the solid ground of known laboratory science, sighting along the back-track of past experience, he launches into the future.

But he may come down in a never-will-be future, because somebody harnessed telepathy, and threw civilization off on an entirely unexpected track. Or because the Supreme Court, currently invalidating 24 out of every 25 patents brought before it, has eliminated the institution of patents. Or because a new social theory has decided that no scientific advance should be permitted for a period of 250 years while a great program of meditation and navel-inspection instead of Naval inspection is pushed forward.

Nevertheless, science-fiction can be not only fun, but an extremely valuable experience. If a friend steps out of a dimly lighted doorway it may provoke a 'Yipe!' of momentary fear, or a casual 'Hi,' dependent entirely on whether or not you expected to meet him there.

The science-fiction reader is a lot less apt to jump in senseless fear and alarm when a new process comes from some unexpected doorway – he'll have been expecting it, and recognize a friend or an enemy – which can be very helpful to survival.

JOHN W. CAMPBELL, JR.

QRM – International code signal meaning 'Interference' of controllable nature, such as man-made static, cross modulation from another channel adjoining or wilful obliteration of signals by an interfering source.

Interference not of natural sources such as electrical storms, common static, et cetera. (Designated by International code as *QRN*.)

–*Handbook, Interplanetary Amateur Radio League*

Korvus, the Magnificent, Nilamo of Yoralen, picked up the telephone in his palace and said: 'I want to talk to Wilneda. He is at the International Hotel in Detroit, Michigan.'

'I'm sorry, sir,' came the voice of the operator. 'Talking is not possible, due to the fifteen-minute transmission lag between here and Terra. However, teletype messages are welcome.'

Her voice originated fifteen hundred miles north of Yoralen, but it sounded as though she might be in the next room. Korvus thought for a moment and then said: 'Take this message: "Wilneda: Add to order for mining machinery one type 56-XXD flier to replace washed-out model. And remember, alcohol and energy will not mix!" Sign that Korvus.'

'Yes, Mr. Korvus.'

'Not *mister*!' yelled the monarch. 'I am Korvus the Magnificent! I am Nilamo of Yoralen!'

'Yes, your magnificence,' said the operator humbly. It was more than possible that she was stifling a laugh, which knowledge made the little man of Venus squirm in wrath. But there was nothing he could do about it, so he wisely said nothing.

To give Korvus credit, he was not a pompous little man. He was large – for a Venusian – which made him small according to the standards set up by the Terrestrians. He, as Nilamo of Yoralen, had extended the once-small kingdom outward to include most of the Palanortis Country which extended from 23.0 degrees North Latitude to 61.7 degrees, and almost across the whole, single continent that was the dry land of Venus.

So Korvus' message to Terra zoomed across the fifteen hundred rocky miles of Palanortis to Northern Landing. It passed high across the thousand-foot-high trees and over the mountain ranges. It swept over open patches of water, and across intervening cities and towns. It went with the speed of light and in a tight beam from Yoralen to Northern Landing, straight as a die and with person-to-person clarity. The operator in the city that lay across the North Pole of Venus clicked on a teletype, reading back the message as it was written.

Korvus told her: 'That is correct.'

'The message will be in the hands of your representative Wilneda within the hour.'

The punched tape from Operator No. 7's machine slid along the line until it entered a coupling machine.

The coupling machine worked furiously. It accepted the tapes from seventy operators as fast as they could write them. It selected the messages as they entered the machine, placing a mechanical preference upon whichever message happened to be ahead of the others on the moving tapes. The master tape moved continuously at eleven thousand words per minute, taking teletype messages from everywhere in the Northern Hemisphere of Venus to Terra and Mars. It was a busy machine; even at eleven thousand words per minute it often got hours behind.

The synchronous-keyed signal from the coupling machine left the operating room and went to the transmission room. It was amplified and sent out of the city to a small, squat building at the outskirts of Northern Landing.

It was hurled at the sky out of a reflector antenna by a thousand kilowatt transmitter. The wave seared against the Venusian Heaviside Layer. It fought and it struggled. And, as is the case with strife, it lost heavily in the encounter. The beam was resisted fiercely. Infiltrations of ionization tore at the radio beam, stripping and trying to beat it down.

But man triumphed over nature. The megawatt of energy that came in a tight beam from the building at Northern Landing emerged from the Heaviside Layer as a weak, piffling signal. It wavered and it crackled. It wanted desperately to lie down and sleep. Its directional qualities were impaired, and it wabbled badly. It arrived at the relay station tired and worn.

One million watts of ultra-high frequency energy at the start, it was measurable in microvolts when it reached a space station, only five hundred miles above the city of Northern Landing.

The signal, as weak and as wabbly as it was, was taken in by eager receptors. It was amplified. It was dehashed, destaticked and deloused. And once again, one hundred decibels stronger and infinitely cleaner, the signal was hurled out on a tight beam from a gigantic parabolic reflector.

Across sixty-seven million miles of space went the signal. Across the orbit of Venus it went in a vast chord. It arrived at the Venus Equilateral Station with less trouble than the original transmission through the Heaviside Layer. The signal was amplified and demodulated. It went into a decoupler machine where the messages were sorted mechanically and sent, each to the proper channel, into other coupler machines. Beams from Venus Equilateral were directed at Mars and at Terra.

The Terra beam ended at Luna. Here it again was placed in the two-compartment beam and from Luna it punched down at Terra's Layer. It emerged into the atmosphere of Terra, as weak and as tired as it had been when it had come out of the Venusian Heaviside Layer. It entered a station in the Bahamas, was stripped of the interference, and put upon the land beams. It entered decoupling machines that sorted the messages as to destination. These various beams spread out across the face of Terra; the one carrying Korvus' message finally coming into a station at Ten Mile Road and Woodward. From this station at the outskirts of Detroit, it went upon land wires downtown to the International Hotel.

The teletype machine in the office of the hotel began to click rapidly. The message to Wilneda was arriving.

And fifty-five minutes after the operator told Korvus that

less than an hour would ensue, Wilneda was saying, humorously, 'So, Korvus was drunk again last night—'

Completion of Korvus' message to Wilneda completes also one phase of the tale at hand. It is not important. There were a hundred and fifty other messages that might have been accompanied in the same manner, each as interesting to the person who likes the explanation of the interplanetary communication service. But this is not a technical journal. A more complete explanation of the various phases that a message goes through in leaving a city on Venus to go to Terra may be found in the Communications Technical Review, Volume XXVII, number 8, pages 411 to 716. Readers more interested in the technical aspects are referred to the article.

But it so happens that Korvus' message was picked out of a hundred-odd messages because of one thing only. At the time that Korvus' message was in transit through the decoupler machines at The Venus Equilateral Relay Station, something of a material nature was entering the air lock of the station.

It was an unexpected visit.

Don Channing looked up at the indicator panel in his office and frowned in puzzlement. He punched a buzzer and spoke into the communicator on his desk.

'Find out who that is, will you, Arden?'

'He isn't expected,' came back the voice of Arden Westland.

'I know that. But I've been expecting someone ever since John Peters retired last week. You know why.'

'You hope to get his job,' said the girl in an amused voice. 'I hope you do. So that someone else will sit around all day trying to make you retire so that he can have your job!'

'Now look, Arden, I've never tried to make Peters retire.'

'No, but when the word came that he was thinking of it, you began to think about taking over. Don't worry, I don't blame you.' There was quite a protracted silence, and then her voice returned. 'The visitor is a gentleman by the name of Francis Burbank. He came out in a flitter with a chauffeur and all.'

'Big shot, hey?'

'Take it easy. He's coming up the office now.'

'I gather that he desires audience with me?' asked Don.

'I think that he's here to lay down the law! You'll have to get out of Peter's office, if his appearance is any guide.'

There was some more silence. The communicator was turned off at the other end, which made Channing fume. He would have preferred to hear the interchange of words between his secretary and the newcomer. Then, instead of having the man announced, the door opened and the stranger entered. He came to the point immediately.

'You're Don Channing? Acting Director of Venus Equilateral?'

'I am.'

'Then I have some news for you, Dr. Channing. I have been appointed Director by the Interplanetary Communications Commission. You are to resume your position as Electronics Engineer.'

'Oh?' said Channing. 'I sort of believed that I would be offered that position.'

'There was a discussion of that procedure. However, the Commission decided that a man of more commercial training would better fill the position. The Communications Division has been operating at too small a profit. They felt that a man of commercial experience could cut expenses and so on to good effect. You understand their reasoning, of course,' said Burbank.

'Not exactly.'

'Well, it is like this. They know that a scientist is not usually the man to consider the cost of experimentation. They build thousand-ton cyclotrons to convert a penny's worth of lead into one and one-tenth cents' worth of lead and gold. And they use three hundred dollars' worth of power and a million-dollar machine to do it with.

'They feel that a man with training like that will not know the real meaning of the phrase, "cutting expenses". A new broom sweeps clean, Dr. Channing. There must be many places where a man of commercial experience can cut expenses. I, as Director, shall do so.'

'I wish you luck,' said Channing.

'Then, there is no hard feeling?'

'I can't say that. It is probably not your fault. I cannot feel against you, but I do feel sort of let down at the decision of the Commission. I have had experience in this job.'

'The Commission may appoint you to follow me. If your work shows a grasp of commercial operations, I shall so recommend.'

'Thanks,' said Channing dryly. 'May I buy you a drink?'

'I never drink. And I do not believe in it. If it were mine to say, I'd prohibit liquor from the premises. Venus Equilateral would be better off without it.'

Don Channing snapped the communicator. 'Miss Westland, will you come in?'

She entered, puzzlement on her face.

'This is Mr. Burbank. His position places him in control of this office. You will, in the future, report to him directly. The report on the operations, engineering projects, and so on that I was to send in to the Commission this morning will, therefore, be placed in Mr. Burbank's hands as soon as possible.'

'Yes, Dr. Channing.' Her eyes held a twinkle, but there was concern and sympathy in them, too. 'Shall I get them immediately?'

'They are ready?'

'I was about to put them on the tape when you called.'

'Then give them to Mr. Burbank.' Channing turned to Burbank. 'Miss Westland will hand you the reports I mentioned.

They are complete and precise. A perusal of them will put you in grasp of the situation here at Venus Equilateral better than will an all-afternoon conference. I'll have Miss Westland haul my junk out of here. You may consider this as your office, it having been used by Dr. Peters. And, in the meantime, I've got to check up on some experiments on the ninth level.' Channing paused. 'You'll excuse me?'

'Yes, if Miss Westland knows where to find you.'

'She will. I'll inform her of my whereabouts.'

'I may want to consult you after I read the reports.'

'That will be all right. The autocall can find me anywhere on Venus Equilateral, if I'm not at the place Miss Westland calls.'

Don Channing stopped at Arden's desk. 'I'm booted,' he told her.

'Leaving Venus Equilateral?' she asked with concern.

'No, blonde and beautiful, I'm just shunted back to my own office.'

'Can't I go with you?' pleaded the girl.

'Nope. You are to stay here and be a nice, good-looking Mata Hari. This bird seems to think that he can run Venus Equilateral like a bus or a factory. I know the type, and the first thing he'll do is to run the place into a snarl. Keep me informed of anything complicated, will you?'

'Sure. And where are you going now?'

'I'm going down and get Walt Franks. We're going to inspect the transparency of a new type of glass.'

'I didn't know that optical investigations come under your jurisdiction.'

'This investigation will consist of a visit to the ninth level.'

'Can't you take me along?'

'Not today,' he grinned. 'Your new boss does not believe in the evils of looking through the bottom of a glass. We must behave with decorum. We must forget fun. We are now operating under a man who will commercialize electronics to a fine art.'

'Don't get stewed. He may want to know where the electrons are kept.'

'I'm not going to drink that much. Walt and I need a discussion,' he said. 'And in the meantime, haul my spinach out of the office, will you, and take it back to the electronics office? I'll be needing it back there.'

'O.K., Don,' she said. 'I'll see you later.'

Channing left to go to the ninth level. He stopped long enough to collect Walt Franks.

Over a tall glass of beer, Channing told Franks of Burbank's visit. And why.

Only one thing stuck in Franks' mind. 'Did you say that he might close Joe's?' asked Franks.

'He said that if it were in his power to do so, he would.'

'Heaven forbid. Where will we go to be alone?'

'Alone?' snorted Channing. The barroom was half filled with people, being the only drinking establishment for sixty-odd million miles.

'Well, you know what I mean.'

'I could smuggle in a few cases of beer,' suggested Don.

'Couldn't we smuggle him out?'

'That would be desirable. But I think he is here to stay. Darn it all, why do they have to appoint some confounded political pal to a job like this? I'm telling you, Walt, he must weigh two hundred if he weighs a pound. He holds his stomach on his lap when he sits down.'

Walt looked up and down Channing's slender figure. 'Well, he won't be holding Westland on his lap if it is filled with stomach.'

'I never hold Westland on my lap—'

'No?'

'—during working hours!' finished Channing. He grinned at

Franks and ordered another beer. 'And how is the Office of Beam Control going to make out under the new regime?'

'I'll answer that after I see how the new regime treats the Office of Beam Control,' answered Franks. 'I doubt that he can do much to bugger things up in my office. There aren't many cheaper ways to direct a beam, you know.'

'Yeah. You're safe.'

'But what I can't understand is why they didn't continue you in that job. You've been handling the business ever since last December when Peters got sick. You've been doing all right.'

'Doing all right just means that I've been carrying over Peters' methods and ideas. What the Commission wants, apparently, is something new. Ergo the new broom.'

'Personally, I like that one about the old shoes being more comfortable,' said Franks. 'If you say the right word, Don, I'll slip him a dose of high voltage. That should fix him.'

'I think that the better way would be to work for the bird. Then when he goes, I'll have his recommendation.'

'Phooey,' snorted Franks. 'They'll just appoint another political pal. They've tried it before and they'll try it again. I wonder what precinct he carries.'

The telephone rang in the bar, and the bartender, after answering, motioned to Walt Franks. 'You're wanted in your office,' said the bartender. 'And besides,' he told Channing, 'if I'm going to get lunch for three thousand people, you'd better trot along, too. It's nearly eleven o'clock, you know, and the first batch of two hundred will be coming in.'

Joe was quite inaccurate as to the figures. The complement of Venus Equilateral was just shy of twenty-seven hundred. They worked in three eight-hour shifts, about nine hundred to a shift. They had their breakfast, lunch, and dinner hours staggered so that at no time were there more than about two hundred people in the big lunchroom. The bar, it may be mentioned, was in a smaller room at one end of the much larger cafeteria.

The Venus Equilateral Relay Station was a modern miracle of engineering if you liked to believe the books. Actually, Venus Equilateral was an asteroid that had been shoved into its orbit about the Sun, forming a practical demonstration of the equilateral triangle solution of the Three Moving Bodies. It was a long cylinder, about three miles in length by about a mile in diameter.

In 1946, the United States Army Signal Corps succeeded in sending forth and receiving in return a radar signal from the moon. This was an academic triumph; at that time such a feat had no practical value. Its value came later when the skies were opened up for travel; when men crossed the void of space to colonize the nearer planets Mars and Venus.

They found then that communications back and forth depended upon the initial experiment in 1946.

But there were barriers, even in deep space. The penetration of the Heaviside Layer was no great problem. That had been done. They found that Sol, our sun, was often directly in the path of the communications beam because the planets all make their way around Sol at different rates of speed.

All too frequently Mars is on the opposite side of the sun from Terra, or Sol might lie between Venus and Mars. Astronomically, this situation where two planets lie on opposite sides of the sun is called Major Opposition, which is an appropriate name even though those who named it were not thinking in terms of communications.

The concept of Sol being between two planets and interfering with communication does not mean a true physical alignment. The Sun is a tremendous generator of radiothermal energy, so that communication begins to fail when the other planet is 15 to 20 degrees from the Sun. Thus from 30 to 40 degree of opposition passage, Venus Equilateral is a necessary relay station.

To circumvent this natural barrier to communications, mankind made use of one of the classic solutions of the problem of the Three Moving Bodies, in which is it stated that three celestial objects at the corners of an equilateral triangle will so remain, rotating about their common center of gravity. The equilateral position between the sun and any planet is called the 'Trojan' position because it has been known for some time that a group of asteroids precede and follow Jupiter around in its orbit. The 'Trojan' comes from the fact that these asteroids bear the well known names of the heroes of the famous Trojan War.

To communicate around the sun, then, it is only necessary to establish a relay station in the Trojan position of the desired planet. This will be either ahead or behind the planet in its orbit; and the planet, the sun, and the station will form an equilateral triangle.

So was born the Venus Equilateral Relay Station.

There was little of the original asteroid. At the present time, the original rock had been discarded to make room for the ever-growing personnel and material that were needed to operate the relay station. What had been an asteroid with machinery was now a huge pile of machinery with people. The insides, formerly of spongy rock, were now neatly cubed off into offices, rooms, hallways, and so on, divided by sheets of steel. The outer surface, once rugged and forbidding, was now all shiny steel. The small asteroid, a tiny thing, was gone, the station having overflowed the asteroid soon after men found that uninterrupted communication was possible between the worlds.

Now the man-made asteroid carried twenty-seven hundred people. There were stores, offices, places of recreation, churches, marriages, deaths, and everything but taxes. Judging by its population, it was a small town.

Venus Equilateral rotated about its axis. On the inner

surface of the shell were the homes of the people – not cottages, but apartmental cubicles, one, two, three, six rooms. Centrifugal force made a little more than one Earth G of artificial gravity. Above this outer shell of apartments, the offices began. Offices, recreation centers, and so on. Up in the central position where the gravity was nil or near-nil, the automatic machinery was placed. The servogyroscopes and their beam finders, the storerooms, the air plant, the hydroponic farms, and all other things that needed little or no gravity for well-being.

This was the Venus Equilateral Relay Station, sixty degrees ahead of the planet Venus, on Venus' orbit. Often closer to Terra than Venus, the relay station offered a perfect place to relay messages through whenever Mars or Terra was on the other side of the sun. It was seldom idle, for it was seldom that Mars and Venus were in such a position that direct communications between all the three planets was possible.

This was the center of Interplanetary Communications. This was the main office. It was the heart of the Solar System's communication line, and as such, it was well manned. Orders for everything emanated from Venus Equilateral. It was a delicate proposition, Venus Equilateral was, and hence the present-on-all-occasions official capacities and office staff.

This was the organization that Don Channing hoped to direct. A closed corporation with one purpose in mind: Interplanetary Communication!

Channing wondered if the summons for Walt Franks was an official one. Returning to the electronics office, Don punched the communicator and asked: 'Is Walt in there?'

Arden's voice came back: 'No, but Burbank is in Franks' office. Wanna listen?'

'Eavesdropper! Using the communicator?'

'Sure.'

'Better shut it off,' warned Don. 'Burbank isn't foolish, you know, and there are pilot lights and warning flags on those things to tell if someone has the key open. I wouldn't want to see you fired for listening-in.'

'All right, but it was getting interesting.'

'If I'm betting on the right horse,' said Channing, 'this will be interesting for all before it is finished.'

Seven days went by in monotonous procession. Seven days in a world of constant climate. One week, marked only by the changing of work shifts and the clocks that marked off the eight-hour periods. Seven days unmarred by rain or cold or heat. Seven days of uninterrupted sunshine that flickered in and out of the sealed viewports with eye-searing brilliance, coming and going as the station rotated.

But in the front offices, things were not serene. Not that monotony ever set in seriously in the engineering department, but that sacred sanctum of all-things-that-didn't-behave-as-they-should found that even their usual turmoil was worse. There was nothing that a person could set his fingers on directly. It was more of a quiet, undercover nature. On Monday Burbank sent around a communiqué removing the option of free messages for the personnel. On Tuesday he remanded the years-long custom of permitting the supply ships to carry, free, packages from friends at home. On Wednesday, Francis Burbank decided that there should be a curfew on the one and only beer emporium. 'Curfew' was a revision made after he found that complete curtailing of all alcoholic beverages might easily lead to a more moral problem; there being little enough to do with one's spare time. On Thursday, he set up a stiff-necked staff of censors for the moving picture house. On Friday, he put a tax on cigarettes and candy. On Saturday, he installed time clocks in all the laboratories and professional offices, where previous to his coming, men had come for work a half hour late and worked an hour overtime at night.

On Sunday—

Don Channing stormed into the Director's office with a scowl on his face.

'Look,' he said, 'for years we have felt that any man, woman, or child that was willing to come out here was worth all the freedom and consideration that we could give them. What about this damned tax on cigarettes? And candy? And who told you to stop our folks from telling their folks that they are still in good health? And why stop them from sending packages of candy, cake, mementoes, clothing, soap, mosquito dope, liquor, or anything else? And did you ever think that a curfew is something that can be applied only when time is one and the same for all? On Venus Equilateral, Mr. Burbank, six o'clock in the evening is two hours after dinner for one group, two hours after going to work for the second group, and mid-sleep for the third. Then this matter of cutting all love scenes, drinking, female vampires, banditry, bedroom items, murders, and sweater girls out of the movies? We are a selected group and well prepared to take care of our morality. Any man or woman going offside would be heaved out quick. Why, after years of personal freedom, do we find ourselves under the authority of a veritable dictatorship?'

Francis Burbank was not touched. 'I'll trouble you to keep to your own laboratory,' he told Channing. 'Perhaps your own laxity in matters of this sort is the reason why the Commission preferred someone better prepared. You speak of many things. There will be more to come. I'll answer some of your questions. Why should we permit our profits to be eaten up by people sending messages, cost-free, to their acquaintances all over the minor planets? Why should valuable space for valuable supplies be taken up with personal favors between friends? And if the personnel wants to smoke and drink, let them pay for the privilege! It will help to pay for the high price of shipping the useless items out from the nearest planet – as well as saving precious storage space!'

'But you're breeding ill will among the employees,' objected Channing.

'Any that prefer to do so may leave!' snapped Burbank.

'You may find it difficult to hire people to spend their lives in a place that offers no sight of a sky or a breath of fresh air. The people here may go home to their own planets to find that smell of fresh, spring air is more desirable than a climate that never varies from the personal optimum. I wonder, occasionally, if it might not be possible to instigate some sort of cold snap or a rainy season just for the purpose of bringing to the members of Venus Equilateral some of the surprises that are to be found in Chicago or New York. Hell, even Canalopsis has an occasional rainstorm!'

'Return to your laboratory,' said Burbank coldly. 'And let me run the station. Why should we spend useful money to pamper people? I don't care if Canalopsis does have an occasional storm, we are not on Mars, we are in Venus Equilateral. You tend to your end of the business and I'll do as I deem fitting for the station!'

Channing mentally threw up his hands and literally stalked out of the office. Here was a close-knit organization being shot full of holes by a screwball. He stamped down to the ninth level and beat upon the closed door of Joe's. The door remained closed.

Channing beat with his knuckles until they bled. Finally a door popped open down the hallway fifty yards and a man looked out. His head popped in again, and within thirty seconds the door to Joe's opened and admitted Channing.

Joe slapped the door shut behind Channing quickly.

'Whatinhell are you operating, Joe – a speakeasy?'

'The next time you want in,' Joe informed him, 'knock on 902 twice, 914 once, and then here four times. We'll let you in. And now, don't say anything too loud.' Joe put a finger to his lips and winked broadly. 'Even the walls listen,' he said in a stage whisper.

He led Channing into the room and put on the light. There was a flurry of people who tried to hide their glasses under the table. 'Never mind,' called Joe. 'It's only Dr. Channing.'

The room relaxed.

'I want something stiff,' Channing told Joe. 'I've just gone three rounds with His Nibs and came out cold.'

Some people within earshot asked about it. Channing explained what had transpired. The people seemed satisfied that Channing had done his best for them. The room relaxed into routine.

The signal knock came on the door and was opened to admit Walt Franks and Arden Westland. Franks looked as though he had been given a stiff workout in a cement mixer.

'Scotch,' said Arden. 'And a glass of brew for the lady.'

'What happened to him?'

'He's been trying to keep to Burbank's latest suggestions.'

'You've been working too hard,' Channing chided him gently. 'This is the wrong time to mention it, I suppose, but did that beam slippage have anything to do with your condition – or was it vice versa?'

'You know that I haven't anything to do with the beam controls personally,' said Franks. He straightened up and faced Channing defiantly.

'Don't get mad. What was it?'

'Mastermind, up there, called me in to see if there were some manner or means of tightening the beam. I told him, sure, we could hold the beam to practically nothing. He asked me why we didn't hold the beam to a parallel and save the dispersed power. He claimed that we could reduce power by two to one if more of it came into the station instead of being smeared all over the firmament. I, foolishly, agreed with him. He's right. You could. But only if everything is immobilized. I've been trying to work out some means of controlling the beam magnetically so that it would compensate for the normal variations due to magnetic influences. So far I've failed.'

'It can't be done. I know, because I worked on the problem for three years with some of the best brains in the system. To date, it is impossible.'

A click attracted their attention. It was the pneumatic tube. A cylinder dropped out of the tube, and Joe opened it and handed the enclosed paper to Franks.

He read:

'WALT:
I'M SENDING THIS TO YOU AT JOE'S BE-
CAUSE I KNOW THAT IS WHERE YOU ARE AND
I THINK YOU SHOULD GET THIS REAL QUICK.
                                            JEANNE S."

Walt smiled wearily and said: 'A good secretary is a thing of beauty. A thing of beauty is admired and is a joy forever. Jeanne is both. She is a jewel.'

'Yeah, we know. What does the letter say?'

'It is another communiqué from our doting boss. He is removing from my control the odd three hundred men I've got working on Beam Control. He is to assume the responsibility for them himself. I'm practically out of a job.'

'Make that two Scotches,' Channing told Joe.

'Make it three,' chimed in Arden. 'I've got to work for him, too!'

'Is that so bad?' asked Channing. 'All you've got to do is to listen carefully and do as you're told. We have to answer to the bird, too.'

'Yeah,' said Arden, 'but you fellows don't have to listen to a dopey guy ask foolish questions all day. It's driving me silly.'

'What I'd like to know,' murmured Franks, 'is what is the

29

idea of pulling me off the job? Nuts, I've been on the Beam Control for years. I've got the finest crew of men anywhere. They can actually foresee a shift and compensate for it, I think. I picked 'em myself and I've been proud of my outfit. Now,' he said brokenly, 'I've got no outfit. In fact, I have darned little crew left at all. Only my dozen lab members. I'll have to go back to swinging a meter myself before this is over.'

It was quite a comedown. From the master of over three hundred highly paid, highly prized, intelligent technicians, Walt Franks was now the superintendent of one dozen laboratory technicians. It was a definite cut in his status.

Channing finished his drink and, seeing that Franks' attention was elsewhere, he told Arden: 'Thanks for taking care of him, but don't use all your sympathy on him. I feel that I'm going to need your shoulder to cry on before long.'

'Anytime you want a soft shoulder,' said Arden generously, 'let me know. I'll come a-running.'

Channing went out. He roamed nervously all the rest of the day. He visited the bar several times, but the general air of the place depressed him. From a place of recreation, laughter and pleasantry, Joe's place had changed to a room for reminiscences and remorse, a place to drown one's troubles – or poison them – or to preserve them in alcohol.

He went to see the local moving picture, a piece advertised as being one of the best mystery thrillers since Hitchcock. He found that all of the interesting parts were cut out and that the only thing that remained was a rather disjointed portrayal of a detective finding meaningless clues and ultimately the criminal. There was a suggestion at the end that the detective and the criminal had fought it out, but whether it was with pistols, field pieces, knives, cream puffs or words was left to the imagination. It was also to be assumed that he and the heroine, who went into a partial blackout every time she sat down, finally got acquainted enough to hold hands after the picture.

Channing stormed out of the theatre after seeing the above and finding that the only cartoon had been barred because it showed an innocuous cow without benefit of shorts.

He troubled Joe for a bottle of the best and took to his apartment in disappointment. By eight o'clock in the evening, Don Channing was asleep with all of his clothing on. The bed rolled and refused to stay on an even keel, but Channing found a necktie and tied himself securely in the bed and died off in a beautiful, boiled cloud.

He woke to the tune of a beautiful hangover. He gulped seven glasses of water and staggered to the shower. Fifteen minutes of iced needles and some coffee brought him part way back to his own, cheerful self. He headed down the hall toward the elevator.

He found a note in his office directing him to appear at a conference in Burbank's office. Groaning in anguish, Don went to the Director's office expecting the worst.

It was bad. In fact, it was enough to drive everyone in the conference to drink. Burbank asked opinions on everything, and then tore the opinions apart with little regard to their validity. He expressed his own opinion many times, which was a disgusted sense of the personnel's inability to do anything of real value.

'Certainly,' he stormed, 'I know you are operating. But have there been any new developments coming out of your laboratory, Mr Channing?'

Someone was about to tell Burbank that Channing had a doctor's degree, but Don shook his head.

'We've been working on a lot of small items,' said Channing. 'I cannot say whether there has been any one big thing that we could point to. As we make developments, we put them into service. Added together, they make quite an honest effort.'

'What, for instance?' stormed Burbank.

31

'The last one was the coupler machine improvement that permitted better than ten thousand words per minute.'

'Up to that time the best wordage was something like eight thousand words,' said Burbank. 'I think that you have been resting too long on your laurels. Unless you can bring me something big enough to advertise, I shall have to take measures.'

'Now you, Mr. Warren,' continued Burbank. 'You are the man who is supposed to be superintendent of maintenance. May I ask why the outer hull is not painted?'

'Because it would be a waste of paint,' said Warren. 'Figure out the acreage of a surface of a cylinder three miles long and a mile in diameter. It is almost eleven square miles! Eleven square miles to paint from scaffolding hung from the outside itself.'

'Use bos'n's chairs,' snapped Burbank.

'A bos'n's chair would be worthless,' Warren informed Burbank. 'You must remember that to anyone trying to operate on the outer hull, the outer hull is a ceiling and directly overhead.

'Another thing,' said Warren, 'you paint that hull and you'll run this station by yourself. Why d'ya think we have it shiny?'

'If we paint the hull,' persisted Burbank, 'it will be more presentable than that nondescript steel color.'

'That steel color is as shiny as we could make it,' growled Warren. 'We want to get rid of as much radiated heat as we can. You slap a coat of any kind of paint on that hull and you'll have plenty of heat in here.'

'Ah, that sounds interesting. We'll save heating costs—'

'Don't be an idiot,' snapped Warren. 'Heating costs, my grandmother's eye. Look, Burbank, did you ever hear of the Uranium Pile? Part of our income comes from refining uranium and plutonium and the preparation of radioisotopes. And — Good Lord, I'm not going to try to explain fission-reacting materials to you; get that first old copy of the Smyth Report and get brought up to date.

'The fact remains,' continued Warren, cooling somewhat after displaying Burbank's ignorance, 'that we have more power than we know what to do with. We're operating on a safe margin by radiating just a little more than we generate. We make up the rest by the old methods of artificial heating.

'But there have been a lot of times when it became necessary to dissipate a lot of energy for divers reasons and then we've had to shut off the heating. What would happen if we couldn't cool off the damned coffee can? We'd roast to death the first time we got a new employee with a body temperature a degree above normal.'

'You're being openly rebellious,' Burbank warned him.

'So I am. And if you persist in your attempt to make this place presentable, you'll find me and my gang out-right mutinous! Good day, sir!'

He stormed out of the office and slammed the door.

'Take a note, Miss Westland. "Interplanetary Communications Commission, Terra. Gentlemen: Michael Warren, superintendent of maintenance at Venus Equilateral, has proven to be unreceptive to certain suggestions as to the appearance and/or operation of Venus Equilateral. It is my request that he be replaced immediately. Signed, Francis Burbank, Director."' He paused to see what effect that message had upon the faces of the men around the table. 'Send that by special delivery!'

Johnny Billings opened his mouth to say something, but shut it with a snap. Westland looked up at Burbank, but she said nothing. Arden gave Channing a sly smile, and Channing smiled back. There were grins about the table, too, for everyone recognized the boner. Burbank had just sent a letter from the interworld communications relay station by special delivery *mail*. It would not get to Terra for better than two weeks; a use of the station's facilities would have the message in the hands of the Commission within the hour.

'That will be all, gentlemen,' Burbank smiled smugly. 'Our next conference will be next Monday morning!'

'Mr. Channing,' chortled the pleasant voice of Arden Westland, 'now that the trifling influence of the boss versus secretary taboo is off, will you have the pleasure of buying me a drink?'

'Can you repeat that word for word and explain it?' grinned Don.

'A man isn't supposed to make eyes at his secretary. A gal ain't supposed to seduce her boss. Now that you are no longer Acting Director, and I no longer your stenog, how about some sociability?'

'I never thought that I'd be propositioned by a typewriter jockey,' said Channing, 'but I'll do it. What time is it? Do we do it openly, or must we sneak over to the apartment and snaffle a snort on the sly?'

'We snaffle. That is, if you trust me in your apartment.'

'I'm scared to death,' Channing informed her. 'But if I should fail to defend my honor, we must remember that it is no dishonor to try and fail.'

'That sounds like a nice alibi,' said Arden with a smile. 'Or a come-on. I don't know which. Or, Mr. Channing, am I being told that my advances might not be welcome?'

'We shall see,' Channing said. 'We'll have to make a careful study of the matter. I cannot make any statements without first making a thorough examination under all sorts of conditions. Here we are. You will precede me through the door, please.'

'Why?' asked Arden.

'So that you cannot back out at the last possible moment. Once I get inside, I'll think about keeping you there!'

'As long as you have some illegal fluid, I'll stay.' She tried to leer at Don but failed because she had had all too little experience in leering. 'Bring it on!'

34

'Here's to the good old days,' toasted Don as the drinks were raised.

'Nope. Here's to the future,' proposed Arden. 'Those good old days – all they were was old. If you were back in them, you'd still have to have the pleasure of meeting Burbank.'

'*Grrrr*,' growled Channing. 'That name is never mentioned in this household.'

'You haven't a pix of the old bird turned to the wall, have you?' asked Arden.

'I tossed it out.'

'We'll drink to that.' They drained glasses. 'And we'll have another.'

'I need another,' said Channing. 'Can you imagine that buzzard asking me to invent something big in seven days?'

'Sure. By the same reasoning that he uses to send a letter from Venus Equilateral instead of just slipping it on the Terra beam. Faulty.'

'Phony.'

The door opened abruptly and Walt Franks entered. 'D'ja hear the latest?' he asked breathlessly.

'No,' said Channing. He was reaching for another glass automatically. He poured, and Walt watched the amber fluid creep up the glass, led by a sheet of white foam.

'Then look!' Walt handed Channing an official envelope. It was a regular notice to the effect that there had been eleven failures of service through Venus Equilateral.

'Eleven! What makes?'

'Mastermind.'

'What's he done?'

'Remember the removal of my jurisdiction over the beam control operators? Well, in the last ten days, Burbank has installed some new features to cut expenses. I think that he hopes to lay off a couple of hundred men.'

'What's he doing, do you know?'

'He's shortening the dispersion. He intends to cut the power by slamming more of the widespread beam into the receptor. The tighter beam makes aiming more difficult, you know, because at seventy million miles, every time little Joey on Mars swings his toy horseshoe magnet on the end of his string, the beam wabbles. And at seventy million miles, how much wabbling does it take to send a narrow beam clear off the target?'

'The normal dispersion of the beam from Venus is over a thousand miles wide. It gyrates and wabbles through most of that arc. That is why we picked that particular dispersion. If we could have pointed the thing like an arrow, we'd have kept the dispersion down.'

'Right. And he's tightened the beam to less than a hundred miles' dispersion. Now, every time a sunspot gets hit amidships with a lady sunspot, the beam goes off on a tangent. We've lost the beam eleven times in a week. That's more times than I've lost it in three years!'

'O.K.,' said Channing. 'So what? Mastermind is responsible. We'll sit tight and wait for developments. In any display of abilities, we can spike Mr. Burbank. Have another drink?'

'Got any more? If you've not, I've got a couple of cases cached underneath the bed in my apartment.'

'I've plenty,' said Channing. 'And I'll need plenty. I have exactly twenty-two hours left in which to produce something comparable to the telephone, the electric light, the airplane, or the expanding universe! Phooey. Pour me another, Arden.'

A knock at the door; a feminine voice interrupted simultaneously. 'May I come in?'

It was Walt's secretary. She looked worried. In one hand she waved another letter.

'Another communiqué?' asked Channing.

'Worse. Notice that for the last three hours, there have been

36

less than twelve percent of messages relayed!'

'Five minutes' operation out of an hour,' said Channing. 'Where's that from?'

'Came out on the Terra beam. It's marked number seventeen, so I guess that sixteen other tries have been made.'

'What has Mastermind tried this time?' stormed Channing. He tore out of the room and headed for the Director's office on a dead run. On the way, he hit his shoulder on the door, caromed off the opposite wall, righted himself, and was gone in a flurry of flying feet. Three heads popped out of doors to see who was making the noise.

Channing skidded into Burbank's office on his heels. 'What gives?' he snapped. 'D'ya realize that we've lost the beam? What have you been doing?'

'It is a minor difficulty,' said Burbank calmly. 'We will iron it out presently.'

'Presently! Our charter doesn't permit interruptions of service of that magnitude. I ask again: What are you doing?'

'You, as electronics engineer, have no right to question me. I repeat, we shall iron out the difficulty presently.'

Channing snorted and tore out of Burbank's office. He headed for the Office of Beam Control, turned the corner on one foot, and slammed the door roughly.

'Chuck!' he yelled. 'Chuck Thomas! Where are you?'

No answer. Channing left the beam office and headed for the master control panels, out near the air lock end of Venus Equilateral. He found Thomas stewing over a complicated piece of apparatus.

'Chuck, for the Love of Michael, what in the devil is going on?'

'Thought you knew,' answered Thomas. 'Burbank had the crew install photoelectric mosaic banks on the beam controls. He intends to use the photomosaics to keep Venus, Terra, and Mars on the beam.'

37

'Great Sniveling Scott! They tried that in the last century and tossed it out three days later. Where's the crew now?'

'Packing for home. They've been laid off!'

'Get 'em back! Put 'em to work. Turn off those darned photomosaics and use the manual again. We've lost every beam we ever had.'

A sarcastic voice came in at this point. 'For what reason do you interfere with my improvements?' sneered the voice. 'Could it be that you are accepting graft from the employees to keep them on the job by preventing the installation of superior equipment?'

Channing turned on his toe and let Burbank have one. It was a neat job, coming up at the right time and connecting sweetly. Burbank went over on his head.

'Get going,' Channing snapped at Thomas.

Charles Thomas grinned. It was not Channing's one-ninety that decided him to comply. He left.

Channing shook Burbank's shoulder. He slapped the man's face. Eyes opened, accusing eyes rendered mute by a very sore jaw, tongue, and throat.

'Now listen,' snapped Channing. 'Listen to every word! Mosaic directors are useless. Know why? It is because of the lag. At planetary distances, light takes an appreciable time to reach. Your beam wobbles. Your planet swerves out of line because of intervening factors; varying magnetic fields, even the bending of light due to gravitational fields will shake the beam microscopically. But, Burbank, a microscopic discrepancy is all that is needed to bust things wide open. You've got to have experienced men to operate the beam controls. Men who can think. Men who can, from experience, reason that this fluctuation will not last, but will swing back in a few seconds, or that this type of swerving will increase in magnitude for a half-hour, maintain the status, and then return, pass through zero and find the same level on the minus side.

'Since light and centimeter waves are not exactly alike in performance, a field that will serve one may not affect the other as much. Ergo your photomosaic is useless. The photoelectric mosaic is a brilliant gadget for keeping a plane in a spotlight or for aiming a sixteen-inch gun, but it is worthless for anything over a couple of million miles.

'So I've called the men back to their stations. And don't try anything foolish again without consulting the men who are paid to think!'

Channing got up and left. As he strode down the stairs to the apartment level, he met many of the men who had been laid off. None of them said a word, but all of them wore bright, knowing smiles.

By Monday morning, however, Burbank was himself again. The rebuff given him by Don Channing had worn off and he was sparkling with ideas. He speared Franks with the glitter in his eyes and said: 'If our beams are always on the center, why is it necessary to use multiplex diversity?'

Franks smiled. 'You're mistaken,' he told Burbank. 'They're not always on the button. They vary. Therefore, we use diversity transmission so that if one beam fails momentarily, one of the other beams will bring the signal in. It is analogous to tying five or six ropes onto a hoisted stone. If one breaks, you have the others.'

'You have them running all the time, then?'

'Certainly. At several minutes of time-lag in transmission, to try and establish a beam failure of a few seconds' duration is utter foolishness.'

'And you disperse the beam to a thousand miles wide to keep the beam centered at any variation?' Burbank shot at Channing.

'Not for any variation. Make that any *normal* gyration and I'll buy it.'

'Then why don't we disperse the beam to two or three thousand miles and do away with diversity transmission?' asked Burbank triumphantly.

'Ever heard of fading?' asked Channing with a grin. 'Your signal comes and goes. Not gyration, it just gets weaker. It fails for want of something to eat, I guess, and takes off after a wandering cosmic ray. At any rate, there are many times per minute that one beam will be right on the nose and yet so weak that our strippers cannot clean it enough to make it usable. Then the diversity system comes in handy. Our coupling detectors automatically select the proper signal channel. It takes the one that is the strongest and subdues the rest within itself.'

'Complicated?'

'It was done in the heyday of radio – 1935 or so. Your two channels come in to a common detector. Automatic volume control voltage comes from the single detector and is applied to all channels. This voltage is proper for the strongest channel, but is too high for the ones receiving the weaker signal; blocking them by rendering them insensitive. When the strong channel fades and the weak channel rises, the detector follows down until the two signal channels are equal and then it rises with the stronger channel.'

'I see,' said Burbank. 'Has anything been done about fading?'

'It is like the weather, according to Mark Twain,' smiled Channing. ' "Everybody talks about it, but nobody does anything about it." About all we've learned is that we can cuss it out and it doesn't cuss back.'

'I think it should be tried,' said Burbank.

'If you'll pardon me, it has been tried. The first installation at Venus Equilateral was made that way. It didn't work, though we used more power than all of our diversity transmitters together. Sorry.'

'Have you anything to report?' Burbank asked Channing.

'Nothing. I've been more than busy investigating the trouble we've had in keeping the beams centered.'

Burbank said nothing. He was stopped. He hoped that the secret of his failure was not generally known, but he knew at the same time that when three hundred men are aware of something interesting, some of them will see to it that all the others involved will surely know. He looked at the faces of the men around the table and saw suppressed mirth in every one of them. Burbank writhed in inward anger. He was a good poker player. He didn't show it at all.

He then went on to other problems. He ironed some out, others he shelved for the time being. Burbank was a good business man. But like so many other businessmen, Burbank had the firm conviction that if he had the time to spare and at the same time was free of the worries and paper work of his position, he could step into the laboratory and show the engineers how to make things hum. He was infuriated every time he saw one of the engineering staff sitting with hands behind head, lost in a gazy, unreal land of deep thought. Though he knew better, he was often tempted to raise hell because the man was obviously loafing.

But give him credit. He could handle business angles to perfection. In spite of his tangle over the beam control, he had rebounded excellently and had ironed out all of the complaints that had poured in. Ironed it out to the satisfaction of the injured party as well as the Interplanetary Communications Commission, who were interested in anything that cost money.

He dismissed the conference and went to thinking. And he assumed the same pose that infuriated him in other men under him; hands behind head, feet upon desk.

The moving picture theater was dark. The hero reached longing arms to the heroine, and there was a sort of magnetic attraction. They approached one another. But the spark misfired. It was blacked out with a nice slice of utter blackness that came from the screen and spread its lightlessness all over the theater. In the ensuing darkness, there were several osculations that were more personal and more satisfying than the censored clinch. The lights flashed on and several male heads moved back hastily. Female lips smiled happily. Some of them parted in speech.

One of them said: 'Why, Mr. Channing!'

'Shut up, Arden,' snapped the man. 'People will think that I've been kissing you.'

'If someone else was taking advantage of the situation,' she said, 'you got gypped. I thought I was kissing you and I cooked with gas!'

'Did you ever try that before?' asked Channing interestedly.

'Why?' she asked.

'I liked it. I merely wondered, if you'd worked it on other men, what there was about you that kept you single.'

'They all died after the first application,' she said. 'They couldn't take it.'

'Let me outta here! I get the implication. I am the first bird that hasn't died, hey?' He yawned luxuriously.

'Company or the hour?' asked Arden.

'Can't be either,' he said. 'Come on, let's break a bottle of beer open. I'm dry!'

'I've got a slight headache,' she told him. 'From what, I can't imagine.'

'I haven't a headache, but I'm sort of logy.'

'What have you been doing?' asked Arden. 'Haven't seen you for a couple of days.'

'Nothing worth mentioning. Had an idea a couple of days ago and went to work on it.'

'Haven't been working overtime or missing breakfast?'

'Nope.'

'Then I don't see why you should be ill. I can explain my headache away by attributing it to eyestrain. Since Billyboy came here, and censored the movies to the bone, the darned things flicker like anything. But eyestrain doesn't create an autointoxication. So, my fine fellow, what have you been drinking?'

'Nothing that I haven't been drinking since I first took to my second bottlehood some years ago.'

'You wouldn't be suffering from a hangover from that hangover you had a couple of weeks ago?'

'Nope. I swore off. Never again will I try to drink a whole quart of Two Moons in one evening. It got me.'

'It had you for a couple of days,' laughed Arden. 'All to itself.'

Don Channing said nothing. He recalled, all too vividly, the rolling of the tummy that ensued after that session with the only fighter that hadn't yet been beaten: Old John Barleycorn.

'How are you coming on with Burbank?' asked Arden. 'I haven't heard a rave for – well, ever since Monday morning's conference. Three days without a nasty dig at Our Boss. That's a record.'

'Give the devil his due. He's been more than busy placating irate citizens. That last debacle with the beam control gave him a real Moscow winter. His reforms came to a stop whilst he entrenched. But he's been doing an excellent job of squirming out from under. Of course, it has been helped by the fact that even though the service was rotten for a few hours, the customers couldn't rush out to some other agency to get communications with the other planets.'

'Sort of: "Take us, lousy as we are?"'

'That's it.'

Channing opened the door to his apartment and Arden went in. Channing followed, and then stopped cold.

'Great Jeepers!' he said in an awed tone. 'If I didn't know—'

'Why, Don! What's so startling?'

'Have you noticed?' he asked. 'It smells like the inside of a chicken coop in here!'

43

Arden sniffed. 'It does sort of remind me of something that died and couldn't get out of its skin.' Arden smiled. 'I'll hold my breath. Any sacrifice for a drink.'

'That isn't the point. This is purified air. It should be as sweet as a baby's breath.'

'Some baby,' whistled Arden. 'What's baby been drinking?'

'It wasn't cow-juice. What I've been trying to put over is that the air doesn't seem to have been changed in here for nine weeks.'

Channing went to the ventilator and lit a match. The flame bent over, flickered, and went out.

'Air intake is O.K.,' he said. 'Maybe it is I. Bring on that bottle, Channing; don't keep the lady waiting.'

He yawned again, deeply and jaw-stretchingly. Arden yawned, to, and the thought of both of them stretching their jaws to the breaking-off point made both of them laugh foolishly.

'Arden, I'm going to break one bottle of beer with you after which I'm going to take you home, kiss you good night, and toss you into your own apartment. Then I'm coming back here and I'm going to hit the hay!'

Arden took a long, deep breath. 'I'll buy that,' she said.

'And tonight, it wouldn't take much persuasion to induce me to snooze right here in this chair!'

'Oh, fine,' cheered Don. 'That would fix me up swell with the neighbors. I'm not going to get shotgunned into anything like that!'

'Don't be silly,' said Arden.

'From the look in your eye,' said Channing, 'I'd say that you were just about to do that very thing. I was merely trying to dissolve any ideas that you might have.'

'Don't bother,' she said pettishly. 'I haven't any ideas. I'm as free as you are, and I intend to stay that way!'

Channing stood up. 'The next thing we know, we'll be fighting,' he observed. 'Stand up, Arden. Shake.'

44

Arden stood up, shook herself, and then looked at Channing with a strange light in her eyes. 'I feel sort of dizzy,' she admitted. 'And everything irritates me.'

She passed a hand over her eyes wearily. Then, with a visible effort, she straightened. She seemed to throw off her momentary ill feeling instantly. She smiled at Channing and was her normal self in less than a minute.

'What is it?' she asked. 'Do you feel funny, too?'

'I do!' he said. 'I don't want that beer. I want to snooze.'

'When Channing would prefer snoozing to boozing he is sick,' she said. 'Come on, fellow, take me home.'

Slowly they walked down the long hallway. They said nothing. Arm in arm they went, and when they reached Arden's door, their good-night kiss lacked enthusiasm. 'See you in the morning,' said Don.

Arden looked at him. 'That was a little flat. We'll try it again – tomorrow or next week.'

Don Channing's sleep was broken by dreams. He was warm. His dreams depicted him in a humid, airless chamber, and he was forced to breathe that same stale air again and again. He awoke in a hot sweat, weak and feeling – lousy!

He dressed carelessly. He shaved hit-or-miss. His morning coffee tasted flat and sour. He left the apartment in a bad mood, and bumped into Arden at the corner of the hall.

'Hello,' she said. 'I feel rotten. But you have improved. Or is that passionate breathing just a lack of fresh air?'

'Hell! That's it!' he said. He snapped up his wrist watch, which was equipped with a stop-watch hand. He looked about, and finding a man sitting on a bench, apparently taking it easy while waiting for someone, Channing clicked the sweep hand into gear. He started to count the man's respiration.

'What gives?' asked Arden. 'What's "It"? Why are you so excited? Did I say something?'

'You did,' said Channing after fifteen seconds. 'That bird's respiration is better than fifty! This whole place is filled to the gills with carbon dioxide. Come on, Arden, let's get going!'

Channing led the girl by several yards by the time that they were within sight of the elevator. He waited for her, and then sent the car upward at a full throttle. Minutes passed, and they could feel that stomach-rising sensation that comes when gravity is lessened. Arden clasped her hands over her middle and hugged. She squirmed and giggled.

'You've been up to the axis before,' said Channing. 'Take long, deep breaths.'

The car came to a stop with a slowing effect. A normal braking stop would have catapulted them against the ceiling.

'Come on,' he grinned at her, 'here's where we make time!'

Channing looked up at the little flight of stairs that led to the innermost level. He winked at Arden and jumped. He passed up through the opening easily. 'Jump,' he commanded. 'Don't use the stairs.'

Arden jumped. She sailed upward, and as she passed through the opening, Channing caught her by one arm and stopped her flight. 'At that speed you'd go right on across,' he said.

She looked up, and there about two hundred feet overhead she could see the opposite wall.

Channing snapped on the lights. They were in a room two hundred feet in diameter and three hundred feet long. 'We're at the center of the station,' Channing informed her. 'Beyond that bulkhead is the air lock. On the other side of the other bulkhead, we have the air plant, the storage spaces, and several rooms of machinery.'

'Come on,' he said. He took her by the hand and with a kick he propelled himself along on a long, curving course to the opposite side of the inner cylinder. He gained the opposite bulkhead as well.

'Now, that's what I call traveling,' said Arden. 'But my

46

tummy goes *whoosh, whoosh* every time we cross the center.'

Channing operated a heavy door. They went in through room full of machinery and into rooms stacked to the center with boxes; stacked from the wall to the center and then packed with springs. Near the axis of the cylinder, things weighed so little that packing was necessary to keep them from floating around.

'I feel giddy,' said Arden.

'High in oxygen,' said he. 'The CO_2 drops to the bottom, being heavier. Then too, the air is thinner up here because centrifugal force swings the whole out to the rim. Out there we are so used to "down" that here, a half mile above – or to the center, rather – we have trouble in saying, technically, what we mean. Watch!'

He left Arden standing and walked rapidly around the inside of the cylinder. Soon he was standing on the steel plates directly over her head. She looked up, and shook her head.

'I know why,' she called, 'but it still makes me dizzy. Come down from up there or I'll be sick.'

Channing made a neat dive from his position above her head. He did it merely by jumping upward from his place toward her place, apparently hanging head down from the ceiling. He turned a neat flip-flop in the air and landed easily beside her. Immediately, for both of them, things became right-side-up again.

Channing opened the door to the room marked: 'Air Plant.' He stepped in, snapped on the lights, and gasped in amazement.

'Hell!' he groaned. The place was empty. Completely empty. Absolutely, and irrevocably vacant. Oh, there was some dirt on the floor and some trash in the corners, and a trail of scratches on the floor to show that the life giving air plant had been removed, hunk by hunk, out through another door at the far end of the room.

'Whoa, Tillie!' screamed Don. 'We've been stabbed! Arden, get on the type and have . . . no wait a minute until we find out a few more things about this!'

They made record time back to the office level. They found Burbank in his office, leaning back, and talking to someone on the phone.

Channing tried to interrupt, but Burbank removed his nose from the telephone long enough to snarl, 'Can't you see I'm busy? Have you no manners or respect?'

Channing, fuming inside, swore inwardly. He sat down with a show of being calm and folded his hands over his abdomen like the famed statue of Buddha. Arden looked at him, and for all the trouble they were in, she couldn't help giggling. Channing, tall, lanky, and strong, looked as little as possible like the popular, pudgy figure of the Sitting Buddha.

A minute passed.

Burbank hung up the phone.

'Where does Venus Equilateral get its air from?' snapped Burbank.

'That's what I want—'

'Answer me, please. I'm worried.'

'So am I. Something—'

'Tell me first, from what source does Venus Equilateral get its fresh air?'

'From the air plant. And that is—'

'There must be more than one,' said Burbank thoughtfully.

'There's only one.'

'There *must* be more than one. We couldn't live if there weren't,' said the Director.

'Wishing won't make it so. There is only one.'

'I tell you, there must be another. Why, I went into the one up at the axis day before yesterday and found that instead of a bunch of machinery, running smoothly, purifying air, and sending it out to the various parts of the station, all there was was a veritable jungle of weeds. Those weeds, Mr. Channing, looked as though they must have been put in there years ago. Now, where did the air-purifying machinery go?'

Channing listened to the latter half of Burbank's speech with his chin at half-mast. He looked as though a feather would knock him clear across the office.

'I had some workmen clear the weeds out. I intend to replace the air machinery as soon as I can get some new material sent from Terra.'

Channing managed to blink. It was an effort. 'You had workmen toss the weeds out—' he repeated dully. 'The weeds—'

There was silence for a minute. Burbank studied the man in the chair as though Channing were a piece of statuary. Channing was just as motionless. 'Channing, man, what ails you—' began Burbank. The sound of Burbank's voice aroused Channing from his shocked condition.

Channing leaped to his feet. He landed on his heels, spun, and snapped at Arden: 'Get on the type. Have 'em slap as many oxy-drums on the fastest ship as they've got! Get 'em here at full throttle. Tell 'em to load up the pilot and crew with gravanol and not to spare the horsepower! Scram!'

Arden gasped. She fled from the office.

'Burbank, what did you think an air plant was?' snapped Channing.

'Why, isn't it some sort of purifying machinery?' asked the wondering Director.

'What better purifying machine is there than a plot of grass?' shouted Channing. 'Weeds, grass, flowers, trees, alfalfa, wheat or anything that grows and uses chlorophyll. We breath oxygen, exhale CO_2. Plants inhale CO_2 and exude oxygen. An air plant means just that. It is a specialized type of Martian sawgrass that is more efficient than anything else in the system for inhaling dead air and revitalizing it. And you've tossed the weeds out!' Channing snorted in anger. 'We've spent years getting that plant so that it will grow just right. It got so good that the CO_2 detectors weren't even needed. The balance was so adjusted that they haven't even been turned on for three or four years. They were just another source of unnecessary expense. Why, save for a monthly inspection, that room isn't even opened, so efficient is the Martian sawgrass. We, Burbank, are losing oxygen!'

The Director grew white. 'I didn't know,' he said.

'Well, you know now. Get on your horse and do something. At least, Burbank, stay out of my way while I do something.'

'You have a free hand,' said Burbank. His voice sounded beaten.

Channing left the office of the Director and headed for the chem lab. 'How much potassium chlorate, nitrate, sulphate, and other oxygen-bearing compounds have you?' he asked. 'That includes mercuric oxide, spare water, or anything else that will give us oxygen if broken down.'

There was a ten-minute wait until the members of the chem lab took a hurried inventory.

'Good,' said Channing. 'Start breaking it down. Collect all the oxygen you can in containers. This is the business! It has priority! Anything, no matter how valuable, must be scrapped if it can facilitate the gathering of oxygen. God knows, there isn't by half enough – not even a tenth. But try, anyway.'

Channing headed out of the chemistry laboratory and into the electronics lab. 'Jimmie,' he shouted, 'get a couple of stone jars and get an electrolysis outfit running. Fling the hydrogen out of a convenient outlet into space and collect the oxygen. Water, I mean. Use tap water, right out of the faucet.'

'Yeah, but—'

'Jimmie, if we don't breathe, what chance have we to go on drinking? I'll tell you when to stop.'

'O.K., Doc,' said Jimmie.

'And look. As soon as you get that running, set up a CO_2 indicator and let me know the percentage at the end of each hour! Get me?'

'I take it that something has happened to the air plant?'

'It isn't functioning,' said Channing shortly. He left the puzzled Jimmie and headed for the beam-control room. Jimmie continued to wonder about the air plant. How in the devil could an air plant cease functioning unless it were – *dead*! Jimmie stopped wondering and began to operate on his electrolysis set-up furiously.

Channing found the men in the beam-control room worried and ill at ease. The fine co-ordination that made them expert in their line was ebbing. The nervous work demanded perfect motor control, excellent perception, and a fine power of reasoning. The perceptible lack of oxygen at this high level was taking its toll already.

'Look, fellows, we're in a mess. Until further notice, take five-minute shifts. We've got about thirty hours to go. If the going gets tough, drop it to three-minute shifts. But, fellows, keep those beams centered until you drop!'

'We'll keep 'em going if we have to call our wives up here to run 'em for us,' said one man. 'What's up?'

'Air plant's sour. Losing oxy. Got a shipload coming out from Terra, be here in thirty hours. But upon you fellows will rest the responsibility of keeping us in touch with the rest of the system. If you fail, we could call for help until hell freezes us all in – and no one would hear us!'

'We'll keep 'em rolling,' said a little fellow who had to sit on a tall stool to get even with the controls.

Channing looked out of the big, faceted plexiglass dome that covered the entire end of the Venus Equilateral Station. 'Here messages go in and out,' he mused. 'The other end brings us

51

things that take our breath away.'

Channing was referring to the big air lock at the other end of the station, three miles away, right through the center.

At the center of the dome, there was a sighting 'scope. It kept Polaris on a marked circle, keeping the station exactly even with the Terrestrial North. About the periphery of the dome, looking out across space, the beam-control operators were sitting, each with a hundred-foot parabolic reflector below his position, outside the dome, and under the rim of the transparent bowl. These reflectors shot the interworld signals across space in tight beams, and the men, half the time anticipating the vagaries of space-warp, kept them centered on the proper, shining speck in that field of stars.

Above his head the stars twinkled. Puny man, setting his will against the monstrous void. Puny man, dependent upon atmosphere. ' "Nature abhors a vacuum," said Descartes,' groaned Channing. 'Nuts! If nature abhorred a vacuum, why did she make so much of it?'

Arden Westland entered the apartment without knocking. 'I'd give my right arm up to here for a cigarette,' she said, marking above the elbow with the other hand.

'Na-hah,' said Channing. 'Can't burn oxygen.'

'I know. I'm tired, I'm cold, and I'm ill. Anything you can do for a lady?'

'Not as much as I'd like to do,' said Channing. 'I can't help much. We've got most of the place stopped off with the airtight doors. We've been electrolyzing water, baking $KCIO_3$ and everything else we can get oxy out of. I've a crew of men trying to absorb the CO_2 content and we are losing. Of course, I've known all along that we couldn't support the station on the meager supplies we have on hand. But we'll win in the end. Our micrcosmic world is getting a shot in the arm in a few hours that will reset the balance.'

'I don't see why we didn't prepare for this emergency,' said Arden.

'This station is well balanced. There are enough people here and enough space to make a little world of our own. We can establish a balance that is pretty darned close to perfect. The imperfections are taken care of by influxes of supplies from the system. Until Burbank upset the balance, we could go on forever, utilizing natural purification of air and water. We grow a few vegetables and have some meat critters to give milk and steak. The energy to operate Venus Equilateral is supplied from the uranium pile. Atomic power, if you please. Why should we burden ourselves with a lot of cubic feet of supplies that would take up room necessary to maintain our balance? We are not in bad shape. We'll live, though we'll all be a bunch of tired, irritable people who yawn in one another's faces.'

'And after it is over?'

'We'll establish the balance. Then we'll settle down again. We can take up where we left off,' said Don.

'Not quite. Venus Equilateral has been seared by fire. We'll be tougher and less tolerant of outsiders. If we were a closed corporation before, we'll be tighter than a vacuum-packed coffee can afterwards. And the first bird that cracks us will get hissed at.'

Three superliners hove into sight at the end of thirty-one hours. They circled the station, signaling by helio. They approached the air lock end of the station and made contact. The air lock was opened and space-suited figures swarmed over the South End Landing Stage. A stream of big oxygen tanks was brought into the air lock, admitted, and taken to the last bulwark of huddled people on the fourth level.

From one of the ships there came a horde of men carrying huge square trays of dirt and green, growing sawgrass.

For six hours, Venus Equilateral was the scene of wild,

53

furious activity. The dead air was blown out of bad areas, and the hissing of oxygen tanks was heard in every room. Gradually the people left the fourth level and returned to their rightful places. The station rang with laughter once more, and business, stopped short for want of breath, took a deep lungful of fresh air and went back to work.

The superliners left. But not without taking a souvenir. Francis Burbank went with them. His removal notice was on the first ship, and Don Channing's appointment as Director of Venus Equilateral was on the second.

Happily he entered the Director's office once more. He carried with him all the things that he had removed just a few short weeks before. This time he was coming to stay.

Arden entered the office behind him. 'Home again?' she asked.

'Yop, he grinned at her. 'Open file B, will you, and break out a container of my favorite beverage?'

'Sure thing,' she said.

There came a shout of glee. 'Break out four glasses,' she was told from behind. It was Walt Franks and Joe.

It was Arden that proposed the toast. 'Here's to a closed corporation,' she said. They drank on that.

She went over beside Don and took his arm. 'You see?' she said, looking up into his eyes. 'We aren't the same. Things have changed since Burbank came, and went. Haven't they?'

'They have,' laughed Channing. 'And now that you are my secretary, it is no longer proper for you to shine up to me like that. People will talk.'

'What's he raving about?' asked Joe.

Channing answered, 'It is considered highly improper for a secretary to make passes at her boss. Think of what people will say; think of his wife and kids.'

'You have neither.'

'People?' asked Channing innocently.

54

'No – you ape – the other.'

'Maybe so,' nodded Don, 'but it is still in bad taste for a secretary—'

'No man can use that tone of voice on me!' stormed Arden with a glint in her eye. 'I resign! You can't call me a secretary!'

'But Arden – darling—'

Arden relaxed in the crook of Channing's arm. She winked at Walt and Joe. 'Me—,' she said, 'I've been promoted!'

Interlude:

Maintaining Communications through the worst of interference was a type of problem in which dire necessity demanded
a solution. Often there are other problems of less demanding
nature. These are sometimes called 'projects' because they may
be desirable but are not born of dire necessity.

Barring interference, the problem of keeping communication
with another planet across a hundred million miles of interplanetary space is partially solved by the fact that you can see
your target! Keeping the cross-hairs in a telescope properly
centered is a technical job more arduous than difficult.

But seeing a spacecraft is another problem. Consider the
relative sizes of spacecraft and planet. Where Terra is eight
thousand miles in diameter, the largest of spacecraft is eight
hundred feet long. Reduced to a common denominator and a
simple ratio, it reads that the earth is 50,000 times as large as
the largest spacecraft. Now go outside and take a look at Venus.
At normal distances, it is a mote in the sky. Yet Venus is only
slightly smaller than the earth. Reduce Venus by fifty thousand
times, and no astronomer would ever suspect its existence.

Then take the invisible mote and place it in a volume of
1,000,000,000,000,000,000 cubic miles and he who found the
needle in a haystack is a piker by comparison.

It could have been lives at stake that drove the job out of the
'project' class and into the 'necessity' stage. The fact that it was
the ebb and flow of a mundane thing like money may lower the
quality of glamor.

But there it was – a problem that cried out for a solution; a
man who was willing to pay for the attempt; and a group of
technicians more than happy to tackle the job.

CALLING THE EMPRESS

The chart in the terminal building at Canalopsis Spaceport, Mars, was a huge thing that was the focus of all eyes. It occupied a thirty-by-thirty space in the center of one wall, and it had a far-flung iron railing about it to keep the people from crowding it too close, thus shutting off the view. It was a popular display, for it helped to drive home the fact that space travel was different from anything else. People were aware that their lives had been built upon going from one fixed place to another place, equally immobile. But on interplanet travel, one left a moving planet for another planet, moving at a different velocity. You found that the shortest distance was not a straight line but a space curve involving higher mathematics.

The courses being traveled at the time were marked, and those that would be traversed in the very near future were drawn upon the chart, too; all appropriately labeled. At a glance, one could see that in fifty minutes and seventeen seconds the *Empress of Kolain* would take off from Mars, which was the red disk on the right, and she would travel along the curve so marked to Venus, which was almost one hundred and sixty degrees clockwise around the Sun. People were glad of the chance to go on this trip because the Venus Equilateral Relay Station would come within a telescope's sight on the way.

The *Empress of Kolain* would slide into Venus on the day side; and a few hours later she would lift again to head for Terra, a few degrees ahead of Venus and about thirty million miles away.

Precisely on the zero-zero, The *Empress of Kolain* lifted upward on four tenuous pillars of dull-red glow and drove a hole in the sky. The glow was almost lost in the bright sun-

57

shine, and soon it died. The *Empress of Kolain* became a little world in itself, and would so remain until it dropped onto the ground at Venus, almost two hundred million miles away.

Driving upward, the *Empress of Kolain* could not have been out of the thin Martian atmosphere when a warning bell rang in the telephone and telespace office at the terminal. The bell caught official ears, and all work was stopped as the personnel of the communications office ran to the machine to see what was so important that the 'immediate attention' signal was rung.

Impatiently the operator waited for the tape to come clicking from the machine. It came, letter by letter, click by click, at fifty words per minute. The operator tore the strip from the machine and read aloud: 'Hold *Empress of Kolain.* Reroute to Terra direct. Will be quarantined at Venus. Whole planet in epidemic of Venusian Fever.'

'Snap answer,' growled the clerk. 'Tell 'em: "Too little and too late. *Empress of Kolain* left thirty seconds before warning bell. What do we do now?" '

The operator's fingers clicked madly over the keyboard. Across space went the signal, across the void to the Relay Station. It ran through the Station's mechanism and went darting to Terra. It clicked out as sent in the offices of Interplanet Transport. A vice president read the message and swore roundly. He swore in three Terran languages, in the language of the Venusians, and even managed to visualize a few choice remarks from the Martian Pictographs that were engraved on the Temples of Canalopsis.

'Miss Deane,' he yelled at the top of his voice. 'Take a message! Shoot a line to Channing on Venus Equilateral. Tell him: "*Empress of Kolain* on way to Venus. Must be contacted and rerouted to Terra direct. Million dollars' worth of Martian Line Moss aboard; will perish under quarantine. Spare no expense." Sign that "Keg Johnson, Interplanet." '

'Yes, Mr. Johnson,' said the secretary. 'Right away.'

More minutes of light-fast communication. Out of Terra to Luna, across space to Venus Equilateral. The machines clicked and tape cleared away from the slot. It was pasted neatly on a sheet of official paper, stamped *rush*, and put in a pneumatic tube.

As Don Channing began to read the message, Williams on Mars was chewing worriedly on his fourth fingernail, and Vice President Keg Johnson was working on his second. But Williams had a head start and therefore would finish first. Both men knew that nothing more could be done. If Channing couldn't do it, nobody could.

Channing finished the 'gram and swore. It was a good-natured swear-word, far from downright villification, though it did consign certain items to the nether regions. He punched a button with some relish, and a rather good-looking woman entered. She smiled at him with more intimacy than a secretary should, and sat down.

'Arden, call Walt, will you?'

Arden Westland smiled. 'You might have done that yourself,' she told him. She reached for the call button with her left hand, and the diamond on her finger glinted like a pilot light.

'I know it,' he answered, 'but that wouldn't give me the chance to see you.'

'Baloney,' said Arden. 'You just wait until next October. I'll be in your hair all the time then.'

'By then I may be tired of you,' said Channing with a smile. 'But until then, take it or leave it.' His face grew serious, and he tossed the message across the table to her. 'What do you think of that?'

Arden read, and then remarked: 'That's a huge order, Don. Think you can do it?'

'It'll cost plenty. I don't know whether we can contact a ship in space. It hasn't been done to date, you know, except for short distances.'

The door opened without a knock and Walt Franks walked in. 'Billing and cooing?' he asked. 'Why do you two need an audience?'

'We don't,' answered Don. 'This was business.'

'For want of evidence, I'll believe that. What's the dope?'

'Walt, what are the chances of hooking up with the *Empress of Kolain*, which is en route from Mars to Venus?'

'About equal to a snowball – you know where,' said Franks looking slyly at Arden.

'Take off your coat, Walt. We've got a job.'

'You mean – Hey! Remind me to quit Saturday.'

'This is dead in earnest, Walt.' Don told the engineer all he knew.

'Boy, this is a job I wouldn't want my life to depend on. In the first place, we can't beam a transmitter at them if we can't see 'em. And in the second place, if we did, they couldn't receive us.'

'We can get a good idea of where they are and how they're going,' said Channing. 'That is common knowledge.'

'Astronomy is an exact science,' chanted Franks. 'But by the time we figure out just where the *Empress of Kolain* is with respect to us at any given instant we'll all be old men with gray beards. She's crossing toward us on a skew curve – and we'll have to beam it past Sol. It won't be easy, Don. And then if we do find them, what do we do about it?'

'Let's find them first and then work out a means of contacting them afterwards.'

'Don,' interrupted Arden, 'what's so difficult?'

Franks fell backward into a chair. Don turned to the girl and asked: 'Are you kidding?'

'No. I'm just ignorant. What is so hard about it? We shoot beams across a couple of hundred million miles of space like nothing and maintain communications at any cost. What should be so hard about contacting a ship?'

'In the first place, we can see a planet, and they can see us, so they can hold their beams. A spaceship might be able to see us, but they couldn't hold a beam on us because of the side sway. We couldn't see them until they are right upon us and so we could not hope to hold a beam on them. Spaceships *might* broadcast, but you have no idea what the square law of radiated power will do to a broadcast signal when millions upon millions of miles are counted in. A half million watts on any planet will not quite cover the planet as a service area on broadcast frequencies. But there's a lot of difference between covering a few stinking miles of planet and a volume the size of the Inner Solar System. So they don't try it. A spaceship may as well be on Rigel as far as contacting her in space goes.

'We might beam a wide-dispersion affair at them,' continued Channing. 'But it would be pretty thin by the time it got there. And, having no equipment, they couldn't hear us.'

'May we amend that?' asked Franks. 'They are equipped with radio. But the things are used only in landing operations where the distance is measured in miles, not Astronomical Units.'

'O.K.,' smiled Channing. 'It's turned off during flight and we may consider the equipment as being non-existent.'

'And, according to the chart, we've got to contact them before the turnabout,' offered Arden. 'They must have time to deflect their course to Terra.'

'You think of the nicest complications,' said Channing. 'I was just about to hope that we could flash them, or grab at 'em with a skeeter. But we can't wait until they pass us.'

'That will be the last hope,' admitted Franks. 'But say! Did any bright soul think of shooting a fast ship after them from Canalopsis?'

'Sure. The answer is the same as Simple Simon's answer to the Pieman: "Alas, they haven't any!"'

'No use asking why,' growled Franks. 'O.K., Don, we'll after 'em. I'll have the crew set up a couple of mass detectors at either end of the station. We'll triangulate, and calculate, and hope to hit the right correction factor. We'll find them and keep them in line. You figure out a means of contacting them, huh?'

'I'll set up the detectors and *you* find the means,' suggested Don.

'No go. You're the director of communications.'

Don sighed a false sigh. 'Arden, hand me my electronics text,' he said.

'And shall I wipe your fevered brow?' cooed Arden.

'Leave him alone,' directed Franks. 'You distract him.'

'It seems to me that you two are taking this rather lightly,' said Arden.

'What do you want us to do? Get down on the floor and chew the rug? You know us better than that. If we can find the answer to contacting a spaceship in flight, we'll add another flower to our flag. But we can't do it by clawing through the first edition of Henney's "Handbook of Radio Engineering." It will be done by the seat of our pants, if at all; a pair of side-cutters, and a spool of wire, a hunk of string and a lump of solder, a—'

'A rag, a bone, and a hank of hair?' asked Franks.

'Leave Kipling out of this. He didn't have to cover the entire Solar System. Let's get cooking.'

Don and Walt left the office just a trifle on the fast side. Arden looked after them, out through the open door, shaking her head until she remembered something that she could do. She smiled and went to her typewriter, and pounded out a message back to Keg Johnson at Interplanet. It read:

'CHANNING AND FRANKS AT WORK ON
CONTACTING THE EMPRESS OF KOLAIN.
WILL DO OUR BEST.
                    VENUS EQUILATERAL.'

Unknowing of the storm, the *Empress of Kolain* sped silently
through the void, accelerating constantly at one G. Hour after
hour she was adding to her velocity, building it up to a speed
that would make the trip in days, and not weeks. Her drivers
flared dull red no more, for there was no atmosphere for the
ionic stream to excite. Her few portholes sparkled with light,
but they were nothing in comparison to the starry curtain of
the background.

Her hull was of a neutral color, and though the sun glanced
from her metal flanks, a reflection from a convex side is not
productive of a beam of light. It spreads according to the
degree of convexity and is lost.

What constitutes an apparent absence? The answer to that
question is the example of a ship in space flight. The *Empress
of Kolain* did not radiate anything detectable in the electromagnetic scale from ultralong waves to ultra-high frequencies;
nothing at all that could be detected at any distance beyond a
few thousand miles. The sweep of her meteor-spotting equipment would pass a spot in micro-micro-seconds at a hundred
miles; at the distance from Venus Equilateral the sweep of the
beam would be so fleeting that the best equipment ever known
or made would have no time to react, thus missing the signal.

Theorists claim a thing unexistent if it cannot be detected.
The *Empress of Kolain* was invisible. It was undetectable to
radio waves. It was in space, so no physical wave could be
transmitted to be depicted as sound. Its mass was inconsider-
able. Its size as cosmic sizes go was comparatively sub-micro-
scopic, and therefore it would occult few, if any, stars.

Therefore, to all intents and purposes, the *Empress of Kolain* was non-existent, and would remain in that state of material-non-being until it came to life again upon its landing at Venus.

Yet the *Empress of Kolain* existed in the minds of the men who were to find her. Like the shot unseen, fired from a distant cannon, the *Empress of Kolain* was coming at them with ever-mounting velocity, its unseen course a theoretical curve.

And the ship, like the projectile, would land if the men who knew of her failed in their purpose.

Don Channing and Walt Franks found their man in the combined dining room and bar – the only one in sixty million miles. They surrounded him, ordered a sandwich and beer, and began to tell him their troubles.

Charles Thomas listened for about three minutes. 'Boy,' he grinned, 'being up in that shiny, plush-lined office has sure done plenty to your think-tank, Don.'

Channing stopped talking. 'Proceed,' he said. 'In what way has my perspective been warped?'

'You talk like Burbank,' said Thomas, mentioning a sore spot of some months past. 'You think a mass detector would work at this distance? Nuts, fellow. It might, if there were nothing else in the place to interfere. But you want to shoot out near Mars. Mars is on the other side of the Sun – and Evening Star to anyone on Terra. You want us to shoot a slap-happy beam like a mass detector out past Sol; and then a hundred and forty million miles beyond in the faint hope that you can triangulate upon a little mite of matter; a stinking six hundred-odd feet of aluminum hull mostly filled with air and some machinery and so on. Brother, what do you think all the rest of the planets will do to your piddling little beam? Retract, or perhaps abrogate the law of universal gravitation?'

'Crushed,' said Franks with a sorry attempt at a smile.

'*Phew!*' agreed Channing. 'Maybe I should know more about mass detectors.'

'Forget it,' said Thomas. 'The only thing that mass detectors are any good for is to conjure up beautiful bubble dreams, which anyone who knows about 'em can break with the cold point of icy logic.'

'What would you do?' asked Channing.

'Darned if I know. We might flash 'em with a big mirror – if we had a big mirror and they weren't heading into the Sun.'

'Let's see,' said Franks, making tubulations on the table-cloth. 'They're a couple of hundred million miles away. In order that your mirror present a recognizable disk, it should be about twice the diameter of Venus as seen from Terra. That's eight thousand miles in – at the least visibility – say, eighty million or a thousand-to-one ratio. The *Empress of Kolain* is heading at us from some two hundred million miles, so at a thousand-to-one ratio our mirror would have to be twenty thousands miles across. Some mirror!'

Don tipped Walt's beer over the edge of the table, and while the other man was busy mopping up and muttering unprintables, Don said to Thomas: 'This is serious and it isn't. Nobody's going to lose their skin if we don't, but a problem has been put to us and we're going to crack it if we have to skin our teeth to do it.'

'You can't calculate their position?'

'Sure. Within a couple of hundred thousand miles we can. That isn't close enough.'

'No, it isn't,' agreed Chuck.

Silence fell for a moment. It was broken by Arden, who came in waving a telegram. She sat down and appropriated Channing's glass, which had not been touched. Don opened the sheet and read: 'Have received information of your effort. I repeat, spare no expense!' It was signed: 'Keg Johnson, Interplanet.'

'Does that latter offer mean anything to you?' asked Arden.

'Sure,' agreed Don. 'But at the same time we're stumped.

Should we be doing anything?'

'Anything, I should think, would be better than what you're doing at present. Or does that dinner-and-beer come under "expenses"?'

Arden stood up, tossed Channing's napkin at him, and started toward the door. Channing watched her go, his hand making motions on the tablecloth. His eyes fell to the table and he took Franks' pencil and drew a long curve from a spot of gravy on one side of the table to a touch of coffee stain on the other. The curve went through a bit of grape jelly near the first stain.

'Here goes the tablecloth strategist,' said Franks. 'What now, little man?'

'That spot of gravy,' explained Don, 'is Mars. The jelly is the *Empress of Kolain*. Coffee stain is Venus, and up here by this cigarette burn is Venus Equilateral. Get me?'

'Yop, that's clear enough.'

'Now it would be the job for seventeen astronomers for nine weeks to predict the movements of this jelly spot with respect to the usual astral standards. But, fellows, we know the acceleration of the *Empress of Kolain*, and we know her position with respect to Mars at the instant of take-off. We can correct for Mars' advance along her – or his – orbit. We can figure the position of the *Empress of Kolain* from her angular distance from Mars! That's the only thing we need know. We don't give a ten-dollar damn about her true position.'

Channing began to write equations on the tablecloth. 'You see, they aren't moving so fast in respect to us. The course is foreshortened as they are coming almost in line with Venus Equilateral, curving outward and away from the Sun. Her course, as we see it from the station here, will be a long radius-upward curve, slightly on the parabolic side. Like all long-range cruises the *Empress of Kolain* will hoist herself slightly above the plane of the ecliptic to avoid the swarm of meteors that follow about the Sun in the same plane as the planets, lifting the highest at the point of greatest velocity.'

'I get it,' said Franks. 'We get the best beam controller we have to keep the planet on the cross hairs. We apply a spiral cam to advance the beam along the orbit. Right?'

'Right.' Don sketched a conical section on the tablecloth and added dimensions. He checked his dimensions against the long string of equations and nodded. 'We'll drive this cockeyed-looking cam with an isochronic clock, and then squirt a beam out there. Thank the Lord for the way our beam transmitters work.'

'You mean the effect of reflected waves?' asked Chuck.

'Sure,' grinned Don. 'There's plenty of radar operating at our transmitting frequencies or near by. So far, no one has ever tried to radar anything as small as a spacecraft at that distance, though getting a radar signal from a planet is duck soup. Yet,' he reflected cheerfully, 'there are a couple of things we have handy out here, and one of them is a plethora of power output. We can soup up one of our beam transmitters and use it with a tightened beam to get a radar fix off of the *Empress of Kolain*.'

'And then?' asked Franks.

'Then we will have left the small end, which I'll give to you, Walt, so that you can have part of the credit.'

Walt shook his head. 'The easy part,' he said uncheerfully. 'By which you mean the manner in which we contact them and make them listen to us?'

'That's her,' said Don with a cheerful smile.

'Fine,' said Thomas. 'Now what do we do?'

'Clear up this mess so we can make the cam. This drawing will do, just grab the tablecloth.'

Joe, the operator of Venus Equilateral's one and only establishment for the benefit of the stomach, came up as the three men began to move their glasses and dishes over to an empty table. 'What makes with the tablecloth?' he asked. 'Want a piece of carbon paper and another tablecloth?'

'No,' said Don nonchalantly. 'This single copy will do.'

'We lose lots of tablecloths that way,' said Joe. 'It's tough, running a restaurant on Venus Equilateral. I tried using paper ones once, but that didn't work. I had 'em printed but when the solar system was on 'em, you fellows drew schematic diagrams for a new coupler circuit. I put all kinds of radio circuits on them, and the gang drew plans for antenna arrays. I gave up and put pads of paper on each table, and the boys used them to make folded paper airplanes and they shot them all over the place. Why don't you guys grow up?'

'Cheer up, Joe. But if this tablecloth won't run through the blueprint machine, we'll squawk!'

Joe looked downcast, and Franks hurried to explain: 'It isn't that bad, Joe. We won't try it. We just want to have these figures so we won't have to run through the math again. We'll return the cloth.'

'Yeah,' said Joe at their retreating figures. 'And for the rest of its usefulness it will be full of curves, drawings, and a complete set of astrogating equations.' He shrugged his shoulders and went for a new tablecloth.

Don, Walt and Chuck took their improvised drawing to the machine shop, where they put it in the hands of the master mechanic.

'This thing has a top requirement,' Don told him. 'Make it as quick as you can.'

Master Mechanic Warren took the cloth and said: 'You forgot the note. You know, "Work to dimensions shown, do not scale this drawing." Lord, Don, this silly looking cam will take a man about six hours to do. It'll have to be right on the button all over, no tolerance. I'll have to cut it to the "T" and then lap it smooth with polishing compound. Then what'll you test it on?'

'Sodium light inferometer. Can you do it in four hours?'

'If nothing goes wrong. Brass all right?'

'Anything you say. It'll only be used once. Anything of sufficient hardness for a single usage will do.'

'I'll use brass then. Or free-cutting steel may be better. If you make it soft you have the chance of cutting too much off with your lapping compound. We'll take care of it, Don. The rest of this stuff isn't too hard. Your framework and so on can be whittled out and pasted together from standard girders, right?'

'Sure. Plaster them together any way you can. And we don't want them painted. As long as she works, phooey to the looks.'

'Fine,' said Warren. 'I'll have the whole business installed in the Beam Control Room in nine hours. Complete and ready to work.'

'That nine hours is a minimum?'

'Absolutely. After we cut and polish that screwball cam, we'll have to check it, and then you'll have to check it. Then the silly thing will have to be installed and its concentricity must be checked to the last wave of cadmium light. That'll take us a couple of hours, I bet. The rest of the works will be ready, checked, and waiting for the ding-busted cam.'

'Yeah,' agreed Franks. 'Then we'll have to get up there with our works and put the electricals on the mechanicals. My guess, Don, is a good, healthy twelve hours before we can begin to squirt our signal.'

Twelve hours is not much in the life of a man; it is less in the life of a planet. The Terran Standard of Gravity is so small that it is expressed in feet per second. But when the two are coupled together as a measure of travel, and the standard Terran G is applied for twelve hours steady, it builds up to almost three hundred miles per second, and by the end of that twelve hours, six million miles have fled into the past.

Now take a look at Mars. It is a small, red mote in the sky, its diameter some four thousand miles. Sol is eight hundred thousand miles in diameter. Six million miles from Mars, then, can be crudely expressed by visualizing a point eight times the diameter of the Sun away from Mars, and you have the distance that the *Empress of Kolain* had come from Mars.

But the ship was heading in at an angle, and the six million miles did not subtend the above arc. From Venus Equilateral, the position of the *Empress of Kolain* was more like two diameters of the Sun away from Mars, slightly to the north, and on the side away from Sol.

It may sound like a problem for the distant future, this pointing a radio beam at a planet, but it is no different from Galileo's attempt to see Jupiter through his Optik Glass. Of course, it has had refinements that have enabled man to make several hundred hours of exposure of a star on a photographic plate. So if men maintain a telescope on a star, night after night, to build up a faint image, they can also maintain a beamed transmission wave on a planet.

All you need is a place to stand; a firm, immobile platform. The three-mile-long, one-mile-diameter mass of Venus Equilateral offered such a platform. It rotated smoothly, and upon its 'business' end a hardened and highly polished set of rails maintained projectors that were pointed at the planets. These were parabolic reflections that focused ultra-high-frequency waves into tight beams which were hurled at Mars, Terra, and Venus for communication.

And because the beams were acted upon by all of the trivia in the Solar System, highly trained technicians stood their tricks at the beam controls. In fifty million miles, even the bending of electromagnetic waves by the Sun's mass had to be considered. Sunspots made known their presence. And the vagaries of land transmission were present in a hundred ways due to the distance and the necessity of concentrating every milliwatt of available power on the target.

70

This problem of the *Empress of Kolain* was different. Spaceships were invisible, therefore the beam-control man must sight on Mars and the mechanical cam would keep the ship in sight of the beam.

The hours went past in a peculiar mixture of speed and slowness. On one hand the minutes sped by swiftly and fleetingly, each tick of the clock adding to the lost moments, never to be regained. Time, being precious, seemed to slip through their fingers like sifting sand.

On the other hand, the time that must be spent in preparation of the equipment went slow. Always it was in the future, that time when their experiment must either prove a success or a failure. Always there was another hour of preparatory work before the parabolic reflector was mounted; and then another hour before it swung freely and perfectly in its new mounting. Then the minutes were spent in anticipation of the instant that the power stage of transmitter was tested and the megawatts of ultra-high-frequency energy poured into the single rod that acted as a radiator.

It was a singularly disappointing sight. The rod glowed not, and the reflector was the same as it was before the rod drew power. But the meters read and the generators moaned, and the pyrometers in the insulators mounted as the small quantity of energy lost was converted into heat. So the rod drew power, and the parabolic reflector beamed that power into a tight beam and hurled it out on a die-true line.

Invisible power that could be used in communications.

Then the cam was installed. The time went by even slower then, because the cam must be lapped and polished to absolute perfection, not only of its own surface but to absolute concentricity to the shaft on which it turned.

But eventually the job was finished, and the men stood back, their eyes expectantly upon Don Channing and Walt Franks.

Don spoke to the man chosen to control the beam. 'You can

start any time now. Keep her knifed clean, if you can.'

The man grinned at Channing. 'If the devils that roam the void are with us we'll have no trouble. We should all pray for a phrase used by some characters in a magazine I read once: "Clear ether!" We could use some right now.'

He applied his eyes to the telescope. He fiddled with the verniers for a brief time, made a major adjustment on a larger handwheel, and then said, without removing his eye from the 'scope, 'That's it, Dr. Channing.'

Don answered: 'O.K., Jim, but you can use the screen now. We aren't going to make you squint through that pipe for the next few hours straight.'

'That's all right. I'll use the screen as soon as you can prove we're right. Ready?'

'Ready,' said Channing.

Franks closed a tiny switch. Below, in the transmitter room, relays clicked and heavy-duty contacts closed with blue fire. Meters began to climb upward across their scales, and the generators moaned in a descending whine. A shielded monitor began to glow, indicating that full power was vomiting from the mouth of the reflector.

And out from the projector there went, like a spearhead, a wavefront of circularly polarized microwaves. Die-true they sped, crossing the void like a line of sight to an invisible spot above Mars and to the left. Out past the Sun, where they bent inward just enough to make Jim's job tough. Out across the open sky they sped at the velocity of light, and taking sixteen minutes to get there.

A half-hour passed. 'Now,' said Channing. 'Are we?'

Ten minutes went by. The receiver was silent save for a constant crackle of cosmic static.

Fifteen minutes passed.

'Nuts,' said Channing. 'Could it be that we aren't quite hitting them?'

'Could be,' admitted Franks. 'Jim, waggle that beam a bit, and slowly. When we hit 'em, we'll know it because we'll hear 'em a half-hour later. Take it easy and slowly. We've used up thirteen of our fifty-odd hours. We can use another thirty or so just in being sure.'

Jim began to make the beam roam around the invisible spot in the sky. He swept the beam in microscopic scans, up and down, and advancing the beam by one-half of its apparent width at the receiver for each sweep.

Two more hours went by. The receiver was still silent of reflected signals.

It was a terrific strain, this necessary wait of approximately a half-hour between each minor adjustment and the subsequent knowledge of failure. Jim gave up the 'scope because of eyestrain, and though Don and Walt had confidence that the beam-control man was competent to use the cross-ruled screen to keep Mars on the beam, Jim was none too sure of himself, and so he kept checking the screen against the 'scope.

At the end of the next hour of abject failure, Walt Franks began to scribble on a pad of paper. Don came over to peer over Franks' shoulder, and because he couldn't read Walt's mind, he was forced to ask what the engineer was calculating.

'I've been thinking,' said Franks.

'Beginner's luck?' asked Don with a wry smile.

'I hope not. Look, Don, we're moving on the orbit of Venus, at Venus' orbital velocity. Oh, all right, say it scientifical: We are circling Sol at twenty-one point seven five miles per second. The reflected wave starts back right through the beam, remember?'

'I get it,' shouted Channing in glee. 'Thirty-two minutes' transmission time at twenty-one point seven five miles per second gives us – ah—'

Walt looked up from his slide rule. 'Fifty-two thousand, two hundred and twenty-four miles,' he said.

'Just what I was about to say,' grinned Don.

'But why do you always get there second with your genius?' complained Walt with a pseudo-hurt whine. 'So how to establish it?'

'Can't use space radar for range,' grunted Channing. 'That would louse up the receiver. We've got everything shut off tight, you know. How about some visual loran?'

'Yipe!' exploded Walt. 'How?'

'I'd suggest an optical range finder excepting that the baseline of three miles – the length of Venus Equilateral – isn't long enough to triangulate for that fifty-two thousand—'

'Two hundred and twenty-four miles,' finished Walt with a grin. 'Proceed, genius, with caution.'

'So we mount a couple of mirrors at either end of the station, and key a beam of light from the center, heading each way. When the pulses arrive at the space flitter at the same time, he's in position. We'll establish original range by radar, of course, but once the proper interval or range is established, the pilot can maintain his own position by watching the pulsed-arrival of the twin-flickers of light. Just like loran, excepting that we'll use light, and we can key it so it will run alternately, top and bottom. To maintain the proper angle, all the pilot will have to do is to keep the light alternating – fluently. And overlapping will show him that he's drifted.'

'Fine!' glowed Walt. 'Now, how the devil long will it take?'

'Ask the boys, Walt,' suggested Don.

Walt made a canvass of the machine shop gang, and came back, saying: 'Couple of hours, God willing.'

The mounting of the mirrors at either end of the station took little time. It was the amount of detailed work that took time; the devising of the interrupting mechanism; and the truing-up of the mirrors that took the time.

Then it became evident that there was more. There were several hundred doorways centered on the axis of Venus Equilateral that must be opened, the space cleared of packing cases, supplies, and in a few cases machinery had to be partially dismantled to clear the way. A good portion of Venus Equilateral's personnel of three thousand were taken off their jobs, haled out of bed for the emergency, or made to work through their play period, depending upon which shift they worked.

The machinery could be replaced, the central storage places could be refilled, and the many doors closed again. But the central room containing the air plant was no small matter. Channing took a sad look at the lush growth of Martian sawgrass and sighed. It was growing nicely now, they had nurtured it into lusty growth from mere sprouts in trays and it was as valuable – precisely – as the lives of the three thousand-odd that lived, loved, and pursued happiness on Venus Equilateral. It was a youthful plant, a replacement brought in a tearing hurry from Mars to replace the former plant that was heaved out by the well-meaning Burbank.

Channing closed his eyes and shuddered in mock horror. 'Chop out the center,' he said.

The 'center' meant the topmost fronds of the long blades; their roots were embedded in the trays that filled the cylindrical floor. Some of the blades would die – Martian sawgrass is tender in spite of the wicked spines that line the edge – but this was an emergency with a capital E.

Cleaning the centermost channel out of the station was no small job. The men who put up Venus Equilateral had no idea that someone would be using the station for a sighting tube some day. The many additions to the station through the years made the layout as regular and as well-planned as the Mammoth Cave in Kentucky.

So for hour upon hour, men swarmed in the central, weightless channel and wielded acetylene torches, cutting steel. Not in all cases, but there were many. In three miles of storage rooms, a lot of doors and bulkheads can be thrown up without

75

crowding the size of the individual rooms.

Channing spoke into the microphone at the north end of Venus Equilateral, and said: 'Walt? We've got a sight. Can you see?'

'Yop,' said Walt. 'And say, what happens to me after that bum guess?'

'That was quite a stretch, Walt. That "hour, God willing," worked itself into four hours, God help us.'

'O.K., so I was optimistic. I thought that those doors were all on the center line.'

'They are supposed to be, but they aren't huge and a little misalignment can do a lot of light-stopping. Can we juggle mirrors now?'

'Sure as shooting. Freddie in the flitter?'

'Yup. He thinks he's at the right distance now. But he's got a light outfit, and this radar can be calibrated to the foot. Is the mirror-dingbat running?'

'We're cooking with glass right now.'

'Brother,' groaned Channing, 'if I had one of those death rays that the boys were crowing about back in the days before space-hopping became anything but a bit of fiction, I'd scorch your ears – or burn 'em off – or blow holes in you – or disintegrate you – depending on what stories you read. I haven't heard such a lousy pun in seventeen years – Hey, Freddie, you're a little close. Run out a couple of miles, huh? – and, Walt, I've heard some doozies.'

There was a click in the phones and a cheerful voice chimed in with: 'Good morning, fellows. What's with the Great Quest?'

Channing answered. 'Hi, Babe, been snoozing?'

'Sure, as any sensible person would. Have you been up all the time?'

'Yeah. We're still up against the main trouble with telephones – the big trouble, same as back in 1887 – our friends have no telephone! You'd be surprised how elusive a spaceship can be in the deep. Sort of a nonexistent, microscopic speck, floating in absolutely nothing. We have a good idea of where they should be, and possibly why and what – but we're really playing with blindfolds, handcuffs, ear plugs, mufflers, nose clamps, and tongue-ties. I am reminded – Hey, Freddie, about three more hundred yards – of the two blind men.'

'Never mind the blind men,' came back the pilot. 'How'm I doing?'

'Fine. Slide out another hundred yards and hold her there.'

'Who – me? Listen, Dr. Channing, you're the bird on the tape line. You have no idea just how insignificant you look from fifty-odd thousand miles away. Put a red-hot on the 'finders and have 'im tell me where the ship sits.'

'O.K., Freddie, you're on the beam and I'll put a guy on here to give you the dope. Right?'

'Right!'

'Right,' echoed Arden breaking in on the phone. 'And I'm going to bring you a slug of coffee and a roll. Or did you remember to eat recently?'

'We didn't,' chimed in Walt.

'You get your own girl,' snorted Channing. 'And besides, you are needed up here. We've got work to do.'

Once again the signal lashed out. The invisible waves drove out and began their swift rush across the void. Time, as it always did during the waiting periods, hung like a Sword of Damocles. The half-hour finally ticked away, and Freddie called in: 'No dice. She's as silent as the grave.'

Minutes added together into an hour. The concentric wave left the reflector and just dropped out of sight.

'Too bad you can't widen her out,' suggested Don.

'I'd like to tighten it down,' objected Walt. 'I think we're losing power and we can't increase the power – but we could tighten the beam.'

77

'Too bad you can't wave it back and forth like a fireman squirting water on a lawn,' said Arden.

'Firemen don't water lawns—' began Walt Franks, but he was interrupted by a wild yell from Channing.

'Something hurt?' asked Arden.

'No, Walt, we can wave the beam.'

'Until we find 'em? We've been trying that. No worky.'

Freddie called in excitedly: 'Something went by just now and I don't think it was Christmas!'

'We might have hit 'em a dozen times in the last ten minutes and we'll never know it,' said Channing. 'But the spaceliners can be caught. Let's shoot at them like popping ducks. Shotgun effect. Look, Walt, we can electronically dance the beam at a high rate of speed, spraying the neighborhood. Freddie can hear us return because we have to hit them all the time and the waver coming on the way back will pass through his position again and again. We'll set up director elements in the reflector, distorting the electrical surface of the parabolic reflector. That'll divert the beam. By making the phases swing right, we can scan the vicinity of the *Empress of Kolain* like a flying spot television camera.'

Walt turned to one of the technicians and explained. The man nodded. He left Franks' laboratory and Walt turned back to his friends.

'Here shoots another couple of hours. I, for one, am going to grab forty winks.'

Jim, the beam-control man, sat down and lighted a cigarette. Freddie let his flitter coast free. And the generators that fed the powerful transmitter came whining to a stop. But there was no sleep for Don and Walt. They kept awake to supervise the work, and to help in hooking up the phase-splitting circuit that would throw out-of-phase radio frequency into the director-elements to swing the beam.

Then once again the circuits were set up. Freddie found the

position again and began to hold it. The beam hurled out again, and as the phase-shift passed from element to element, the beam swept through an infinitesimal arc that covered thousands of miles of space by the time the beam reached the position occupied by the *Empress of Kolain.*

Like a painter, the beam painted in a swipe a few hundred miles wide and swept back and forth, each sweep progressing ahead of the stripe before by less than its width. It reached the end of its arbitrary wall and swept back to the biginning again, covering space as before. Here was no slow, irregular swing of mechanical reflector, this was the electronically controlled wavering of a stable antenna.

And this time the half hour passed slowly but not uneventfully. Right on the tick of the instant, Freddie called back: 'Got 'em!'

It was a weakling beam that came back in staccato surges. A fading, wavering, spotty signal that threatened to lie down on the job and sleep. It came and it went, often gone for seconds and never strong for so much as a minute. It vied and almost lost completely, with the constant crackle of cosmic static. It fought with the energies of the Sun's corona and was more than once the underdog. Had this returning beam carried intelligence of any sort it would have been wasted. About all that could be carried on a beam as sorry as this was the knowledge that there was a transmitter – and that it was transmitting.

But its raucous note synchronized with the paint-brush wiping of the transmitter. There was no doubt.

Don Channing put an arm around Arden's waist and grinned at Walt Franks. 'Go to work, genius. I've got the *Empress of Kolain* on the pipe. You're the bright-eyed lad that is going to wake them up! We've shot almost twenty hours of our allotted fifty. Make with the megacycles, Walter. Arden and I will take in a steak, a moom pitcher, and maybe a bit of woo. Like?' he asked the girl.

'I like,' she answered.

Walt Franks smiled and stretched lazily. He made no move to the transmitter. 'Don't go away,' he cautioned them. 'Better call up Joe and order beer and sandwiches for the boys in the back room. On you!'

'Make with the signals first,' said Channing. 'And lay off the potables until we finish this silly job.'

'You've got it. Is there a common, garden variety, transmitting key in the place?'

'Probably. We'll have to ask. Why?'

'Ask me.'

Don removed his arm from Arden's waist. He picked up a spanner and advanced on Franks.

'Na!' objected Arden. 'Poison him – I can't stand the sight of blood. Or better, bamboo splinters under the fingernails. He knows something simple, the big bum!'

'Beer and sandwiches?' asked Walt.

'Beer and sandwiches,' agreed Don. 'Now, Tom Swift, what gives?'

'I want to key the beam. Y'see, Don, we're using the same frequency, by a half dozen megacycles, as their meteor spotter. I'm going to retune the beam to their frequency and key it. Realize what'll happen?'

'Sure,' agreed Don, 'but you're still missing the boat. You can't transmit keyed intelligence with an intermittent contact.'

'In words, what do you mean, Don?' asked Arden.

'International Code is a series of dots and dashes, you may know. Our wabbling beam is whipping through the area in which the *Empress of Kolain* is passing. Therefore the contact is intermittent. And how could you tell a dot from a dash?'

'Easy,' bragged Walt Franks. 'We're not limited to the speed of deviation, are we?'

'Yes – limited by the speed of the selsyn motors that transfer the phase-shifting circuits to the director radiators. Yeah, I get it, Edison, and we can wind them up to a happy six or eight thousand r. p. m. Six would get us a hundred cycles per second – a nice, low growl.'

'And how will they receive that kind of signal on the meteor spotter?' asked Arden.

'The officer of the day will be treated to the first meteor on record that has intermittent duration – it is there only when it spells in International Code!'

Prying the toy transmitting key from young James Burke was a job only surpassed in difficulty by the task of opening the vault of the Interplanetary Bank after working hours. But Burke, Junior, was plied with soda pop, ice cream, and candy. He was threatened, cajoled, and finally bribed. And what Venus Equilateral paid for the toy finally would have made the toy manufacturer go out and look for another job. But Walt Franks carried the key to the scene of operations and set it on the bench to look at it critically.

'A puny gadget, at that,' he said, clicking the key. 'Might key a couple of hundred watts with it – but not too long. She'd go up like a skyrocket under our load!'

Walt opened up a cabinet and began to pull out parts. He piled several parts on a bread board, and in an hour had a very husky thyraton hooked into a circuit that was simplicity itself. He hooked the thyraton into the main power circuit and tapped the key gingerly. The transmitter followed the keyed thyraton and Don took a deep breath.

'Do you know code?' he asked.

'Used to. Forgot it when I came to Venus Equilateral. Used to hold a ham ticket on Terra. But there's no use hamming on the station here where you can wake somebody by yelling at the top of your voice. The thing to ask is, "Does anyone know code on board the *Empress of Kolain*?"'

They forgot their keying circuit and began to adjust the transmitter to the frequency used by the meteor spotter. It was a job. But it was done, all the way from the master oscillator stage through the several frequency doubler stages and to the big power-driver stage. The output stage came next, and then a full three hours of tinkering with files and hacksaws were required to adjust the length of the main radiator and the director elements so that their length became right for the changed frequency.

Finally Walt took the key and said: 'Here goes!'

He began to rattle the key. In the power room the generators screamed and the lights throughout the station flickered just a bit at the sudden surges.

Don Channing said to Arden: 'If someone of the *Empress of Kolain* can understand code—'

The *Empress of Kolain* was zipping along in its silent passage through the void. It was an unseen, undetected, unaware bit of human manufacture marking man's will among the stars. In all the known universe it moved against the forces of celestial mechanics because some intelligent mote that infested the surface of a planet once had the longing to visit the stars. In all the Solar System, most of the cosmic stuff was larger than it – but it alone defied the natural laws of space.

Because it alone possessed the required *outside* force spoken of in Newton's 'Universal Laws'.

And it was doing fine.

Dinner was being served in the dining room. A group of shapely girls added grace to the swimming pool on the promenade deck. The bar was filled with a merry crowd which in turn were partly filled with liquor. A man in uniform, the Second Officer, was throwing darts with a few passengers in the playroom, and there were four oldish ladies on sabbatical leave who were stricken with *mal-de-void*.

The passage up to now had been uneventful. A meteor or two had come to make the ship swing a bit – but the swerve was less than the pitch of an ocean vessel in a moderate sea and it did not continue as did an ocean ship. Most of the time the *Empress of Kolain* seemed as steady as solid rock.

Only the First Officer, on the bridge, and the Chief Pilot, far below in the Control Room, knew just how erratic their course truly was. But they were not worried. They were not a shell, fired from a gun; they were a spaceship, capable of steering themselves into any port on Venus when they arrived and the minute wobbulations in their course could be corrected when the time came. For nothing had ever prevented a ship of space from seeing where it was going.

Yes, it was uneventful.

Then the meteor screen flashed into life. A circle of light appeared in the celestial globe and the ship's automatic pilot swerved ever so little. The dot of light was gone.

Throughout the ship, people laughed nervously. A waiter replaced a glass of water that had been set too close to the edge of the table and a manly-looking fellow dived into the swimming pool to haul a good-looking blonde to the edge again. She'd been in the middle of a swan dive when the swerve came and the ship had swerved without her. The resounding smack of feminine stomach against the water was of greater importance than the meteor, now so many hundred miles behind.

The flash of light returned and the ship swerved again. Upon the third swerve, the First Officer was watching the celestial globe with suspicion. He went white. It was conceivable that the *Empress of Kolain* was about to encounter a meteor shower.

And that was bad.

He marked the place and set his observation telescope in synchronism with the celestial globe. He searched the sky. There was nothing but the ultimate starry curtain in the background. He snapped a switch and the voice of the pilot came out of a speaker in the wall.

'You called, Mr. Hendall?'

'Tony, take the levers, will you please? Something is rotten in the State of Denmark.'

'O.K., sir. I'm riding personal.'

'Kick out the meteor-spotting coupling circuits and forget the alarm.'

'Right, Mr Hendall, but will you confirm that in writing?'

Hendall scribbled on the telautograph and then abandoned the small 'scope. The flashing in the celestial globe continued, but the ship no longer danced in its path. Hendall went up into the big dome.

The big twenty-inch Cassegrain showed nothing at all, and Hendall returned to the bridge scratching his head. Nothing on the spotting 'scope and nothing on the big instrument.

That intermittent spot was large enough to mean a huge meteor. But wait. At the speed of the *Empress*, it should have retrogressed in the celestial globe unless it was so huge and so far away – but Sol didn't appear on the globe and it was big and far away, bigger by far. Nothing short of a planet at less-than-planetary distances would do this.

Not even a visible change in the position of the spot.

'Therefore,' thought Hendall, 'this is no astral body that makes this spot!'

Hendall went to a cabinet and withdrew a cable with a plug on either end. He plugged one end into the test plug on the meteor spotter and the opposite end into the speaker. A low humming emanated from the speaker in synchronism with the flashing of the celestial globe.

It hit a responsive chord.

Hendall went to the main communication microphone and spoke. His voice went all over the *Empress of Kolain* from pilot room and cargo spaces to swimming pool and infirmary.

'Attention!' he said in a formal voice. 'Attention to official orders!'

Dancers stopped in midstep. Swimmers paused and then made their way to the edges of the pool and sat with their feet dangling in the warm water. Diners sat with their forks poised foolishly.

'Official orders!' meant an emergency.

Hendall continued: 'I believe that something never before tried is being attempted. I am forced against my better knowledge to believe that some agency is trying to make contact with us; a spaceship in flight! This is unknown in the annals of space flying and is, therefore, indicative of something important. It would not have been tried without preparations unless an emergency exists.

'However, the requirements of an officer of space do not include a knowledge of code because of the lack of communication with the planets while in space. Therefore, I request that any person with a working knowledge of International Morse will please present himself to the nearest officer.'

Minutes passed. Minutes during which the flashing lights continued.

Then the door of the bridge opened and Third Officer Jones entered with a thirteen-year-old youngster at his heels. The boy's eyes went wide at the sight of the instruments on the bridge, and he looked around in amazed interest.

'This is Timmy Harris,' said Jones. 'He knows code!'

'Go to it, Mr. Harris,' said Hendall.

The boy swelled visibly. You could almost hear him thinking: 'He called me "mister"!'

Then he went to the table by the speaker and reached for pencil and paper. 'It's code all right,' he said. Then Timmy winked at Jones. 'He has a lousy fist!'

Timmy Harris began to write.

'—course and head for Terra direct' – the beam faded for

seconds – 'Venusian fever and you will be quarantined.

'Calling CQ, calling CQ, calling CQ. Calling *Empress of Kolain* . . . empowered us to contact you and convey . . . message – you are requested to correct your course and head . . . a plague of Venusian fever and you – Johnson of Interplanet has empowered us . . . the following message: "You are requested to correct your . . . head for Terra direct." Calling CQ . . .'

'Does that hash make sense to you?' asked Jones of Hendall.

'Sure,' smiled Hendall, 'it is fairly plain. It tells us that Keg Johnson of Interplanet wants us to head for Terra direct because of a plague of Venusian fever that would cause us to stay in quarantine. That would ruin the Line Moss. Prepare to change course, Mr. Jones!'

'Who could it be?' asked Jones foolishly.

'There is only one outfit in the Solar System that could possibly think of a stunt like this. And that is Channing and Franks. This signal came from Venus Equilateral!'

'Wait a minute,' said Timmy Harris. 'Here's some more.'

' "As soon as this signal – intelligible – at right angles to your course for ten minutes. That will take – out of – beam and reflected – will indicate to us – left the area and know of our attempt." '

'They're using a beam of some sort that indicates to them that we are on the other end but we can't answer. Mr. Jones, and Pilot Canton, ninety degrees north for ten minutes! Call the navigation officer to correct our course. I'll make the announcement to the passengers. Mr. Harris, you are given the freedom of the bridge for the remainder of the trip.'

Mr. Harris was overwhelmed. He'd learn plenty – and that would help him when he applied for training as a space officer; unless he decided to take a position with Venus Equilateral when he grew up.

The signal faded from the little cruiser and silence prevailed.

Don spoke into the microphone and said: 'Run her up a millisecond,' to the beam controller. The beam wiped the space above the previous course for several minutes and Franks was sending furiously:

'You have answered our message. We'll be seeing you!'

Channing told the man in the cruiser to return. He kicked the main switch and the generators whined down the scale and coasted to a stop. Tube filaments darkened and meters returned to zero.

'O.K., Warren. Let the spinach lay. Get the next crew to clean up the mess and polish the set-up into something presentable. I'll bet a cooky that we'll be chasing spaceships all the way to Pluto after this. We'll work it into a fine thing and perfect our technique. Right now I owe the gang a dinner.'

Interlude:

When necessity dictates a course of action and the course of action proves valuable, it is but a short step to the inclusion of the answer into the many facets of modern technical civilization. Thus it was that not many months after Venus Equilateral successfully established planet-to-planet communications with the 'Empress of Kolain' that all course constants were delivered to the relay station and thereafter messages were transmitted as a part of the regular business of Interplanetary Communications.

This, of course, offered another problem. Ships in space were in the position of being able to catch messages but were not able to answer back. It would take, perhaps, another emergency to set up conditions which demanded the reverse of the problem of contacting a ship in space.

But there was a more immediate problem. Spacecraft were protected from meteors by means of radar that was coupled to the steering panels of the ships; when a meteor threatened, the ship merely turned aside by that fraction of a degree that gave it safety.

It took, however, but a few meteors, and the resulting few fractions of a degree to shut the swiftly moving ship out of the coverage-area of the ship-seeking beams from Venus Equilateral. Then the power and ingenuity of Venus Equilateral was wasted on vacant space and the messages intended for the ships went undelivered.

Since the ship must avoid meteors, and the meteors could not be diverted from their courses, there was but one answer: Swerve the ship and let the messages go hang, for a message is of no use to a riddled spacecraft!

But, thought several people, if the meteor cannot be steered, perhaps it might be removed. . . .

Walter Franks sat in the director's office; his feet on the director's desk. He was smoking one of the director's cigarettes. He was drinking the director's liquor, filched shamelessly from the director's private filing cabinet where it reposed in the drawer marked 'S'. Drawer 'B' would have given beer, but Walt preferred Scotch.

He leaned forward and dropped the director's cigarette into the director's wastebasket and then he pressed the button on the desk and looked up.

But it was not the director's secretary who entered. It was his own, but that did not disturb Franks. He knew that the director's ex-secretary was off on Mars enjoying a honeymoon with the director.

Jeanne entered and smiled. 'Must you call me in here to witness you wasting the company's time?' she asked in mock anger.

'Now look, Jeanne, this is what Channing does.'

'No dice. You can't behave as Don Channing behaves. The reason is my husband.'

'I didn't call to have you sit on my lap. I want to know if the mail is in.'

'I thought so,' she said. 'And I brought it in with me. Anything more?'

'Not until you get a divorce,' laughed Franks.

'You should live so long,' she said with a smile. She stuck her tongue out at him.

Walt thumbed his way through the mail, making notations on some, and setting others aside for closer reading. He came to one and tossed it across the desk to Jeanne. She took the message and read:

DEAR ACTING DIRECTOR:
HAVING A WOMDERFUL HONEYMOON; GLAD
YOU AREN'T HERE.   DON AND ARDEN.

'Wonderful stuff, love,' smiled Franks.

'It is,' agreed Jeanne. A dreamy look came into her eyes.

'Scram, Jeanne. There are times when you can't work worth a darn. Mostly when you're thinking of that husband of yours. What's he got that I haven't?'

'Me,' said Jeanne slyly. She arose and started for the door. 'Oh,' she said, 'I almost forgot. Warren phoned and said that the turret is ready for a try-out.'

'Fine,' said Walt. 'Swell.' He unfolded himself from the chair with alacrity and almost beat the girl to the door.

'My,' she laughed, 'you can move after all.'

'Sure,' he grinned. 'Now that I have something for which to live.'

'I hope it's worth it. You've sunk a lot of change into that bug-house.'

'I know, but we can stand it. After all, since Don took over this affair, Venus Equilateral is an up and running business. We're out of the Government subsidy class now, and are making money. If this works, we'll make more. It's worth a gamble.'

'What are you trying to build?' asked Jeanne.

'Why, since this business of contacting ships-at-space has become so universally liked, we have a tough time keeping ships on the mobile beam. That's because they are always ducking out of the way of loose meteorites and stuff, and that screws up their course. We can't see 'em, and must take their position on the basis of their expected course. We never know whether we hit 'em until they land.

'Now, I've been trying to devise a space gun that will blast meteors directly instead of avoiding them by coupling the meteor detector to the autopilot.'

'Gonna shoot 'em out of existence?'

'Not exactly. Popping at them with any kind of a rifle would be like trying to hit a flying bird with a spitball. Look, Jeanne, speed on the run from Mars to Terra at major opposition is up among the thousands of miles per second at the turnover. A meteor itself may be blatting along at fifty miles per second. Now a rifle, shooting a projectile at a few thousand feet per second, would be useless. You have the meteor in your lap and out of the other side while the projectile is making up its mind to move forward and relieve the pressure that is building up behind it due to the exploding powder.

'I've designed an electron gun. It is a superpowered, over-sized edition of the kind they used to use in kinescope tubes, oscilloscope tubes, and electron microscopes. Since the dingbat is to be used in space, we can leave the works of the gun open and project a healthy stream of electrons at the offending object without their being slowed and dispersed by an impending atmosphere.'

'But that sounds like shooting battleships with a toy gun.'

'Not so fast on the objections, gal,' said Franks. 'I've seen a simple oscilloscope tube with a hole in the business end. It was burned right through a quarter inch of glass because the fellows were taking pix and had the intensity turned up high. The sweep circuit blew a fuse and the beam stopped on one spot. That was enough to puncture the screen.'

'I see. That was just a small affair.'

'A nine-inch tube. The electron gun in a nine-inch kinescope tube is only about four inches long and three-quarters of an inch in diameter. Mine, out there in the turret, is six feet in diameter and thirty feet long. I can fire out quite a bundle of electrons from a tube of that size.'

'It sounds as though you mean business.'

'I do. This is the right place to do research of that kind. Out here on Venus Equilateral, we're in a natural medium for an electron gun, and we've the power requirements to run it. I can't think of any place in the system that offers better chances.'

'When are you going to try it out?'

'As soon as a meteor comes over the pile, as long as Warren says we're ready.'

Jeanne shook her head. 'I wish Channing were here. Things are wild enough when you are both working on something screwball, but I could get scared something fierce at the thought of either one of you working without the other.'

'Why?'

'You two sort of act as balance wheels to one another's craziness. Oh, don't take that word to heart. Everybody on the relay station thinks the world of you two, myself included. *Craziness* in this case means a sort of friendly description of the way your brains work. Both of you dash off on tangents now and then, and when either one of you get off the beam, the other one seems to swing the weight required to bring the lost one back to the fold.'

'That's a real mess of mixed metaphors, Jeanne. But I am going to surprise Don hairless when he gets back here and finds that I've done what people claimed couldn't be done. I'm going to be the bird whose bust sits in the Hall of Fame in between Edison, Einstein, Alexander Graham Bell, S. F. B. Morse, and—'

'Old Man River, Jack Frost, and Little Boy Blue,' laughed Jeanne. 'I hope it's not a bust, Walt.'

'You mean I should have a whole statue?'

'I mean, I hope your dream is not a bust.'

Jeanne left, with Walt right behind her. Franks did not remain at the desk, however, but made his way from the office level to the outer skin of the relay station by way of a not-often-used stairway that permitted him to drop to the outer skin. Above his head were the first levels of apartmental cubicles occupied by the personnel of Venus Equilateral. Out here, Walt had but a scant thickness of steel between him and the void of space.

Franks came to a room built from outer skin to inner skin and about fifty feet in diameter. He unlocked the door with a key on his watch chain, and entered. Warren was waiting for him.

'Hi, ordnance expert. We're ready as soon as they are.'

'How's she working?'

'I should know? We've been squirting ropes of electrons out to blank space for hours. She gets rid of them all right. But have we done any good? I dunno.'

'Not a meteor in sight, I suppose.'

'The detector hasn't blinked once. But when she does, your electron gun will pick it up a thousand miles before it gets here, and will follow the darned thing until it gets a half thousand miles out of sight.'

'That sounds fine. It's a good thing that we don't have to swivel that mess of tube around a whole arc in actual use. It would take too long. But we'll put one in each quadrant of a spaceship and devise it so that its working arc will be small enough to make it work. Time enough to find that out after we know if it works.'

'That's something that I've been wondering about,' said Warren, 'Why didn't we build a small one out here and evacuate the skin for a few hundred feet? We could set up a few chunks of iron and squirt electrons at them.'

'And have the folks upstairs screaming? Nope. I've a hunch that when this beam hits something hard, it will create quite a ruckus. It would be fine to have a hunk blown right off the skin, wouldn't it?'

'Guess you're right,' admitted Warren.

The meteor alarm flashed, and a bell dinged once.

'Here's our chance,' snapped Walt. 'We've about fifteen seconds to work on this one.'

He looked out of a tiny window, and saw that the big tube

had lined up with the tiny model that was a monitor for the big tube. He sighted through the model, which in itself was a high-powered telescope, and he saw the jagged meteor rushing forward at an angle to the station. It would miss by many miles, but it would offer a good target.

'Cathode's hot,' said Warren.

Walt Franks grasped the power switch and thrust it down part way. Meters leaped up their scales and from somewhere there came the protesting whine of tortured generators. Through the window, nothing very spectacular was happening. The cathode glowed slightly brighter due to the passage of current through its metal and out of the coated surface. But the electrostatic stresses that filled the gaps between the accelerator and focussing anodes was no more visible than the electricity that runs a toy motor. Its appearance had not changed a bit, but from the meters, Walt Franks knew that megawatts of electronic power, in the shape of high-velocity electrons, were being poured from the cathode, accelerated by the ring anodes; and focussed to a narrow beam by the focussing anodes. And from the end of the framework that supported these anodes, a stream of high-velocity electrons poured forth, twelve inches in diameter.

Through the telescope, the meteor did not seem to be disturbed. It exploded not, neither did it melt. It came on inexorably, and if the inanimate nickel and iron of a meteor can be said to have such, it came on saucily and in utter disregard for the consequences.

Frantically, Walt cranked the power up higher and higher, and the lights all over the station dimmed as the cathode gun drained the resources of the station.

Still no effect.

Then in desperation, Walt slammed the lower lever down to the bottom notch. The girders strained in the tube from the terrific electrostatic stresses, and for a second, Walt was not certain that the meteor was not finally feeling the effects of the electron bombardment.

He was not to be sure, for the experiment came to a sudden stop.

An insulator arced where it led the high-voltage lines that fed the anodes through the wall. Immediately it flashed over, and the room filled to the brim with the pungent odor of burning insulation. A medium-voltage anode shorted to one of the high-voltage anodes, and the stress increased in the tube. They broke from the moorings, these anodes, and plunged backward, down the tube toward the cathode. They hit, and it was enough to jar the whole tube backward on the gimbals.

The shock warped the mounting of the tube, and it flexed slightly, but sufficiently to bring the farthermost and highest voltage anode into the electron stream. It glowed redly, and the secondary emission raved back through the series of electrodes, heating them and creating more warpage.

Then the pyrotechnics stopped. Great circuit breakers crashed open up in the power room hundreds of feet above them, high in the station.

Walt Franks looked out through the window at the tangled mess that had been a finely machined piece of equipment. He saw the men looking quizzically at him as he turned away from the window, and with a smile that cost him an effort, he said: 'All right, so Marconi didn't WLW on his first try, either. Come on, fellows, and we'll clean up this mess.'

With the utter disregard that inanimate objects show toward the inner feelings of the human being, the meteor alarm blinked again and the bell rang. The pilot tube swiveled quickly to one side, lining up with the spot in the celestial globe of the meteor detector. In the turret that housed the big tube, motors strove against welded commutators and the big tube tried to follow.

Walt looked at the pointing tube and said: 'Bah! Go ahead and point!'

*   *   *

95

Don Channing smiled at Arden. 'Mrs. Channing,' he said, 'must you persist in keeping me from my first love?'

Arden smiled winningly. 'Naturally. That's what I'm here for. I intend to replace your first love entirely and completely.'

'Yeah,' drawled Don, 'and what would we live on?'

'I'll permit you to attend to your so-called first love during eight hours every day, provided that you remember to think of me every half-hour.'

'That's fine. But you really aren't fair about it. We were on Terra for two weeks. I was just getting interested in a program outlined by one of the boys that works for Interplanet, and what happened? You hauled me off to Mars. We stayed for a week at the Terraland Hotel at Canalopsis and the first time that Keg Johnson came to see us with an idea and a sheaf of papers, you rushed me off to Lincoln Head. Now I'm scared to death that some guy will try to open a blueprint here; at which I'll be rushed off to Palanortis Country until someone finds us there. Then it'll be the Solar Observatory on Mercury or the Big Glass on Luna.'

Arden soothed Don's ruffled feelings by sitting on his lap and snuggling. 'Dear,' she said in a voice that positively dripped, 'we're on a honeymoon, remember?'

Don stood up, dumping Arden to the floor. 'Yeah,' he said, 'but this is the highest velocity honeymoon that I ever took!'

'And it's the first one I was ever on where the bridegroom took more time admiring beam installations than he took to whisper sweet nothings to his gal. What has a beam transmitter got that I haven't got?'

'One: Its actions can be predicted. Two: It can be controlled. Three: It never says anything original, but only repeats what it has been told. Four: It can be turned off.'

'Yeah?' Drawled Arden, grinning wisely. 'And how about this rumor?'

'Rumor?' asked Channing innocently.

'Yes – rumor!' stormed Arden with a chuckle. 'Keep you from your first love, me eye. I'll play second fiddle to nothing, Donald. I'll just replace your original first love, but I'm too stinking bright to make you forget it entirely. That, my sweet, is why I've brought you here. You can go chase the rumor whilst I do a bit of shopping. May I borrow your checkbook?'

'Rumor?' repeated Channing with some puzzlement, 'What rumor?'

'Rumor has it,' said Arden in hyperbolic tones, 'that two gentlemen, by name James Baler and Bernard Carroll, who have spent years digging up and studying the ancient Martian Artifacts, have recently uncovered a large and strange type of vacuum tube that seems to have been used by the Martians as a means of transmitting power. Since I felt that the time had come for the honeymooners to spend at least eight minutes apart, I insisted upon Lincoln Head for our next stop because Lincoln Head happens to have been the scene of some rare happenings, if rumor—'

'Oh, nuts,' grinned Channing. 'That's no rumor—'

'And you let me ramble on,' cried Arden.

She caught Don on the point of the chin with a pillow and effectively smothered him. She followed her advantage with a frontal attack that carried him backward across the bed, where she landed on top viciously and proceeded to lambaste him with the other pillow.

It was proceeding according to plan, this private, good-natured war, until a knock on the door brought a break in operations. Channing struggled out from beneath Arden and went to the door, trying to comb his hair by running spread fingers through it. He went with a sense of failure caused by Arden's quiet laugh and the statement that he resembled a bantam rooster.

The man at the door apologized, and then said: 'I'm Doug Ferris of the *Triworld News*.'

'Come in,' said Don, 'and see if you can find a place to sit.'

'Thanks.'

'I didn't know that *Triworld News* was interested in the wedded life of the Channings. Why doesn't *Triworld* wait until we find out about it ourselves?'

'*Triworld* does not care to pry into the private life of the newly wed Channing family,' laughed Doug. 'We, and the rest of the system, do not give a damn whether Mrs. Channing calls you Bunny-bit or Sugar-pie—'

'Sweetums,' corrected Arden with a gleam in her eye.

'—we've got something big to handle. I can't get a thing out of the gang at Canalopsis, they're all too busy worrying.'

'And so you came here? What do you expect to get out of us? We're not connected in any way with Canalopsis.'

'I know,' said Doug, 'but you do know space. Look, Channing, the *Solar Queen* has been missing since yesterday morning!'

Don whistled.

'See what I mean? What I want to know is this: What is your opinion on the matter? You've lived in space for years, on Venus Equilateral and you've had experience beyond anybody I can reach.'

'Missing since yesterday morning,' mused Channing. 'That means trouble.'

'That's what I thought. Now if you were running the space-port at Canalopsis, what would your own private opinion be?'

'I don't know whether I should speak for publication,' said Don.

'It won't be official. I'll corroborate anything you say before it is printed, and so on. But I want an unofficial opinion, too. If you want this withheld, say so, but I still want a technical deduction to base my investigation on. I don't understand the ramifications and the implications of a missing ship. It is enough to make Keg Johnson's hair turn gray overnight, though, and I'd like to know what is so bad before I start to turn stones.'

'Well, keep it off the record until Canalopsis gives you the go-ahead. I can give you an opinion, but I don't want to sound official.'

'O.K. Do you suppose she was hit by a meteor shower?'

'Doubt it like the devil. Meteor detectors are many and inter-connected on a spaceship, as well as being alarmed and fused to the nth degree. Any trouble with them will bring a horde of ringing bells all through the ship which would bring the personnel a-running. They just don't go wrong for no reason at all.'

'Suppose that so many meteors came from all directions that the factors presented to the autopilot—'

'No dice. The possibility of a concentration of meteors from all directions all about to pass through a certain spot in space is like betting on two Sundays in a row. Meteors don't just run in all directions, they have a general drift. And the meteor detecting equipment would have been able to pick up the centroid of any group of meteors soon enough to lift the ship around it. Why, there hasn't been a ship hit by a meteor in ten years.'

'But—'

'And if it had been,' continued Channing, 'the chances are more than likely that the ship wouldn't have been hit badly enough to make it impossible to steer, or for the crew to shoot out message tubes which would have landed on Canalopsis.'

'Look, there's one thing I don't understand,' said Doug. 'Spacecraft are always dodging meteors, yet Venus Equilateral seems immune.'

'It's the velocity,' explained Don. 'Venus Equilateral is traveling at the same speed as Venus, of course. A spacecraft hits it up in the hundreds of miles per second. Say two hundred and seventy miles per second, which is about ten times the orbital velocity of Venus Equilateral. Then with a given dispersion of meteors throughout space, any spacecraft has ten times the possible chances of encounter because the ship covers ten times the volume in the same time. Besides, truly missing meteors is a hypothetical problem.'

'How so?'

'To avoid only those whose courses will intersect yours would demand some sort of course predicting gear that would read the course of the oncoming meteor and apply it in a space problem to the predicted course of the ship. That's just too much machinery, Doug. So spacecraft merely turn aside for anything that even *looks* close. They don't take any chances at all,' said Don Channing. 'They can't afford to.'

'Suppose that the ship ducked a big shower and it went so far out of course that they missed Mars?'

'That's out, too,' laughed Channing.

'Why?'

'A standard ship of space is capable of hitting it up at about four G all the way from Terra to Mars at major opposition and end up with enough power and spare cathodes to continue to Venus in quadrature. Now the velocity of the planets in their orbits is a stinking matter of miles per second, while the top speed of a ship in even the shortest passage runs up into four figures per second. You'd be surprised at what velocity you can attain at one G for ten hours.'

'Yes?'

'It runs to slightly less than two hundred and fifty miles per second, during which you've covered only four million miles. In the shortest average run from Venus to Terra at conjunction, a skimpy twenty-five million miles, your time of travel is a matter of twenty-five hours odd running at the standard two G. Your velocity at turnover – or the halfway point where the ship stops going *up* from Terra and starts to go *down* to Venus – is a good cool five hundred miles per second. So under no condition would the ship miss its objective badly enough to cause its complete loss. Why, this business is run so quickly that were it not for the saving in time and money that amounts to a small percentage at the end of each flight, the pilot could head for his planet and approach the planet asymptotically.'

'You know what you're doing, don't you?' asked the reporter.

'I think so.'

'You're forcing my mind into accepting something that has never happened before, and something that has no basis for its—'

'You mean piracy? I wonder. We've all read tales of the Jolly Roger being painted on the side of a sleek ship of space while the pirate, who is a fine fellow at heart though uninhibited, hails down the cruiser carrying radium. He swipes the stuff and kisses all the women whilst menacing the men with a gun-hand full of searing, coruscating, violently lethal ray pistol. But that sounds fine in stories. The trick is tougher than it sounds, Douglas. You've got to catch your rabbit first.'

'Meaning?'

'Meaning that finding a ship in space to prey upon is somewhat less difficult than juggling ten billiard balls whilst riding a horse blindfolded. Suppose you were to turn pirate. This is what would happen:

'You'd get the course of the treasure ship from the spaceport, fine and good, by resorting to spies and such. You'd lie in wait out there in the blackness of space, fixing your position by the stars and hoping that your error in fix was less than a couple of hundred thousand miles. The time comes. You look to your musket, sharpen your cutlass, and see to the priming of your derringers that are thrust into the red sash at your waist. You are right on the course, due to your brilliant though lawless navigator who was tossed out of astrogato's school for filching the teacher's whiskey. Then the treasure ship zoops past at a healthy hundred miles per second and you decide that since she is hitting it up at two G, you'd have had to start from scratch at a heck of a lot better to catch her within the next couple of light years.'

'But suppose you took the course as laid and applied the same acceleration? Suppose you followed on the heels of your quarry until you were both in space? You could do it then, couldn't you?'

'Gosh,' said Channing, 'I never thought of that. That's the only way a guy could pirate a ship – unless he planted his men on board and they mutinied.'

'Then it might be pirates?'

'It might be,' admitted Channing. 'It'd have to occur near beginning or end, of course, though. I can't think of anything being shot at out of a gun of any kind while both crates are hitting it up at a couple of hundred miles per second and at a distance of a few miles apart. It would be all right if you were both running free, but at two G acceleration, you'd have to do quite a bit of ballistic gymnastics to score a hit.'

'Or run in front of your quarry and sow a bouquet of mines.'

'Except that the meteor detector would show the position of the pirate craft in the celestial globe and the interconnecting circuits would cause the treasure ship to veer off at a sharp angle. Shucks, Doug, this thing has got too many angles to it. I can't begin to run it off either way. No matter how difficult it may sound, there are still ways and means to do it. The only thing that stands out like a sore thumb is the fact that the *Solar Queen* has turned up missing. Since no inanimate agency could cause failure, piracy is the answer.'

'You're sure of that?'

'Not positive. There are things that might cause the ship to founder. But what they are depends on too many coincidences. It's like hitting a royal flush on the deal, or filling a full house from two pairs.'

'Well, thanks, Channing. I'm heading back to Canalopsis right now. Want to come along?'

Channing looked at Arden, who was coming from the dressing room carrying her coat and he nodded. 'The gal says yes,' he grinned. 'Annoy her until I find my shoes, will you?'

Arden wrinkled her nose at Don. 'I'll like that,' she said to Doug.

The trip from Lincoln Head to Canalopsis was a fast one. Doug drove the little flier through the thin air of Mars at a breakneck speed and covered the twelve hundred miles in just shy of an hour. At the spaceport, Channing found that he was not denied entrance as the reporter had been. He was ushered into the office of Keg Johnson, and he and the manager of the Canalopsis Spaceport greeted Don with a worried expression on his face.

'Still gone,' said Johnson cryptically. 'Like the job of locating her?'

Don shook his head with a sympathetic smile. 'Like trying to find a grain of sand on a beach – a specified grain, I mean. Wouldn't know how to go about it.'

Keg nodded. 'I thought as much. That leaves her out of the picture. Well, up to now space travel has been about as safe as spending the evening in your easy-chair. Hello, Arden, how's married life?'

'Can't tell yet,' she said with a twinkle. 'I've got to find out whether I can break him of a dozen bad habits before I'll commit myself.'

'I wish you luck, Arden, although from that statement, it's Don that needs the luck.'

'We came to see if there was anything we could do about the *Solar Queen*,' offered Channing.

'What can anybody do?' asked Keg, with spread hands. 'About all we can do is to put it down in our remembrances and turn to tomorrow. Life goes on, you know,' said Keg in a resigned tone, 'and either we keep up or we begin to live in the past. Are you going to stay here for a day or two?'

'Was thinking about it,' said Don.

'Well, suppose you register at the Terraland and meet me back here for lunch. If anything occurs, I'll shoot you a quickie.' Keg looked at his watch and whistled. 'Lordy,' he said ruefully. 'I didn't know how late it was. Look, kids, I'll run downtown myself, and we'll all have lunch at the Terraland. How's that?'

'Sounds better,' admitted Channing. 'My appetite, you know.'

'I know,' laughed Arden. 'Come on, meat-eater, and we'll peel a calf.'

It was during lunch that a messenger raced into the dining room and handed Keg a letter. Keg read, and then swore roundly. He tossed the letter across the table to Don and Arden.

TO THE OPERATORS OF ALL SPACELINES:

IT HAS COME TO MY ATTENTION THAT YOUR SHIPS NEED PROTECTION. THE ABSENCE OF THE SOLAR QUEEN IS PROOF ENOUGH THAT YOUR EFFORTS ARE INSUFFICIENT TO INSURE THE ARRIVAL OF A SPACESHIP AT ITS DESTINATION.

I AM CAPABLE OF OFFERING PROTECTION AT THE REASONABLE RATE OF ONE DOLLAR SOLARIAN FOR EVERY GROSS TON, WITH THE RETURN OF TEN DOLLARS SOLARIAN IF ANY SHIP FAILS TO COME THROUGH SAFELY. I THINK THAT YOU MAY FIND IT NECESSARY TO SUBSCRIBE TO MY INSURANCE, SINCE WITHOUT MY PROTECTION I CANNOT BE RESPONSIBLE FOR FAILURES.

ALLISON (HELLION) MURDOCH.

'Why the dirty racketeer,' stormed Arden. 'Who is he, anyway?'

'Hellion Murdoch is a man of considerable ability as a surgeon and a theoretical physicist,' explained Don. 'He was sentenced to the gas chamber ten years ago for trying some of his theories out on human beings without their consent. He escaped with the aid of fifteen or twenty of his cohorts who had stolen the *Hippocrates* right out of the private spaceport of the Solarian Medical Research Institute.'

'And they headed for the unknown,' offered Keg. 'Wonder where they've been for the last ten years?'

'I'll bet a hat that they've been in the Melapalan Jungle, using the machine shop of the *Hippocrates* to fashion guns. That machine shop was a dilly, if I remember correctly.'

'It was. The whole ship was just made to be as self-sustaining as it could be. They used to run all over the System in it, you know, chasing bugs. But look, Don, if I were you, I'd begin worrying about Venus Equilateral. That's where he'll hit next.'

'You're right. But what are you going to do?'

'Something that will drive him right out to the relay station,' said Keg in a sorrowful tone. 'Sorry, Don, but when I put an end to all space shipping for a period of six weeks, Hellion Murdoch will be sitting in your lap.'

'He sure will,' said Channing nervously. 'Arden, are you willing to run a gauntlet?'

'Sure,' she answered quickly. 'Are you sure that there will be no danger?'

'Reasonably sure, or I wouldn't take you with me. Unless Murdoch has managed to build himself a couple of extra ships, we've got a chance in three that he'll be near one of the other two big spaceports. So we'll slide out of here unannounced and at a peculiar time of day. We'll load up with gravanol and take it all the way to the station at six G.'

'He may have two or three ships,' said Keg. 'A man could

cover all the standard space shipping in three, and he might not have too bad a time with two, especially if he were only out looking for those which weren't paid for. But, look, I wouldn't check out of the Terraland if I were you. Keep this under cover. Your heap is all ready to take sky from Canalopsis Spaceport and you can leave directly.'

'Hold off on your announcement as long as possible,' Don asked Keg.

Johnson smiled and nodded. 'I'll give you time to get there anyway. But I've no control over what will be done at Northern Landing or Mojave. They may kick over the traces.'

'Arden, we're moving again,' laughed Don. 'Keg, ship us our duds as soon as this affair clears up.' Channing scribbled a message on the back of Murdoch's letter. 'Shoot this off to Walt Franks, will you? I won't wait for an answer, that'll take about fifty minutes, and by that time I'll have been in space for twenty.'

They paused long enough to stop at the nurse's office at the spaceport for a heavy shot of gravanol and a thorough bracing with wide adhesive tape. Then they made their way to the storage space of the spaceport where they entered their small ship. Channing was about to send the power lever home when the figure of Keg Johnson waved him to stop.

Keg ran up the space lock and handed in a paper.

'You're it,' he said. 'Good luck, Channings.'

It was another message from Hellion Murdoch. It said, bluntly:

TO DONALD A. CHANNING, PH.D:
DIRECTOR OF COMMUNICATIONS:
  CONSIDERABLE DIFFICULTY HAS BEEN EX-
PERIENCED IN TRANSMITTING MESSAGES TO
THE INTERESTED PARTIES. I DESIRE A FREE

HAND IN TELLING ALL WHO CARE THE PARTI-
CULARS OF MY INSURANCE.

SINCE YOUR RELAY STATION IS IN A POSI-
TION TO CONTROL ALL COMMUNICATIONS BE-
TWEEN THE WORLDS, I AM OFFERING YOU THE
OPTION OF EITHER SURRENDERING THE STA-
TION TO ME, OR OF FIGHTING ME FOR ITS
POSSESSION. I AM CONFIDENT THAT YOU WILL
SEE THE INTELLIGENT COURSE: AN UNARMED
STATION IN SPACE IS NO MATCH FOR A FULLY
ARMED AND EXCELLENTLY MANNED CRUISER.

YOUR ANSWER WILL BE EXPECTED IN FIVE
DAYS.

ALLISON (HELLION) MURDOCH.

Channing snarled and thrust the power lever down to the
last notch. The little ship leaped upward at five G, and was
gone from sight in less than a minute.

Arden shook her head. 'What was that message you sent
to Franks?' she asked.

'I told him that there was a wild-eyed pirate on the loose, and
that he might take a stab at the station. We are coming in as
soon as we can get there and to be on the lookout for us on the
landing communications radio, and also for anything untoward
in the nature of space vessels.'

'Then this is not exactly a shock,' said Arden, waving the
message from Murdoch.

'Not exactly,' said Channing dryly. 'Now look, Arden, you
go to sleep. This'll take hours and hours, and gabbing about it
will only lay you out cold.'

'I feel fine,' objected Arden.

'I know, but that's the gravanol, not you. The tape will keep
you intact, and the gravanol will keep you awake without
nausea. But you can't get something for nothing, Arden, and

when that gravanol wears off, you'll spend ten times as long with one-tenth of the trouble you might have had. So take it easy for yourself now and later you'll be glad that you aren't worse.'

The sky blackened, and Channing knew that they were free in space. Give them another fifteen minutes and the devil himself couldn't find them. With no flight plan scheduled and no course posted, they might as well have been in the seventeenth dimension. As they emerged from the thin atmosphere, there was a fleeting flash of fire from several miles to the east, but Channing did not pay particular attention to it. Arden looked through a telescope and thought she saw a spaceship circling, but she could not be sure.

Whatever it was, nothing came of it.

The trip out to the station was a monotonous series of un-eventful hours, proceeding along one after the other. They dozed and slept most of the time, eating sparingly and doing nothing that was not absolutely necessary.

Turnabout was accomplished and then the deceleration be-gan, equally long and equally monotonous. It was equally inactive. Channing tried to plan, but it failed because he could not plan without talking and discussing the affair with his men. Too much depended upon their cooperation. He fell into a morose, futile feeling that made itself evident in grousing; Arden tried to cheer him, but Don's usually bubbling spirit was doused too deep. Also, Arden herself was none too happy, which is necessary before one can cheer another.

Then they sighted the station and Channing's ill-spirit left. A man of action, what he hated most was the no-action busi-ness of just sitting in a little capsule waiting for the relay station to come up out of the sky below. Once it was sighted, Channing foresaw action, and his grousing stopped.

They zipped past the station at a distance of ten miles, and Channing opened the radio.

'Walt Franks! Wake up, you slumberhead.'

The answer came inside of half a minute. 'Hello, Don. Who's asleep?'

'Where are you? In Joe's?'

'Joe has declared a drought for the duration,' said Franks with a laugh. 'He thinks we can't think on Scotch.'

'We can't. Have you seen the boys?'

'Murdoch's crew? Sure, they're circling at about five miles, running around in the plane of the ecliptic. Keep running on the colure and the chances are that you won't even see 'em. But, Don, they can hear us!'

'How about the landing stage at the south end?'

'There are two of them running around the station at different heights from north to south. The third is circling in a four-mile circle on a plane five miles south of the station. We've picked up a few HE shells, and I guess that, if you try to make a landing there, you'll be shot to bits. That devil is using the meteor detector for a gun pointer.'

'Walt, remember the visual loran?'

'Y'mean the one we used to find the *Empress*?'

'Uh-huh. Rig it without the mirrors? Get me? D'you know what I want to do?'

'Yop. All we have to do is clear away some of the saw grass again. Not too much, though, because it hasn't been too long since we cut it before. I get you all right.'

'Fine. How soon?'

'I'm in the beam control north. I've got a portable mike, and I walk over to the mirror and begin to tinker with the screws. *Ouch!* I've skun me a knuckle. Now look, Don, I'm going inside and crack the passage end. I've broadcast throughout the station that it is to be cracked, and the men are swarming all over the axis of the station doing just that. Come – a-running!'

Channing circled the little ship high to the north and came down toward the axis of the station. He accelerated fiercely for a portion of the time, and then made a slam-bang turnabout. A pilot light on the instrument panel gleamed, indicating that some of the plates were strained and that the ship was leaking air. Another light lit, indicating that the automatic pressure control was functioning, and that the pressure was maintained, though it might not long be.

Then in deceleration, Channing fought the ship on to a die-straight line with the open door at the north end. He fixed the long, long passageway in the center of his sights, and prayed.

The ship hit the opening squarely, and only then did their terrific speed become apparent. Past bulkhead after bulkhead they drove, and a thin scream came to their ears as the atmosphere down in the bowels of the station was compressed by the tiny ship's passage.

Doors slammed behind the ship as it passed, and air locks were opened, permitting the station's center to fill to its normal pressure once more.

Then the rocketing ship slowed. Channing saw a flash of green and knew that the Martian saw grass was halfway down the three-mile length of the station. He zipped past storerooms and rooms filled with machinery, and then the ship scraped lightly against one of the bulkheads.

It caromed from this bulkhead against the next, hitting it in a quartering slice. From side to side the ship bounced, crushing the bulkheads and tearing great slices from the flanks of the ship.

It slowed, and came to rest against a large room full of packing cases, and was immediately swarmed over by the men of Venus Equilateral.

They found Channing partly conscious. His nose was bleeding but otherwise he seemed all right. Arden was completely out, though a quick check by the station's medical staff assured Don that she would be all right as soon as they gave her a workout. He was leaving the center of the station when Franks came puffing up the stairway from the next lowest level.

'Gosh,' he said. 'It's a real job trying to guess where you stopped. I've been hitting every hundred feet and asking. Well, that was one for the book.'

'Yeah,' groaned Don. 'Come along, Walt. I want a shower. You can give the resumé of the activities while I'm showering and trying to soak this adhesive off. Arden, lucky girl, will be unconscious when Doc rips it off; I never liked the way they remove tape.'

'There isn't much to tell,' said Franks. 'But what there is, I'll tell you.'

Channing was finishing the shower when Walt mentioned that it was too bad that they hadn't started his electron gun a few weeks sooner.

Don shut off the water, fumbled for a towel, and said: 'What?'

Franks repeated.

Again Channing said: 'What? Are you nuts?'

'No. I've been tinkering with an idea of mine. If we had another month to work on it, I think we might be able to clip Murdoch's ears.'

'Just what are you using in this super weapon, chum?'

Franks explained.

'Mind if I put in an oar?' asked Channing.

'Not at all. So far we might be able to fry a smelt at twenty feet, or we could cook us a steak. But I haven't been able to do a thing yet. We had it working once, and I think we heated a meteor somewhat, but the whole thing went blooey before we finished the test. I've spent the last week and a half fixing the thing up again, and would have tried it out on the next meteor, but your message brought a halt to everything but cleaning up the mess and making ready just in case we might think of something practical.'

'I'll put in my first oar by seeing the gadget. Wait till I find my pants, and I'll go right along.'

Don inspected the installation and whistled. 'Not half bad, sonny, not half bad.'

'Except that we haven't been able to make it work.'

'Well, for one thing, you've been running on the wrong track. You need more power.'

'Sure,' grinned Walt. 'More power, he says. I don't see how we can cram any more soup into this can. She'll melt.'

'Walt, what happens in a big gun?'

'Powder burns; expanding products of combustion push—'

'Functionally, what are you trying to accomplish? Take it on the basis of a solid shot, like they used to use back in the sailing ship days.'

'Well,' said Walt thoughtfully, 'I'd say they were trying to heave something large enough to do damage.'

'Precisely. Qualifying that statement a little, you might say that the projectile transmits the energy of the powder charge to its objective.'

'Right,' agreed Walt.

'And it is possible to transmit that energy mechanically. I think if we reason this idea out in analogy, we might be able to do it electrically. First, there is the method. There is nothing wrong with your idea, functionally. Electron guns are as old as radio. They—'

The door opened and Arden entered. 'Hi, fellows,' she said. 'What's cooking?'

'Hi, Arden. Like marriage?' Walt asked.

'How long do people have to be married before people stop asking that darn fool question?' asked Arden.

'O.K., how about your question?'

'I meant that. I ran into Warren, who told me that the

brains were down here tinkering on something that was either a brilliant idea or an equally brilliant flop – he didn't know which. What goes?'

'Walt has turned Buck Rogers and is now about to invent a ray gun.'

'No!'

'Yes!'

'Here's where we open a psychopathic ward,' said Arden sadly. 'So far, Venus Equilateral is the only community that hasn't had a village idiot. But no longer are we unique. Seriously, Walt?'

'Sure enough,' said Channing. 'He's got an idea here that may work with a little tinkering.'

'Brother Edison, we salute you,' said Arden. 'How does it work?'

'Poorly. Punk. Lousy.'

'Well, sound recording has come a long way from the tin-foil cylinder that scratched out: "Mary had a little lamb!" And transportation has come along swell from the days of sliding sledges. You may have the nucleus of an idea, Walt. But I meant its operation instead of its efficiency.'

'We have an electron gun of super size,' explained Walt. 'The cathode is a big affair six feet in diameter and capable of emitting a veritable storm of electrons. We accelerate them by means of properly spaced anodes of the proper voltage level, and we focus them into a nice bundle by means of electro-static lenses—'

'Whoah, Tillie, you're talking like the venerable Buck Rogers himself. Say that in words of one cylinder, please,' chuckled Arden.

'Well, any voltage gradient between electrodes of different voltage acts as a prism, sort of. When you have annular electrodes of the proper size, shape, and voltage difference, they act as a lens.'

'In other words, the ring-shaped electrodes are electrostatic lenses?'

'Nope. It is the space between them. With light or electrons a convex lens will converge the light no matter which direction the light is coming from.'

'Uh-huh. I see in a sort of vague manner. Now, fellows, go on from there. What's necessary to make this dingbat tick?'

'I want to think out loud,' said Channing.

'That's nothing unusual,' said Arden. 'Can't we go into Joe's? You can't think without a tablecloth, either.'

'What I'm thinking is this, Walt. You've been trying to squirt electrons like a fireman runs a hose. Walt, how long do you suppose a sixteen-inch rifle would last if the explosives were constantly replaced and the fire burned constantly?'

'Not long,' admitted Walt.

'A gun is an overloaded machine,' said Don. 'Even a little one. The life of a gun barrel is measured in seconds; totalling up the time of transit of all the rounds from new gun to worn barrel gives a figure expressed in seconds. Your electron gun, Walt, whether it be fish, flesh, or fowl, must be overloaded for an instant.'

'Is overload a necessary requirement?' asked Arden. 'It seems to me that you might be able to bore a sixteen-inch gun for a twenty-two. What now, little man?'

'By the time we get something big enough to do more than knock paint off, we'll have something bigger than a twenty-two,' grinned Channing. 'I was speaking in terms of available strength versus required punch. In the way that a girder will hold tremendous overloads for brief instants, a gun is overloaded for milliseconds. We'll have a problem—'

'O.K., aside from that, have you figured out why I haven't been able to do more than warm anything larger than a house brick?'

'Sure,' laughed Channing. 'What happens in a multigrid

radio tube when the suppressor grid is hanging free?'

'Charges negative and blocks the electron stream . . . hey! That's it!'

'What?' asked Arden.

'Sure,' said Walt. 'We fire off a batch of electrons, and the first contingent that arrives charges the affair so that the rest of the beam sort of wriggles out of line.'

'Your meteor is going to take on a charge of phenomenal negative value, and the rest of your beam is going to be deflected away, just as your electron lenses deflect the original beam,' said Channing. 'And now another thing, old turnip. You're squirting out a lot of electrons. That's much amperage. Your voltage – velocity – is nothing to rave about even though it sounds high. Watts is what you want, to corn a phrase.'

'*Phew*,' said Walt. 'Corn, he says. Go on, prodigy, and make with the explanations. I agree, we should have more voltage and less quantity. But we're running the stuff at plenty of voltage now. Nothing short of a Van Der Graf generator would work – and while we've got one up on the forty-ninth level, we couldn't run a supply line down here without reaming a fifty-foot hole through the station, and then I don't know how we'd get that kind of voltage down here without . . . that kind of stuff staggers the imagination. You can't juggle a hundred million volts on a wire. She'd squirt off in all directions.'

'Another thing, whilst I hold it in my mind,' said Channing, thoughtfully, 'You go flinging electrons off the station in basketful after basketful, and the next bird that drops a ship on the landing stage is going to spot-weld himself right to the south end of Venus Equilateral. It wouldn't be long before the station would find itself being pulled into Sol because of the electrostatic stress – if we didn't run out of electrons first!'

'I hardly think that we'd run out – but we might have a tough time flinging them away after a bit. Could it be that we should blow out a fist full of protons at the same time?'

'Might make up a concentric beam and wave positive ions at the target,' said Channing. 'Might help.'

'But this space-charge effect. How do we get around that?'

'Same way we make the electron gun work. Fire it off at a devilish voltage. Run your electron velocity up near the speed of light; the electrons at that speed will acquire considerable mass, in accordance with Lorenz's equation which shows that as the velocity of a mass reaches the speed of light, its mass becomes infinite. With a healthy mass built up by near-light velocities, the electrons with not be as easy to deflect. Then, too, we can do the damage we want before the charge can be built up that will deflect the stream. We ram 'em with a bundle of electrons moving so fast that the charging effect can not work; before the space charge can build up to the level required for self-nullification of our beam, the damage is done.'

'And all we need is a couple of trillion volts. Two times ten to the twelfth power. *Grrr.*'

'I can see that you'll need a tablecloth,' said Arden. 'You birds can think better over at Joe's. Come along and feed the missus, Don.'

Channing surveyed the instrument again, and then said: 'Might as well, Walt. The inner man must be fed, and we can wrangle at the same time. Argument assists the digestion – and vice versa.'

'Now,' said Channing as the dishes were pushed aside, clearing a space on the table. 'What are we going to do?'

'That's what I've been worrying about,' said Walt. 'Let's list the things that make our gun ineffective.'

'That's easy. It can't dish out enough. It's too dependent upon mobility. It's fundamentally inefficient because it runs out of ammunition too quick, by which I mean that it is a sort of gun with antiseptic bullets. It cures its own damage.'

'Prevents,' said Arden.

'All right, it acts as its own shield, electrostatically.'

'About this mobility,' said Walt, 'I do not quite agree with that.'

'You can't whirl a hunk of tube the size and weight of a good-sized telescope around fast enough to shoot holes in a racing spaceship,' said Channing. 'Especially one that is trying to dodge. We've got to rely upon something that can do the trick better. Your tube did all right following a meteor that runs in a course that can be predicted, because you can set up your meteor spotter to correct for the mechanical lag. But in a spaceship that is trying to duck your shot, you'll need something that works with the speed of light. And, since we're going to be forced into something heavy and hard hitting, its inertia will be even more so.'

'Heavy and hard hitting means exactly what?'

'Cyclotron, betatron or synchrotron. One of those dinguses that whirls nucleons around like a stone on a string until the string breaks and sends the stone out at terrific speed. We need a velocity that sounds like a congressional figure.'

'We've got a cyclotron.'

'Yeah,' drawled Channing. 'A wheezy old heap that cries out in anguish every time the magnets are charged. I doubt that we could move the thing without it falling apart. The betatron is the ticket.'

'But the cyclotron gives out with a lot more soup.'

'If I had to increase the output of either one, I could do it a lot quicker with the betatron,' said Channing. 'In a cyclotron, the revolution of the ions in their acceleration period is controlled by an oscillator, the voltage output of which is impressed on the D chambers. In order to speed up the ion stream, you'd have to do two things. One: Build a new oscillator that will dish out more power. Two: Increase the strength of the magnets.

'But in the betatron, the thing is run differently. The magnet

117

is built for A.C. and the electron gun runs off the same. As your current starts up from zero, the electron gun squirts a bouquet of electrons into a chamber built like a pair of angel's food cake tins set rim to rim. The magnet's field begins to build up at the same time, and the resulting increase in field strength accelerates the electrons and at the same time, its increasing field keeps the little devils running in the same orbit. Shoot it with two-hundred-cycle current, and in the half cycle your electrons are made to run around the center a few million times. That builds up a terrific velocity – measured in six figures, believe it or not. Then the current begins to level off at the top of the sine wave, and the magnet loses its increasing phase. The electrons, still in acceleration, begin to whirl outward. The current levels off for sure and begins to slide down – and the electrons roll off at a tangent to their course. This stream can be collected and used. In fact, we have a two-hundred-cycle beam of electrons at a couple of billion volts. That, brother, ain't hay!'

'Is that enough?'

'Nope.'

'Then how do you hope to increase this velocity? If it is easier to run this up than it would be the cyclotron, how do we go about it?'

Channing smiled and began to draw diagrams on the tablecloth. Joe looked over with a worried frown, and then shrugged his shoulders. Diagrams or not, this was an emergency – and besides, he thought, he needed another lesson in high powered gadgetry.

'The nice thing about this betatron,' said Channing, 'is the fact that it can and does run both ends on the same supply. The current and voltage phases are correct so that we do not require two supplies which operate in a carefully balanced condition. The cyclotron is one of the other kinds; though the one supply is strictly D.C., the strength of the field must be controlled separately from the supply to the oscillator that runs the D plates. You're sitting on a fence, juggling knobs and stuff all the time you are bombarding with a cyc.

'Now let us inspect the supply of the betatron. It is sinusoidal. There is the catch. There is the thing that makes it possible. That single fact makes it easy to step the power up to terrific quantities. Since the thing is fixed by nature so that the output is proportional – electron gun initial velocity versus magnetic field strength – if we increase the input voltage, the output voltage goes up without having to resort to manipulistic gymnastics on the part of the operator.'

'Go on, Professor Maxwell.'

'Don't make fun of a great man's name,' said Arden. 'If it wasn't for Clerk Maxwell, we'd still be yelling out of the window at one another instead of squirting radio beams all over the Solar System.'

'Then make him quit calling me Tom Swift.'

'Go on, Don, Walt and I will finish this argument after we finish Hellion Murdoch.'

'May I?' asked Channing with a smile. He did not mind the interruption; he was used to it in the first place and he had been busy with his pencil in the second place. 'Now look, Walt, what happens when you smack a charged condenser across an inductance?'

'You generate a damped cycle of the amplitude of the charge on the condenser, and of frequency equal to the L, C constants of the condenser and inductance. The amplitude decays according to the factor Q, following the equation for decrement—'

'Never mind, I've got it here on my whiteboard,' smiled Channing, pointing to the tablecloth. 'You are right. And the purity of the wave?'

'Sinusoidal . . . hey! That's it!' Walt jumped to his feet and went to the telephone.

'What's "it"?' asked Arden.

'The betatron we have runs off a five-hundred-volt supply,' chuckled Channing. 'We can crank that up ten to one without running into any difficulty at all. Five-hundred-volt insulation is peanuts, and the stuff they put on wires nowadays is always good for ten times that just because it wouldn't be economical to try to thin the installation down so that it only protects five hundred. I'll bet a crank that he could crank the input up to fifty thousand volts without too much sputtering – though I wouldn't know where to lay my lunch hooks on a fifty-thousand-volt condenser of any appreciable capacity. Well, stepping up the rig ten to one will dish us out just shy of a couple of thousand million volts, which, as Brother Franks says, is not hay!'

Walt returned after a minute and said: 'Warren's measuring the inductance of the betatron magnet. He will then calculate the value of C required to tune the thing to the right frequency and start to achieve that capacity by mazing up whatever high-voltage condensers we have on the station. Now, Don, let's calculate how we're going to make the thing mobile.'

'That's a horse of a different color. We'll have to use electromagnetic deflection. From the constants of the electron stream out of our souped-up Suzy, we'll have to compute the necessary field to deflect such a beam. That'll be terrific, because the electrons are hitting it up at a velocity approaching that of light – maybe a hundred and seventy thousand miles per – and their mass will be something fierce. That again will help to murder Murdoch; increasing mass will help to keep the electrons from being deflected, since it takes more to turn a heavy mass – et cetera, see Newton's law of inertia for complete statement. Have 'em jerk the D plates out of the cyc and bring the magnet frame down here – to the turret, I mean – and set 'em up on the vertical. We'll use that to run the beam up and down, we can't possibly get one hundred and eighty degree deflection, of course, but we can run the deflection over considerable range. It should be enough to catch a spaceship that is circling the station. For the horizontal deflection, what have we got?'

'Nothing. But the cyc magnet is a double pole affair. We could break the frame at the D plates and set one winding sidewise to the other and use half on each direction.'

'Sure. Have one of Warren's gang fit the busted pole pieces up with a return-magnetic frame so that the field will be complete. He can weld some girders on and around in an hour. That gives us complete deflection properties up and down; left and right. We should be able to cover a ninety-degree cone from your turret.'

'That'll cover all of Murdoch's ships,' said Walt.

'Too bad we haven't got some U-235 to use. I'd like to plate up one of his ships with some positive ions of U-235 and then change the beam to slow neutrons. That might deter him from his life of crime.'

'Variations, he wants,' said Arden. 'You're going to impale one ship on a beam of electrons; one ship on a beam of U-235 ions; and what will you have on the third?'

'I'll think of something,' said Channing. 'A couple of hundred pounds of U-235 should make things hum, though.'

'More like making them disappear,' said Franks. '*Swoosh!* No ship. Just an incandescent mass falling into the Sun. I'm glad we haven't any purified U-235 or plutonium in any quantity out here. We catch a few slow neutrons now and then, and I wouldn't be able to sleep nights. The things just sort of wander right through the station as though it weren't here at all; they stop just long enough to register on the counter upstairs and then they're gone.'

'Well, to work, people. We've got a job to do in the next three and a half days.'

Those days were filled with activity. Hauling the heavy parts down to the turret was no small job, but it was accomplished after a lot of hard work and quite a bit of tinkering with a cutting torch. The parts were installed in the outer skin, and the crew with the torch went back over the trail and replaced the gaping holes they left in the walls and floors of Venus Equilateral. The engineering department went to work, and for some hours the place was silent save for the clash of pencil on paper and the scratching of scalps. The most popular book in the station became a volume on nuclear physics, and the second most popular book was a table of integrals. The stenographic force went to work combing the library for information pertaining to electronic velocities, and a junior engineer was placed in as buffer between the eager stenographers and the harried engineering department. This was necessary because the stenographers got to the point where they'd send anything at all that said either 'electrons' or 'velocity' and one of the engineers read halfway through a text on atomic structure before he realized that he had been sold a bill of goods. Wire went by the mile down to the turret, and men proceeded to blow out half of the meters in the station with the high-powered beam. Luckily, the thing was completely nonspectacular, or Murdoch might have gained an inkling of their activities. The working crew manipulated constants and made haywire circuits, and finally announced that the beam would deflect – if the calculations were correct.

'They'd better be,' said Channing. He was weary. His eyes were puffed from lack of sleep, and he hadn't had his clothing off in three days.

'They are,' said Franks. He was in no better shape than Don.

'They'd better be right,' said Channing ominously. 'We're asking for a kick in the teeth. The first bundle of stuff that leaves our gun will energize Murdoch's meteor spotter by sheer electrostatic force. His gun mounts, which you tell me are coupled to the meteor detector for aiming, will swivel to cover the turret out here. Then he'll let us have it right in the betatron. If we don't get him first, he'll get us second.'

'Don,' said Walt in a worried voice. 'How are we going to replace the charge on the station? Like the bird who was tossing baseballs out of the train – he quit when he ran out of them. Our gun will quit cold when we run out of electrons – or when the positive charge gets so high that the betatron can't overcome the electrostatic attraction.'

'Venus Equilateral is a free grid,' smiled Channing. 'As soon as we shoot off electrons, Old Sol becomes a hot cathode and our station collects 'em until the charge is equalized again.'

'And what is happening to the bird who is holding on to something when we make off with a million volts? Does he scrape himself off the opposite wall in a week or so – after he comes to – or can we use him for freezing ice cubes? Seems to me that it might be a little bit fatal.'

'Didn't think of that,' said Channing. 'There's one thing, their personal charge doesn't add up to a large quantity of electricity. If we insulate 'em and put 'em in their spacesuits, they'll be all right as long as they don't try to grab anything. They'll be on the up and down for a bit, but the resistance of the spacesuit is high enough to keep 'em from draining out all their electrons at once. I recall the experiments with early Van Der Graf generators at a few million volts – the operator used to sit in the charged sphere because it was one place where he couldn't be hit by man-made lightning. It'll be rough, but it won't kill us. Spacesuits, and have 'em sit in plastic chairs, the feet of which are insulated from the floor by china dinner plates. This plastic wall covering that we have in the apartments is a blessing. If it were all bare steel, every room would be a miniature hell. Issue general instructions to that effect. We've been having emergency drills for a long time; now's the time to use the grand collection of elastomer spacesuits. Tell 'em we give 'em an hour to get ready.'

Hellion Murdoch's voice came over the radio at exactly the

second of the expiration of his limit. He called Channing and said:

'What is your answer, Dr. Channing?'

Don squinted down the pilot tube of the meteor spotter and saw the *Hippocrates* passing. It was gone before he spoke, but the second ship came along, and the pilot tube leaped into line with it. Don checked meters on the crude panel before him, and then pressed the plastic handle of a long lever.

There was the crash of heavy-duty oil switch.

Crackles of electricity flashed back and forth through the station, and the smell of ozone arose. Electric light filaments leaned over crazily, trying to touch the inner walls of the glass. Panes of glass ran blue for an instant, and the nap of the carpets throughout the station stood bolt upright. Hair stood on end, touched the plastic helmet dome, discharged, fell to the scalp, raised again and discharged, fell once more, and then repeated this raising and falling, again and again and again. Electric clocks ran crazily, and every bit of electronic equipment on the station began to act in an unpredictable manner.

Then things settled down again as the solar emission charged the station to equilibrium.

Aboard the ship, it was another story. The celestial globe of the meteor spotter blazed once in a blinding light and then went completely out of control. It danced with pinpoints of light, and the coupler that was used to direct the guns went crazy. Turrets tried to swivel, but the charge raised hob with the electronic controls, and the guns raised once, and then fell, inert. One of them belched flame, and the shell went wild. The carefully balanced potentials in the driver tubes were upset, and the ship lost headway. The heavy ion stream from the driving cathode bent and spread, touching the dynodes in the tubes. The resulting current brought them to a red heat, and they melted down and floated through the evacuated tube in round droplets. Instruments went wild, and gave every possible answer, and the ship became a bedlam of ringing bells and flashing danger lights.

But the crew was in no shape to appreciate this display. From metal parts in the ship there appeared coronas that reached for the unprotected men, and seared their flesh. And since their gravity-apparent was gone, they floated freely through the air, and came in contact with highly charged walls, ceilings and floors; to say nothing of the standard metal furniture.

It was a sorry bunch of pirates that found themselves in a ship-without-motive-power that was beginning to leave their circular course on a tangent that would let them drop into the Sun.

'That's my answer, Murdoch!' snapped Channing. 'Watch your second ship!'

'You young devil!' snarled Murdoch. 'What did you do?'

'You never thought that it would be an electronics engineer that made the first energy gun, did you, Murdoch? I'm now going to take a shot at No. 3!'

No. 3's turret swiveled around and from the guns flashes of fire came streaming. Channing punched his lever savagely, and once again the station was tortured by the effects of its own offensive.

Ship No. 3 suffered the same fate as No. 2.

Then, seconds later, armor-piercing shells began to hit Venus Equilateral. They hit, and because of the terrific charge, they began to arc at the noses. The terrible current passed through the fuses, and the shells exploded on contact instead of boring in before detonation. Metal was bent and burned, but only a few tiny holes resulted. As the charge on the station approached equilibrium once more, men ran with torches to seal these holes.

'Murdoch,' said Channing, 'I want you!'

'Come and get me!'

'Land – or die!' snapped Channing in a vicious tone. 'I'm no humanitarian, Murdoch. You'd be better off dead!'

'Never!' said Hellion Murdoch.

Channing pulled the lever for the third time, but as he did, Murdoch's ship leaped forward under several G. The magnets could not change in field soon enough to compensate for this change in direction, and the charge failed to connect as a bull's eye. It did expend some of its energy on the tail of the ship. Not enough to cripple the *Hippocrates*, but the vessel took on a charge of enough value to make things hard on the crew.

Metal sparked, and instruments went mad. Meters wound their needles around the end pegs. The celestial globe glinted in a riot of color and then went completely dead. Gun servers dropped their projectiles as they became too heavily charged to handle, and they rolled across the turret floors, creating panic in the gun crews. The pilot fought the controls, but the charge on his driver tubes was sufficient to make his helm completely unpredictable. The panel sparked at him and seared his hands, spoiling his nervous control and making him heavy-handed.

'Murdoch,' cried Channing in a hearty voice, 'that was a miss! Want a hit?'

Murdoch's radio was completely dead. His ship was yawing from side to side as the static charges raced through the driver tubes. The pilot gained control after a fashion, and decided that he had taken enough. He circled the station warily and began to make a shaky landing at the south end.

Channing saw him coming, and with a glint in his eye, he pressed the lever for the fourth and last time.

Murdoch's ship touched the landing stage just after the charge had been driven out into space. The heavy negative charge on the *Hippocrates* met the heavy positive charge on Venus Equilateral. The ship touched, and from that contact, there arose a cloud of incandescent gas. The entire charge left the ship at once, and through that single contact. When the cloud dissipated, the contact was a crude but efficient welded

126

joint that was gleaming white-hot.

Channing said to Walt: 'That's going to be messy.'

Inside of the *Hippocrates*, men were frozen to their hand-holds. It was messy, and cleaning up the *Hippocrates* was a job not relished by those who did it.

But cleaning up Venus Equilateral was no small matter, either.

A week went by before the snarled-up instruments were repaired. A week in which the captured *Hippocrates* was repaired, too, and used to transport prisoners to and material and special supplies from Terra, and Venus, and Mars. A week in which the service from planet to planet was erratic.

Then service was restored, and life settled down to a reasonable level. It was after this that Walt and Channing found time to spend an idle hour together. Walt raised his glass and said: 'Here's to electrons!'

'Yeah,' grinned Channing, 'here's to electrons. Y'know, Walt, I was a little afraid that space might become a sort of Wild West show, with the ships bristling with space guns and betatrons and stuff like that. In which case you'd have been a stinking benefactor. But if the recoil is as bad as the output – and Newton said that it must be – I can't see ships cluttering up their insides with stuff that'll screw up their instruments and driver tubes. But the thing that amuses me about the whole thing is the total failure you produced.'

'Failure?' asked Walt. 'What failed?'

'Don't you know? Have you forgotten? Do you realize that spaceships are still ducking around meteors instead of blasting them out of the way with the Franks Electron Gun? Or did you lose sight of the fact that this dingbat started out in life as a meteor-sweeper?'

Walt glared over the rim of his glass, but he had nothing to say.

Interlude:

Once the threat of piracy was over, Don Channing returned to his major problem: How to devise two-way communication between ship and planet, or better, from ship to ship. It was not to come easily.

But it is not hard to come to the mistaken conclusion that nothing much was taking place outside of Venus Equilateral; that all of the science of communication was centred there. The truth is different. For uncounted centuries earlier, on the now-arid plains of Mars, a highly civilized culture developed sophisticated equipment and then died away, leaving some of their gear to be puzzled over, not by engineers, but by archaeologists.

LOST ART

Sargon of Akkad was holding court in all of his spendor in the Mesopotamia area, which he thought to be the center of the Universe. The stars to him were but holes in a black bowl which he called the sky. They were beautiful then, as they are now, but he thought that they were put there for his edification only; for was he not the ruler of Akkadia?

After Sargon of Akkad, there would come sixty centuries of climbing before men reached the stars and found not only that there had been men upon them, but that a civilization on Mars had reached its peak four thousand years before Christ and was now but a memory and a wealth of pictographs that adorned the semipreserved Temples of Canalopsis.

And sixty centuries after, the men of Terra wondered about the ideographs and solved them sufficiently to piece together the wonders of the long-dead Martian Civilization.

Sargon of Akkad did not know that the stars that he beheld carried on them wonders his mind would not, could not, accept.

Altas, the Martian, smiled tolerantly at his son. The young man boasted on until Altas said: 'So you have memorized the contents of my manual? Good, Than, for I am growing old and I would be pleased to have my son fill my shoes. Come into the workshop that I may pass upon your proficiency.'

Altas led Than to the laboratory that stood at the foot of the great tower of steel; Altas removed from a cabinet a replacement element from the great beam above their heads, and said: 'Than, show me how to hook this up!'

Than's eyes glowed. From other cabinets he took small auxiliary parts. From hooks upon the wall, Than took lengths of wire. Working with a brilliant deftness that was his heritage as a Martian, Than spent an hour attaching the complicated circuits. After he was finished, Than stepped back and said: 'There – and believe it or not, this is the first time you have permitted me to work with one of the beam elements.'

'You have done well,' said Altas with that same cryptic smile. 'But now we shall see. The main question is: Does it work?'

'Naturally,' said Than in youthful pride. 'Is it not hooked up exactly as your manual says? It will work.'

'We shall see,' repeated Altas. 'We shall see.'

Barney Carroll and James Baler cut through the thin air of Mars in a driver-wing flier at a terrific rate of speed. It was the only kind of flier that would work on Mars with any degree of safety since it depended upon the support of its drivers rather than the wing surface. They were hitting it up at almost a thousand miles per hour on their way from Canalopsis to Lincoln Head; their trip would take an hour and a half.

As they passed over the red sand of Mars, endlessly it seemed, a glint of metal caught Barney's eye, and he shouted.

'What's the matter, Barney?' asked Jim.

'Roll her over and run back a mile or so,' said Barney. 'I saw something down there that didn't belong in this desert.'

Jim snapped the plane around in a sharp loop that nearly took their heads off, and they ran back along their course.

'Yop,' called Barney, 'there she is!'

'What?'

'See that glint of shiny metal? That doesn't belong in this mess of erosion. Might be a crash.'

'Hold tight,' laughed Jim. 'We're going down.'

They did. Jim's piloting had all the aspects of a daredevil racing pilot's, and Barney was used to it. Jim snapped the nose of the little flier down and they power-dived to within a few yards of the sand before he set the plane on its tail and skidded flatwise to kill speed. He leveled off, and the flier came scream-ing in for a perfect landing not many feet from the glinting object.

'This is no crash,' said Baler. 'This looks like the remains of an air-lane beacon of some sort.'

'Does it? Not like any I've ever seen. It reminds me more of some of the gadgets they find here and there – the remnants of the Ancients. They used to build junk like this.'

'Hook up the sand-blower,' suggested Jim Baler. 'We'll clear some of this rubble away and see what she really looks like. Can't see much more than what looks like a high-powered searchlight.'

Barney hauled equipment out of the flier and hitched it to a small motor in the plane. The blower created a small storm for an hour or so, its blast directed by suitclad Barney Carroll. Working with experience gained in uncovering the remains of a dozen dead and buried cities, Barney cleared the shifting sand from the remains of the tower.

The head was there, preserved by the dry sand. Thirty feet below the platform, the slender tower was broken off. No delv-ing could find the lower portion.

'This is quite a find,' said Jim. 'Looks like some of the carv-ings on the Temple of Science at Canalopsis – that little house on the top of the spire with the three-foot runway around it; then this dingbat perched on top of the roof. Never did figure out what it was for.'

'We don't know whether the Martians' eyes responded as our do,' suggested Barney. 'This might be a searchlight that puts out with Martian visible spectrum. If they saw with infrared, they wouldn't be using Terran fluorescent lighting. If they saw with long heat frequencies, they wouldn't waste power with even a tungsten filament light, but would have invented some-thing that cooked its most energy in the visible spectrum, just as we have in the last couple of hundred years.'

'That's just a guess, of course.'

'Naturally,' said Barney. 'Here, I've got the door cracked. Let's be the first people in this place for six thousand years Terran. Take it easy, this floor is at an angle of thirty degrees.'

'I won't slide. G'wan in. I'm your shadow.'

They entered the thiry-foot circular room and snapped on their torches. There was a bench that ran almost around the entire room. It was empty save for a few scraps of metal and a Martian book of several hundred metal pages.

'Nuts,' said Barney, 'we would have to find a thing like this but empty. That's our luck. What's the book, Jim?'

'Some sort of text, I'd say. Full of diagrams and what seems to be mathematics. Hard to tell, of course, but we've established the fact that mathematics is universal, though the characters cannot possibly be.'

'Any chance of deciphering it?' asked Barney.

'Let's get back in the flier and try. I'm in no particular hurry.'

'Nor am I. I don't care whether we get to Lincoln Head to-night or the middle of next week.'

'Now let's see that volume of diagrams,' he said as soon as they were established in the flier.

Jim passed the book over, and Barney opened the book to the first page. 'If we never find anything else,' he said, 'this will make us famous. I am now holding the first complete volume of Martian literature that anyone has ever seen. The darned thing is absolutely complete, from cover to cover!'

'That's a find,' agreed Jim. 'Now go ahead and transliterate it – you're the expert on Martian pictographs.'

For an hour, Barney scanned the pages of the volume. He made copious notes on sheets of paper which he inserted between the metal leaves of the book. At the end of that time, during which Jim Baler had been inspecting the searchlight-thing on top of the little house, he called to his friend, and Jim entered the flier lugging the thing on his shoulders.

'What'cha got?' he grinned. 'I brought this along. Nothing else in that shack, so we're complete except for the remnants of some very badly corroded cable that ran from this thing to a flapping end down where the tower was broken.'

Barney smiled and blinked. It was strange to see this big man working studiously over a book; Barney Carroll should have been leading a horde of Venusian engineers through the Palanortis country instead of delving into the artifacts of a dead civilization.

'I think that this thing is a sort of engineer's handbook,' he said. 'In the front there is a section devoted to mathematical tables. You know, a table of logs to the base twelve which is because the Martians had six fingers on each hand. There is what seems to be a table of definite integrals – at least if I were writing a handbook I'd place the table of integrals at the last part of the math section. The geometry and trig is absolutely recognizable because of the designs. So is the solid geom and the analyt for the same reason. The next section seems to be devoted to chemistry; the Martians used a hexagonal figure for a benzene ring, too, and so that's established. From that we find the key to the Periodic Chart of the Atoms which is run vertically instead of horizontally, but still unique. These guys were sharp, though; they seem to have hit upon the fact that isotopes are separate elements though so close in grouping to one another that they exhibit the same properties. Finding this will uncover a lot of mystery.'

'Yeah,' agreed Baler, 'from a book of this kind we can decipher most anything. The keying on a volume of physical constants is perfect and almost infinite in number. What do they use for Pi?'

'Circle with a double dot inside.'

'And Plank's Constant?'

'Haven't hit that one yet. But we will. But to get back to the meat of this thing, the third section deals with something strange. It seems to have a bearing on this gadget from the top of the tower. I'd say that the volume was a technical volume on the construction, maintenance, and repair of the tower and its functions – whatever they are.'

Barney spread the volume out for Jim to see. 'That dingbat is some sort of electronic device. Or, perhaps subelectronic. Peel away that rusted side and we'll look inside.'

Jim peeled a six-inch section from the side of the big metal tube, and they inspected the insides. Barney looked thoughtful for a minute and then flipped the pages of the book until he came to a diagram.

'Sure,' he said exultantly, 'this is she. Look, Jim, they draw a cathode like this, and the grids are made with a series of fine parallel lines. Different, but more like the real grid than our symbol of a zigzag line. The plate is a round circle instead of a square, but that's so clearly defined that it comes out automatically. Here's your annular electrodes, and the . . . call 'em deflection plates. I think we can hook this do-boodle up as soon as we get to our place in Lincoln Head.'

'Let's go then. Not only would I like to see this thing work, but I'd give anything to know what it's for!'

'You run the crate,' said Barney, 'and I'll try to decipher this mess into voltages for the electrode-supply and so on. Then we'll be in shape to go ahead and hook her up.'

The trip to Lincoln Head took almost an hour. Barney and Jim landed in their landing yards and took the book and the searchlight-thing inside. They went to their laboratory, and called for sandwiches and tea. Jim's sister brought in the food a little later and found them tinkering with the big beam tube.

'What have you got this time?' she groaned.

'Name it and it's yours,' laughed Barney.

'A sort of gadget that we found on the Red Desert.'

'What does it do?' asked Christine Baler.

'Well,' said Jim, 'it's a sort of a kind of a dingbat that does things.'

'Uh-huh,' said Christine. 'A dololly that plings the inghams.'

'Right!'

'You're well met, you two. Have your fun. But for Pete's sake don't forget to eat. Not that you will, I know you, but a girl has got to make some sort of attempt at admonishment. I'm going to the moom-picher. I'll see you when I return.'

'I'd say stick around,' said Barney. 'But I don't think we'll have anything to show you for hours and hours. We'll have something by the time you return.'

Christine left, and the men applied themselves to their problem. Barney had done wonders in unraveling the unknown. Inductances, he found, were spirals; resistances were dotted lines; capacitances were parallel squares.

'What kind of stuff do we use for voltages?' asked Jim.

'That's a long, hard trail,' laughed Barney. 'Basing my calculations on the fact that their standard voltage cell was the same as ours, we apply the voltage as listed on my schematic here.'

'Can you assume that their standard is the same as ours?'

'Better,' said Barney. 'The Terran Standard Cell – the well-known Weston Cell – dishes out what we call 1.0183 volts at twenty degrees C. Since the Martian description of their Standard Cell is essentially the same as the Terran, they are using the same thing. Only they use sense and say that a volt is the unit of a standard cell, period. Calculating their figures on the numerical base of twelve is tricky, but I've done it.'

'You're doing fine. How do you assume their standard is the same?'

'Simple,' said Barney in a cheerful tone. 'Thank God for their habit of drawing pictures. Here we have the well-known H tube. The electrodes are signified by the symbols for the elements used. The Periodic Chart in the first section came in handy here. But look, master mind, this dinky should be evacuated don't you think?'

'If it's electronic or subelectronic, it should be. We can solder up this breach here and apply the hyvac pump. Rig us up a power supply whilst I repair the blowout.'

'Where's the BFO?'

'What do you want with that?' asked Jim.

'The second anode takes about two hundred volts worth of eighty-four cycles,' explained Barney. 'Has a sign that seems to signify "In Phase", but I'll be darned if I know with what. Y'know, Jim, this dingbat looks an awful lot like one of the drivers we use in our spaceships and driver-wing fliers.'

'Yeah,' drawled Jim. 'About the same recognition as the difference between Edison's first electric-light and a twelve-element, electron multiplier, power output tube. Similarly: They both have cathodes.'

'Edison didn't have a cathode—'

'Sure he did. Just because he didn't hang a plate inside of the bottle doesn't stop the filament from being a cathode.'

Barney snorted. 'A monode, hey?'

'Precisely. After which come diodes, triodes, tetrodes, pentodes, hexodes, heptodes—'

'—and the men in the white coats. How's your patching job?'

'Fine. How's your power-supply job?'

'Good enough,' said Barney. 'This eighty-four cycles is not going to be a sine wave at two hundred volts; the power stage of the BFO overloads just enough to bring in a bit of second harmonic.'

'A beat-frequency-oscillator was never made to run at that level,' complained Jim Baler. 'At least, not this one. She'll tick on a bit of second, I think.'

'Are we ready for the great experiment?'

'Yup, and I still wish I knew what the thing was for. Go ahead, Barney. Crack the big switch!'

Altas held up a restraining hand as Than grasped the main power switch. 'Wait,' he said. 'Does one stand in his sky flier and leave the ground at full velocity? Or does one start an internal combustion engine at full speed?'

'No,' said the youngster. 'We usually take it slowly.'

'And like the others, we must tune our tube. And that we cannot do under full power. Advance your power lever one-tenth step and we'll adjust the deflection anodes.'

'I'll get the equipment,' said Than. 'I forgot that part.'

'Never mind the equipment,' smiled Altas. 'Observe.'

Altas picked up a long screwdriverlike tool and inserted it into the maze of wiring that surrounded the tube. Squinting in one end of the big tube, he turned the tool until the cathode surface brightened slightly. He adjusted the instrument until the cathode was at its brightest, and then withdrew the tool.

'That will do for your experimental set-up,' smiled Altas. 'The operation in service is far more critical and requires equipment. As an experiment, conducted singly, the accumulative effect cannot be dangerous, though if the deflection plates are not properly served with their supply voltages, the experiment is a failure. The operation of the tube depends upon the perfection of the deflection-plate voltages.'

'No equipment is required, then?'

'It should have been employed,' said Altas modestly. 'But in my years as a bcam-tower attendant, I have learned the art of aligning the plates by eye. Now, son, we may proceed from there.'

Barney Carroll took a deep breath and let the power switch fall home. Current meters swung across their scales for an instant, and then the lights went out in the house!

137

'Fuse blew,' said Barney shortly. He gumbled his way through the dark house and replaced the fuse. He returned smiling. 'Fixed that one,' he told Jim. 'Put a washer behind it.'

'O.K. Hit the switch again.'

Barney cranked the power over, and once more the meters climbed up across the scales. There was a groaning sound from the tube, and the smell of burning insulation filled the room. One meter blew with an audible sound as the needle hit the end stop, and immediately afterward the lights in the entire block went out.

'Fix that one by hanging a penny behind it,' said Jim with a grin.

'That's a job for Martian Electric to do,' laughed Barney.

Several blocks from there, an attendant in the substation found the open circuit-breaker and shoved it in with a grim smile. He looked up at the power-demand meter and grunted. High for this district, but not dangerous. Duration, approximately fifteen seconds. Intensity, higher than usual but not high enough to diagnose any failure of the wiring in the district. 'Ah, well,' he thought, 'we can crank up the blow-point on this breaker if it happens again.'

He turned to leave and the crashing of the breaker scared him out of a week's growth. He snarled and said a few choice words not fit for publication. He closed the breaker and screwed the blow-point control up by two-to-one. 'That'll hold 'em,' he thought, and then the ringing of the telephone called him to his office, and he knew that he was in for an explanatory session with some people who wanted to know why their lights were going on and off. He composed a plausible tale on his way to the phone. Meanwhile, he wondered about the unreasonable demand and concluded that one of the folks had just purchased a new power saw or something for their home workshop.

'Crack the juice about a half,' suggested Barney. 'That'll keep us on the air until we find out what kind of stuff this thing takes. The book claims about one tenth of the current-drain for this unit. Something we've missed, no doubt.'

'Let's see that circuit,' said Jim. After a minute, he said: 'Look, guy, what are these screws for?'

'They change the side plate voltages from about three hundred to about three hundred and fifty. I've got 'em set in the middle of the range.'

'Turn us on half voltage and diddle one of 'em.'

'That much of a change shouldn't make the difference,' objected Barney.

'Brother, we don't know what this thing is even for,' reminded Jim. 'Much less do we know the effect of anything on it. Diddle, I say.'

'O.K., we diddle.' Barney turned on half power and reached into the maze of wiring and began to tinker with one of the screws. 'Hm-m-m,' he said after a minute. 'Does things, all right. She goes through some kind of resonance point or something. There is a spot of minimum current here. There! I've hit it. Now for the other one.'

For an hour, Barney tinkered with first one screw and then the other one. He found a point where the minimum current was really low; the two screws were interdependent and only by adjusting them alternately was he able to reach the proper point on each. Then he smiled and thrust the power on full. The current remained at a sane value.

'Now what?' asked Barney.

'I don't know. Anything coming out of the business end?'

'Heat.'

'Yeah, and it's about as lethal as a sun lamp. D'ye suppose the Martians used to artificially assist their crops by synthetic sunshine?'

Barney applied his eye to a spectroscope. It was one of the newer designs that encompassed everything from short ultra-violet to long infrared by means of fluorescent screens at the invisible wave lengths. He turned the instrument across the spectrum and shook his head. 'Might be good for a chest cold,' he said, 'but you wouldn't get a sunburn off of it. It's all in the infra. Drops off like a cliff just below the deep red. Nothing at all in the visible or above. Gee,' he said with a queer smile, 'you don't suppose that they died off because of a pernicious epidemic of colds and they tried chest-cooking *en masse*?'

'I'd believe anything if this darned gadget were found in a populated district,' said Jim. 'But we know that the desert was here when the Martians were here, and that it was just as arid as it is now. They wouldn't try farming in a place where iron oxide abounds.'

'Spinach?'

'You don't know a lot about farming, do you?' asked Jim.

'I saw a cow once.'

'That does not qualify you as an expert on farming.'

'I know one about the farmer's daughter, and—'

'Not even an expert on dirt farming,' continued Jim. 'Nope, Barney, we aren't even close.'

Barney checked the book once more and scratched his nose.

'How about that eighty-four cycle supply,' asked Jim.

'It's eighty-four, all right. From the Martian habit of using twelve as a base, I've calculated the number to be eighty-four.'

'Diddle that, too,' suggested Jim.

'O.K.,' said Barney. 'It doesn't take a lot to crank that one around from zero to about fifteen thousand c.p.s. Here she goes!'

Barney took the main dial of the beat-frequency oscillator and began to crank it around the scale. He went up from eighty-four to the top of the dial and then returned. No effect. Then he passed through eighty-four and started down toward zero.

He hit sixty cycles and the jackpot at the same time!

At exactly sixty cycles, a light near the wall dimmed visibly.

The wallpaper scorched and burst into a smoldering flame on a wall opposite the dimmed light.

Barney removed the BFO from the vicinity of sixty cycles and Jim extinguished the burning wallpaper.

'Now we're getting somewhere,' said Barney.

'This is definitely some sort of weapon,' said Jim. 'She's not very efficient right now, but we can find out why and then we'll have something hot.'

'What for?' asked Barney. 'Nobody hates anybody any more.'

'Unless the birds who made this thing necessary return,' said Jim soberly. His voice was ominous. 'We know that only one race of Martians existed, and they were all amicable. I suspect an inimical race from outer space—'

'Could be. Some of the boys are talking about an expedition to Centauri right now. We could have had a visitor from somewhere during the past.'

'If you define eternity as the time required for everything to happen once, I agree. In the past or in the future, we have been or will be visited by a super race. It may have happened six thousand years ago.'

'Did you notice that the electric light is not quite in line with the axis of the tube?' asked Barney.

'Don't turn it any closer,' said Jim. 'In fact, I'd turn it away before we hook it up again.'

'There she is. Completely out of line with the light. Now shall we try it again?'

'Go ahead.'

Barney turned the BFO gingerly, and at sixty cycles the thing seemed quite sane. Nothing happened. 'Shall I swing it around?'

'I don't care for fires as a general rule,' said Jim. 'Especially in my own home. Turn it gently, and take care that you don't focus the tube full on that electric light.'

Barney moved the tube slightly, and then with a cessation of noise, the clock on the wall stopped abruptly. The accustomed ticking had not been noticed by either man, but the unaccustomed lack-of-ticking became evident at once. Barney shut off the BFO immediately and the two men sat down to a head-scratching session.

'She's good for burning wallpaper, dimming electric lights, and stopping clocks,' said Barney. 'Any of which you could do without a warehouse full of cockeyed electrical equipment. Wonder if she'd stop anything more powerful than a clock.'

'I've got a quarter-horse motor here. Let's wind that up and try it.'

The motor was installed on a bench nearby, and the experiment was tried again. At sixty cycles the motor groaned to a stop, and the windings began to smolder. But at the same time the big tube began to exhibit the signs of strain. Meters raced up their scales once more, reached the stops and bent. Barney shut off the motor, but the strains did not stop in the tube. The apparent overload increased linearly and finally the lights went out all over the neighborhood once more.

'Wonderful,' said Barney through the darkness. 'As a weapon, this thing is surpassed by everything above a fly swatter.'

'We might be able to cook a steak with it – if it would take the terrific overload,' said Jim. 'Or we could use it as an insect exterminator.'

'We'd do better by putting the insect on an anvil and hitting it firmly with a five-pound hammer,' said Barney. 'Then we'd only have the anvil and hammer to haul around. This thing is like hauling a fifty-thousand-watt radio transmitter around. Power supplies, BFO, tube, meters, tools, and a huge truck full of spare fuses for the times when we miss the insect. Might be good for a central heating system.'

'Except that a standard electric unit is more reliable and

considerably less complicated. You'd have to hire a corps of engineers to run the thing.'

The lights went on again, and the attendant in the substation screwed the blow-point control tighter. He didn't know it, but his level was now above the rating for his station. But had he known it he might not have cared. At least, his station was once more in operation.

'Well,' said Barney, getting up from the table, 'what have we missed?'

Altas said: 'Now your unit is operating at its correct level. But, son, you've missed one thing. It is far from efficient. Those two leads must be isolated from one another. Coupling from one to the other will lead to losses.'

'Gosh,' said Than, 'I didn't know that.'

'No, for some reason the books assume that the tower engineer has had considerable experience in the art. Take it from me, son, there are a lot of things that are not in the books. Now isolate those leads from one another and we'll go on.'

'While you're thinking,' said Jim, 'I'm going to lockstitch these cables together. It'll make this thing less messy.' Jim got a roll of twelve-cord from the cabinet and began to bind the many supply leads into a neat cable.

Barney watched until the job was finished, and then said: 'Look, chum, let's try that electric-light trick again.'

They swung the tube around until it was in the original position, and turned the juice on. Nothing happened.

Barney looked at Jim, and then reached out and pointed the big tube right at the electric light.

Nothing happened.

'Check your anode voltages again.'

'All O.K.'

'How about that aligning job?'

143

Barney fiddled with the alignment screws for minutes, but his original setting seemed to be valid.

'Back to normal,' said Barney. 'Rip out your cabling.'

'Huh?'

'Sure. You did something. I don't know what. But rip it out and fan out the leads. There is something screwy in the supply lines. I've been tied up on that one before; this thing looks like electronics, as we agree, and I've had occasion to remember coupling troubles.'

'All right,' said Jim, and he reluctantly ripped out his lock-stitching. He fanned the leads and they tried it again.

Obediently the light dimmed and the wallpaper burned.

'Here we go again,' said Jim, killing the circuits and reaching for a small rug to smother the fire. 'No wonder the Martians had this thing out in the middle of the desert. D'ye suppose that they were trying to find out how it works, too?'

'Take it easier this time and we'll fan the various leads,' said Barney. 'There's something tricky about the lead placement.'

'Half power,' announced Barney. 'Now, let's get that sixty cycles.'

The light dimmed slightly and a sheet of metal placed in front of the tube became slightly warm to the touch. The plate stopped the output of the tube, for the wallpaper did not scorch. Jim began to take supply line after supply line from the bundle of wiring. About halfway through the mess he hit the critical lead, and immediately the light went out completely, and the plate grew quite hot.

'Stop her!' yelled Barney.

'Why?'

'How do we know what we're overloading this time?'

'Do we care?'

'Sure. Let's point this thing away from that light. Then we can hop it up again and try it at full power.'

'What do you want to try?'

'This energy-absorption thing.'

'Wanna burn out my motor?'

'Not completely. This dingbat will stop a completely mechanical gadget, like a clock. It seems to draw power from electric lights. It stops electromechanical power. I wonder just how far it will go toward absorbing power. And also I want to know where the power goes.'

The tube was made to stop the clock again. The motor groaned under the load put upon it by the tube. Apparently the action of the tube was similar to a heavy load being placed on whatever its end happened to point to. Barney picked up a small metal block and dropped it over the table.

'Want to see if it absorbs the energy of a falling object— Look at that!'

The block fell until it came inside of the influence of the tube. Then it slowed in its fall and approached the table slowly. It did not hit the table, it touched and came to rest.

'What happens if we wind up a spring and tie it?' asked Jim. They tried it. Nothing happened.

'Works on kinetic energy, not potential energy,' said Barney.

He picked up a heavy hammer and tried to hit the table. 'Like swinging a club through a tub of water,' he said.

'Be a useful gadget for saving the lives of people who are falling,' said Jim thoughtfully.

'Oh, sure. Put it on a truck and rush it out to the scene of the suicide.'

'No. How about people jumping out of windows on account of fires? How about having one of the things around during a flier-training course? Think of letting a safe down on one of these beams, or taking a piano from the fifth floor of an apartment building.'

'The whole apartment full of furniture could be pitched out of a window,' said Barney.

'Mine looks that way now,' said Jim, 'and we've only moved

a couple of times. No, Barney, don't give 'em any ideas.'

Jim picked up the hammer and tried to hit the table. Then, idly, he swung the hammer in the direction of the tube's end.

Barney gasped. In this direction there was no resistance. Jim's swing continued, and the look on Jim's face indicated that he was trying to brake the swing in time to keep from hitting the end of the tube. But it seemed as though he were trying to stop an avalanche. The swing continued on and on and finally ended when the hammer head contacted the end of the tube.

There was a burst of fire. Jim swung right on through, whirling around off balance and coming to a stop only when he fell to the floor. He landed in darkness again. The burst of fire emanated from the insulation as it flamed under the heat of extreme overload.

This time the lights were out all over Lincoln Head. The whole city was in complete blackout!

Candles were found, and they inspected the tube anxiously. It seemed whole. But the hammer head was missing. The handle was cut cleanly, on an optically perfect surface.

Where the hammer head went, they couldn't say. But on the opposite wall there was a fracture in the plaster that Jim swore hadn't been there before. It extended over quite an area, and after some thought, Barney calculated that if the force of Jim's hammer blow had been evenly distributed over that area on the wall, the fracturing would have been just about that bad.

'A weapon, all right,' said Barney.

'Sure. All you have to do is to shoot your gun right in this end and the force is dissipated over quite an area out of that end. In the meantime you blow out all of the powerhouses on the planet. If a hammer blow can raise such merry hell, what do you think the output of a sixteen-inch rifle would do? Probably stop the planet in its tracks. D'ye know what I think?'

'No, do you?'

'Barney, I think that we aren't even close as to the operation and use of this device.'

'For that decision, Jim, you should be awarded the Interplanetary Award for Discovery and Invention – posthumously!'

'So what do we do now?'

'Dunno. How soon does this lighting situation get itself fixed?'

'You ask me . . . I don't know either.'

'Well, let's see what we've found so far.'

'That's easy,' said Jim. 'It might be a weapon, but it don't weap. We might use it for letting elevators down easy, except that it would be a shame to tie up a room full of equipment when the three-phase electric motor is so simple. We could toast a bit of bread, but the electric toaster has been refined to a beautiful piece of breakfast furniture that doesn't spray off and scorch the wallpaper. We could use it to transmit hammer blows, or to turn out electric lights, but both of those things have been done very simply; one by means of sending the hammerer to the spot, and the other by means of turning the switch. And then in the last couple of cases, there is little sense in turning out a light by short circuiting the socket and blowing all the fuses.

'That is the hard way,' smiled Barney. 'Like hitting a telephone pole to stop the car, or cutting the wings off a plane to return it to the ground.'

'So we have a fairly lucid book that describes the entire hookup of the thing except what it's for. It gives not only the use of this device, but also variations and replacements. Could we figure it out by sheer deduction?'

'I don't see how. The tower is in the midst of the Red Desert. There is nothing but sand that assays high in iron oxide between Canalopsis, at the junction of the Grand Canal and

Lincoln Head. Might be hid, of course, just as this one was, and we'll send out a crew of expert sub-sand explorers with under-surface detectors to cover the ground for a few hundred miles in any direction from the place where we found this. Somehow, I doubt that we'll find much.'

'And how do you . . . ah, there's the lights again . . . deduce that?' asked Jim.

'This gadget is or was of importance to the Martians. Yet in the Temple of Science and Industry at Canalopsis, there is scant mention of the towers.'

'Not very much, hey?'

'Very little, in fact. Of course the pictographs on the Temple at Canalopsis shows one tower between what appear two cities. Wavy lines run from one city to the tower and to the other city. Say! I'll bet a cooky that this is some sort of signaling device!'

'A beam transmitter?' asked Jim skeptically. 'Seems like a lot of junk for just signaling. Especially when such a swell job can be done with standard radio equipment. A good civilization – such as the Martians must have had – wouldn't piddle around with relay stations between two cities less than a couple of thousand miles apart. With all the juice this thing can suck, they'd be more than able to hang a straight broadcast station and cover halfway around the planet as ground-wave area. What price relay station?'

'Nevertheless, I'm going to tinker up another one of these and see if it is some sort of signaling equipment.'

The door opened and Christine Baler entered. She waved a newspaper before her brother's eyes and said. 'Boy, have you been missing it!'

'What?' asked Barney.

'Pixies or gremlins loose in Lincoln Head.'

'Huh-huh. Read it,' said Jim.

148

'Just a bunch of flash headlines. Fire on Manley Avenue. Three planes had to make dead-tube landings in the center of the city; power went dead for no good reason for about ten minutes. Façade of the City Hall caved in. Power plants running wild all over the place. Ten thousand dollars' worth of electrical equipment blown out. Automobiles stalled in rows for blocks.'

Jim looked at Barney. 'Got a bear by the tail,' he said.

'Could be,' admitted Barney.

'Are you two blithering geniuses going to work all night?' asked Christine.

'Nope. We're about out of ideas. Except the one that Barney had about the gadget being some sort of signaling system.'

'Why don't you fellows call Don Channing? He's the signaling wizard of the Solar System.'

'Sure, call Channing. Every time someone gets an idea, everyone says, "Call Channing!" He gets called for everything from Boy Scout wigwag ideas to super-cyclotronic-electron-stream beams to contact the outer planets. Based upon the supposition that people will eventually get there, of course.'

'Well?'

'Well, I . . . we, I mean . . . found this thing and we're jolly well going to tinker it out. In spite of the fact that it seems to bollix up everything from electric lights to moving gears. I think we're guilty of sabotage. Façade of the City Hall, et cetera. Barney, how long do you think it will take to tinker up another one of these?'

'Few hours. They're doggoned simple things in spite of the fact that we can't understand them. In fact, I'm of the opinion that the real idea would be to make two; one with only the front end for reception, one for the rear end for transmission, and the one we found for relaying. That's the natural bent, I believe.'

'Could be. Where are you going to cut them?'

149

'The transmitter will start just before the cathode and the receiver will end just after the . . . uh, cathode.'

'Huh?'

'Obviously the cathode is the baby that makes with the end product. She seems to be a total intake from the intake end and a complete output from the opposite end. Right?'

'Right, but it certainly sounds like heresy.'

'I know,' said Barney thoughtfully, 'but the thing is obviously different from anything that we know today. Who knows how she works?'

'I give up.'

Christine, who had been listening in an interested manner, said: 'You fellers are the guys responsible for the ruckus that's been going on all over Lincoln Head?'

'I'm afraid so.'

'Well, brother warlocks, unless you keep your activities under cover until they're worth mentioning, you'll both be due for burning at the stake.'

'O.K., Chris,' said Jim. 'We'll not let it out.'

'But how are you going to tinker up that transmitter-relay-receiver system?'

'We'll take it from here to Barney's place across the avenue and into his garage. That should do it.'

'O.K., but now I'm going to bed.'

'Shall we knock off, too?' asked Jim.

'Yup. Maybe we'll dream a good thought.'

'So long then. We'll leave the mess as it is. No use cleaning up now, we'll only have to mess it up again tomorrow with the same junk.'

'And I'll have that – or those – other systems tinkered together by tomorrow noon. That's a promise,' said Barney. 'And you,' he said to Christine, 'will operate the relay station.'

Altas said to Than: 'Now that your system is balanced properly, and we have proved the worth of this tube as a replacement, we shall take it to the roof and install it. The present tube is about due for retirement.'

'I've done well, then?' asked Than.

'Considering all, you've done admirably. But balancing the device in the tower, and hooked into the circuit as an integral part is another thing. Come, Than. We shall close the line for an hour whilst replacing the tube.'

'Is that permissible?'

'At this time of the night the requirements are small. No damage will be done; they can get along without us for an hour. In fact, at this time of night, only the people who are running the city will know that we are out of service. And it is necessary that the tube be maintained at full capability. We can not chance a weakened tube; it might fail when it is needed the most.'

Than carried the tube to the top of the tower, and Altas remained to contact the necessary parties concerning the shut-off for replacement purposes. He followed Than to the top after a time and said: 'Now disconnect the old tube and put it on the floor. We shall replace the tube immediately, but it will be an hour before it is properly balanced again.'

It was not long before Than had the tube connected properly. 'Now,' said Altas, 'turn it on one-tenth power and we shall align it.'

'Shall I use the meters?'

'I think it best. This requires perfect alignment. We've much power and considerable distance, and any losses will create great amounts of heat.'

'All right,' said Than. He left the tower top to get the meters.

Barney Carroll spoke into a conveniently placed microphone. 'Are you ready?' he asked.

'Go ahead,' said Christine.

'We're waiting,' said Jim.

'You're the bird on the transmitter,' said Barney to Jim. '*You* make with the juice.'

Power rheostats were turned up gingerly, until Jim shouted to stop. His shout was blotted out by cries from the other two. They met in Barney's place to confer.

'What's cooking?' asked Jim.

'The meters are all going crazy in my end,' said Barney. 'I seem to be sucking power out of everything in line with my tube.'

'The so-called relay station is firing away at full power and doing nothing but draining plenty of power from the lne,' complained Christine.

'And on my end, I was beginning to scorch the wallpaper again. I don't understand it. With no receiver-end, how can I scorch wallpaper?'

'Ask the Martians. They know.'

'You ask 'em. What shall we do, invent a time machine and go back sixty centuries?'

'Wish we could,' said Barney. 'I'd like to ask the bird that left this textbook why they didn't clarify it more.'

'Speaking of Don Channing again,' said Jim, 'I'll bet a hat that one of his tube-replacement manuals for the big transmitters out on Venus Equilateral do not even mention that the transmitter requires a receiver before it is any good. We think we're modern. We are, and we never think that some day some poor bird will try to decipher our technical works. Why, if Volta himself came back and saw the most perfect machine ever invented – the transformer – he'd shudder. No connection between input and output, several kinds of shorted loops of wire; and instead of making a nice simple electromagnet, we short the lines of force and on top of that we use a lot of laminations piled on top of one another instead of a nice, soft iron core. We completely short the input, et cetera, but how do we make with a gadget like that?'

'I know. We go on expecting to advance. We forget the simple past. Remember the lines of that story: "How does one chip the flint to make the best arrowhead?" I don't know who wrote it any more than I know how to skin a boar, but we do get on without making arrowheads or skinning boars or trimming birch-bark canoes.'

'All right, but there's still this problem.'

'Remember how we managed to align this thing? I wonder if it might not take another alignment to make it work as a relay.'

'Could be,' said Jim. 'I'll try it. Christine, you work these screws at the same time we do, and make the current come out as low as we can.'

They returned to their stations and began to work on the alignment screws. Jim came out first on the receiver. Christine was second on the transmitter, wnile Barney fumbled for a long time with the relay tube.

Then Christine called: 'Fellows, my meter readings are climbing up again. Shall I diddle?'

'Wait a minute,' said Barney. 'That means I'm probably taking power out of that gadget you have in there. Leave 'em alone.'

He fiddled a bit more, and then Jim called: 'Whoa, Nellie. Someone just lost me a milliammeter. She wound up on the far end.'

'Hm-m-m,' said Barney, 'so we're relaying.'

'Go ahead,' said Jim. 'I've got a ten-ampere meter on here now.'

Barney adjusted his screws some more.

'Wait a minute,' said Jim. 'I'm going to shunt this meter up to a hundred amps.'

'What?' yelled Barney.

'Must you yell?' asked Christine ruefully. 'These phones are plenty uncomfortable without some loud-mouthed bird screaming.'

'Sorry, but a hundred amps . . . *whoosh!* What have we got here, anyway?'

'Yeah,' said Christine. 'I was about to say that my input meter is running wild again.'

'Gone?'

'Completely. You shouldn't have hidden it behind that big box. I didn't notice it until just now, but she's completely gone.'

'I'll be over. I think we've got something here.'

An hour passed, during which nothing of any great importonce happened. By keying the transmitter tube, meters in the receiver tube were made to read in accordance. Then they had another conclave.

'Nothing brilliant,' said Jim. 'We could use super-output voice amplifiers and yell halfway across the planet if we didn't have radio. We can radio far better than this cockeyed system of signaling.'

'We might cut the power.'

'Or spread out quite a bit. I still say however, that this is no signaling system.'

'It works like one.'

'So can a clothesline be made to serve as a transmitter of intelligence. But its prime function is completely different.'

'S'pose we have a super-clothesline here?' asked Christine.

'The way that hammer felt last night, I'm not too sure that this might not be some sort of tractor beam,' said Jim.

'Tractor beams are mathematically impossible.'

'Yeah, and they proved conclusively that a bird cannot fly,' said Jim. 'That was before they found the right kind of math. Up until Clerk Maxwell's time, radio was mathematically impossible. Then he discovered the electromagnetic equations, and we're squirting signals across the Inner System every day. And when math and fact do not agree, which changes?'

'The math. Galileo proved that. Aristotle said that a heavy stone will fall faster. Then Galileo changed the math of that by heaving a couple of boulders off the Leaning Tower. But what have we here?'

'Has anyone toyed with the transmission of power?'

'Sure. A lot of science-fiction writers have their imaginary planets crisscrossed with transmitted power. Some broadcast it, some have it beamed to the consumer. When they use planes, they have the beam coupled to an object-finder so as to control the direction of the beam. I prefer the broadcasting, myself. It uncomplicates the structure of the tale.'

'I mean actually?'

'Oh, yes. But the losses are terrific. Useful power transmission is a minute percentage of the total output of the gadget. Absolutely impractical, especially when copper and silver are so plentiful to string along the scenery on steel towers. No good.'

'But look at this cockeyed thing. Christine puts in a couple of hundred amps; I take them off my end. Believe it or not, the output meter at my end was getting a lot more soup than I was pouring in.'

'And my gadget was not taking anything to speak of,' said Barney.

'Supposing it was a means of transmitting power. How on Mars did they use a single tower there in the middle of the Red Desert? We know there was a Martian city at Canalopsis, and another one not many miles from Lincoln Head. Scribbled on the outer cover of this book is the legend: "Tower Station, Red Desert," and though the Martians didn't call this the "Red Desert," the terminology will suffice for nomenclature.'

'Well?' asked Jim.

'You notice they did not say: "Station No. 1," or "3" or "7."

That means to me that there was but one.'

'Holy Smoke! Fifteen hundred miles with only one station? On Mars the curvature of ground would put such a station below the electrical horizon—' Jim thought that one over for a minute and then said: 'Don't tell me they bent the beam?'

'Either they did that or they heated up the sand between,' said Barney cryptically. 'It doesn't mind going through non-conducting walls, but a nice, fat ground . . . blooey, or I miss my guess. That'd be like grounding a high line.'

'You're saying that they did bend – *Whoosh*, again!'

'What was that alignment problem? Didn't we align the deflecting anodes somehow?'

'Yeah, but you can't bend the output of a cathode ray tube externally of the deflection plates.'

'But this is not electron-beam stuff,' objected Barney. 'This is as far ahead of cathode-ray tubes as they are ahead of the Indian signal drum or the guy who used to run for twenty-six miles from Marathon to Athens.'

'That one was from Athens to Sparta,' explained Christine, 'the Ghent to Aix journey was a-horse-back, and some thousand-odd years after.'

'Simile's still good,' said Barney. 'There's still a lot about this I do not understand.'

'A masterpiece of understatement, if I ever heard one,' laughed Jim. 'Well, let's work on it from that angle. Come on, gang, to horse!'

'Now,' said Altas, 'you will find that the best possible efficiency is obtained when the currents in these two resistances are equal and opposite in direction. That floats the whole tube on the system, and makes it possible to run the tube without any external power source. It requires a starter-source for aligning and for standby service, and for the initial surge; then it is self-sustaining. Also the in-phase voltage can not better be

156

obtained than by exciting the phasing anode with some of the main-line power. That must always be correctly phased. We now need the frequency generator no longer, and by increasing the power rheostat to full, the tube will take up the load. Watch the meters, and when they read full power, you may throw the cut-over switch and make the tube self-sustaining. Our tower will then be in perfect service, and you and I may return to our home below.'

Than performed the operations, and then they left, taking the old tube with them.

And on Terra, Sargon of Akkad watched ten thousand slaves carry stone for one of his public buildings. He did not know that on one of the stars placed in the black bowl of the evening sky for his personal benefit, men were flinging more power through the air than the total output of all of his slaves combined. Had he been told, he would have had the teller beheaded for lying because Sargon of Akkad couldn't possibly have understood it—

'You know, we're missing a bet,' said Jim. 'This in-phase business here. Why shouldn't we hang a bit of the old wall-socket juice in here?'

'That might be the trick,' said Barney.

Jim made the connections, and they watched the meters read up and up and up – and from the street below them a rumbling was heard. Smoke issued from a crevasse in the pavement, and then with a roar, the street erupted and a furrow three feet wide and all the way across the street from Jim Baler's residence to Barney Carroll's garage lifted out of the ground. It blew straight up and fell back, and from the bottom of the furrow the smoldering of burned and tortured wiring cast a foul smell.

'*Wham!*' said Barney, looking at the smoking trench. 'What was that?'

'I think we'll find that it was the closest connection between our places made by the Electric Co.,' said Jim.

'But what have we done?'

'I enumerate,' said Christine, counting off on her fingers. 'We've blasted in the façade of the City Hall. We've caused a couple of emergency flier-landings within the city limits. We've blown fuses and circuit breakers all the way from here to the main powerhouse downtown. We've stalled a few dozen automobiles. We've torn or burned or cut the end off one hammer and have fractured the wall with it . . . where did that go, anyway, the hammerhead? We've burned wallpaper. We've run our electric bill up to about three hundred dollars, I'll bet. We've bunged up a dozen meters. And now we've ripped up a trench in the middle of the street.'

'Somewhere in this set-up, there is a return circuit,' said Jim thoughtfully. 'We've been taking power out of the line, and I've been oblivious of the fact that a couple of hundred amperes is too high to get out of our power line without trouble. What we've been doing is taking enough soup out of the public utility lines to supply the losses only. The power we've been seeing on our meters is the build-up, recirculated!'

'Huh?'

'Sure. Say we bring an amp in from the outside and shoot it across the street. It goes to the wires and comes back because of some electrical urge in our gadgets here, and then goes across the street in-phase with the original. That makes two amps total crossing our beam. The two come back and we have two plus two. Four come back, and we double again and again until the capability of our device is at saturation. All we have to do is to find the ground-return and hang a load in there. We find the transmitter-load input, and supply that with a generator. Brother, we can beam power all the way from here to Canalopsis on one relay tower!'

Barney looked at his friend. 'Could be.'

'Darned right. What other item can you think of that fits this tower any better? We've run down a dozen ideas, but this works. We may be arrested for wrecking Lincoln Head, but we'll get out as soon as this dingbat hits the market. Brother, what a find!'

'Fellows, I think you can make your announcement now,' smiled Christine. 'They won't burn you at the stake if you can bring electric power on a beam of pure nothing. This time you've hit the jackpot!'

It is six thousand Terran Years since Sargon of Akkad held court that was lighted by torch. It is six thousand years, Terran, since Than and Altas replaced the link in a power system that tied their cities together.

It is six thousand years since the beam tower fell into the Red Desert and the mighty system of beamed power became lost as an art. But once again the towers dot the plains, not only of Mars, but of Venus and Terra, too.

And though they are of a language understood by the peoples of three worlds, the manuals of instruction would be as cryptic to Than as his manual was to Barney Carroll and Jim Baler.

People will never learn.

Interlude:

Don Channing's initial problem was to develop ship to planet communication, if not ship to ship. And since, as a general rule, anything that could be used to transmit power could also be used to transmit information, Channing went to Mars to seek out Messrs Baler and Carroll.

Strangely enough, the problem of communicating from planet to ship was not solved – nor would it be complete until some means of returning messages was devised. For the cams that kept the ship beams pointed to the place where the invisible spaceship was supposed to be had no way of knowing when the ship might swerve to miss a meteor. Many were the messages that went into space – undelivered – because a ship dodged a meteor that might have been dangerous. Postulating the rather low possibility of danger made little difference. Misdirected messages were of less importance than even the remote danger of death in the skies.

But Don Channing's luck was running low. On arrival at Lincoln Head, he discovered that Baler and Carroll had packed up their tube and left for Terra. Keg Johnson knew about it; he informed Channing that the foremost manufacturer of electrical apparatus had offered a lucrative bid for the thing as it stood and that Big Jim Baler had grinned, saying that the money that the Terran Electric Company was tossing around would permit the two of them, Carroll and himself, to spend the rest of their lives digging around the artifacts of Mars in style.

So Channing sent word to Venus Equilateral and told them to get in touch with either the Baler-Carroll combine or Terran Electric and make dicker.

Then he started to make the journey back to Venus Equilateral on the regular spacelanes. . . .

OFF THE BEAM

Thirty hours out of Mars for Terra, the *Ariadne* sped along her silent, invisible course. No longer was she completely severed from all connection with the planets of the inner system; the trick cams that controlled the beams at Venus Equilateral kept the ship centered by sheer mathematics in spite of her thirty hours at two G, which brought her velocity to eleven hundred miles per second.

What made this trip ironic was the fact that Don Channing was aboard. The beams had been bombarding the *Ariadne* continually ever since she left Mars with messages for the Director of Communications. In one sense, it seemed funny that Channing was for once on the end of a communications line where people could talk to him but from which he could not talk back. On the other hand, it was a blessing in disguise, for the Director of Communications was beginning to paper-talk himself into some means of contacting Venus Equilateral from a spaceship.

A steward found Channing in the salon and handed him a 'gram. Channing smiled, and the steward returned the smile and added: 'You'll fix these ships to talk back one day. Wait till you read that one – you'll burn from here to Terra!'

'Reading my mail?' asked Channing cheerfully. The average spacegram was about as secret as a postcard, so Channing didn't mind. He turned the page over and read:

HOPE YOU'RE WELL FILLED WITH GRAVANOL
AND ADHESIVE TAPE FOR YOUR JUMP FROM
TERRA TO STATION. SHALL TAKE GREAT DE-
LIGHT IN RIPPING ADHESIVE TAPE OFF YOUR
MEASLY BODY. LOVE,
                                                    ARDEN

'She will, too,' grinned Don. 'Well, I'd like to toss her one back, but she's got me there. I'll just fortify myself at the bar and think up a few choice ones for when we hit Mojave.'

'Some day you'll be able to answer those,' promised the steward. 'Mind telling me why it's so tough?'

'Not at all,' smiled Channing. 'The problem is about the same as encountered by the old-time cowboy. It's a lot easier to hit a man on a moving horse from a nice, solid rock than it is to hit a man on a nice, solid rock from a moving horse. Venus Equilateral is quite solid as things go. But a spaceship's course is fierce. We're wabbling a few milliseconds here and a few there, and by the time you use that arc to swing a line of a hundred million miles, you're squirting quite a bit of sky. We're tinkering with it right now, but so far we have come up with nothing. Ah, well, the human race got along without electric lights for a few million years, we can afford to tinker with an idea for a few months. Nobody is losing lives or sleep because we can't talk with the boys back home.'

'We've been hopping from planet to planet for quite a number of years, too,' said the steward. 'Quite a lot of them went by before it was even possible to contact a ship in space.'

'And that was done because of an emergency. Probably this other thing will go on until we hit an emergency; then we shall prove that old statement about a loaf of bread being the maternal parent of a locomotive.' Channing lit a cigarette and puffed deeply. 'Where do we stand?'

'Thirty hours out,' answered the steward. 'About ready for turnover. I imagine that the power engineer's gang is changing cathodes about now.'

'It's a long drag,' said Channing. He addressed himself to his glass and began to think of a suitable answer for his wife's latest thrust.

Bill Hadley, of the power engineer's gang, spoke to the pilot's

162

greenhouse below the ship. 'Hadley to the pilot room; cathodes 1 and 3 ready.'

'Pilot Greenland to Engineer Hadley: Power fadeover from even to odd now under way. Tubes 2 and 4 now dead; load on 1 and 3. You may enter 2 and 4.'

'Check!'

Hadley cracked an air valve beside a circular air door. The hiss of entering air crescendoed and died, and then Hadley cracked the door that opened in upon the huge driver tube. With casual disregard for the annular electrodes that would fill the tube with sudden death if the pilot sent the driving power surging into the electrodes, Hadley climbed to the top of the tube and used a spanner to remove four huge bolts. A handy differential pulley permitted him to lower the near-exhausted cathode from the girders to the air door, where it was hauled to the deck. A fresh cathode was slung to the pulley and hoisted to place. Hadley bolted it tight and clambered back into the ship. He closed the air door and the valve, and then opened the valve that led from the tube to outer space. The tube evacuated and Hadley spoke once more to the pilot room.

'Hadley to Greenland: Tube 4 ready.'

'Check.'

The operation was repeated on tube 2, and then Pilot Greenland said: 'Fade-back beginning. Power diminishing on 1 and 3, increasing on 2 and 4. Power equalized, acceleration two G as before. Deviation from norm: two-tenths G.'

Hadley grinned at the crew. 'You'd think Greenland did all that himself, the way he talks. If it weren't for autopilots, we'd have been all over the sky.'

Tom Bennington laughed. He was an old-timer, and he said in a reminiscent tone: 'I remember when we did that on manual. There were as many cases of *mal-de-void* during

163

cathode change as during turnover. Autopilots are the nuts — look! We're about to swing right now, and I'll bet a fiver that the folks below won't know a thing about it.'

A coincidence of mammoth proportions occurred at precisely that instant. It was a probability that made the chance of drawing a royal flush look like the chances of tomorrow coming on time. It was, in fact, one of those things that they said couldn't possibly happen, which went to prove only how wrong they were. It hadn't happened yet and probably wouldn't happen again for a million million years, but it did happen once.

Turnover was about to start. A relay circuit that coupled the meteor-spotter to the autopilot froze for a bare instant, and the coincidence happened between the freezing of the relay contacts and the closing of another relay whose purpose it was to shunt the coupler circuits through another line in case of relay failure. In the conceivably short time between the failure and the device that corrected failure, the *Ariadne* hit a meteor head-on.

It is of such coincidence that great tragedies and great victories are born.

The meteor, a small one as cosmic objects go, passed in through the broad observation dome at the top of the ship. Unhampered, it zipped through the central well of the *Ariadne* and passed out through the pilot's greenhouse at the bottom of the ship. Its speed was nothing worth noting; a scant twenty miles per second almost sunward. But the eleven hundred miles per second of the *Ariadne* made the passage of the meteor through the six hundred feet of the ship's length of less duration than the fastest camera shutter.

In those microseconds, the meteor did much damage.

It passed through the main pilot room cable and scrambled those circuits which it did not break entirely. It tore the elevator system from its moorings. It entered as a small hole in the observation dome and left taking the entire pilot's greenhouse and all of the complex paraphernalia with it.

The lines to the driver tubes were scrambled, and the ship shuddered and drove forward at 10 gravities. An inertia switch tried to function, but the resetting solonoid had become shorted across the main battery and the weight could not drop.

Air doors clanged shut, closing the central well from the rest of the ship and effectively sealing the well from the crew.

The lights in the ship flickered and died. The cable's shorted lines grew hot and fire crept along its length and threatened the continuity. The heat opened fire-quenching vents and a cloud of CO_2 emerged together with some of the liquid gas itself. The gas quenched the fire and the cold liquid cooled the cable. Fuses blew in the sorted circuits—

And the *Ariadne* continued to plunge on and on at 10 gravities: the maximum speed possible out of her driving system.

The only man who remained aware of himself aboard the *Ariadne* was the man who was filled with gravanol and adhesive tape. No other person expected to be hammered down by high acceleration. Only Channing, intending to leave Terra in his own little scooter, was prepared to withstand high G. He, with his characteristic haste of doing anything slowly, was ready to make the Terra to Venus Equilateral passage at five or six gravities.

It might as well have caught him, too. With all of the rest unconscious, hurt, or dead, he was alone and firmly fastened to the floor of the salon under eighteen hundred pounds of his own, helpless weight.

And as the hours passed, the *Ariadne* was driving farther and farther from the imaginary spot that was the focus of the communicator beams from Venus Equilateral.

The newly replaced cathodes in the driving tubes were capable of driving the ship for about two hundred G-hours at one G, before exhaustion to the point of necessary replacement for safety purposes. The proportion is not linear, nor is it a square-law, but roughly it lies in the region just above linear, so that the *Ariadne* drove on and on through space for ten hours at ten G before the cathodes died for want of emitting surface. They died, not at once, but in irregular succession so that when the last erg of power was gone from the drivers it was zooming on a straight line tangent from its point of collision but rolling in a wild gyration through the void.

And twenty-five hundred miles per second, added to her initial velocity of eleven hundred miles per second summed up to thirty-six hundred miles per second. She should have had about seventy-five million miles to go at minus two G to reach Terra in thirty hours from the halfway point, where she turned ends to go into deceleration. Instead, the *Ariadne* after ten hours of misdirected ten-G acceleration was thirty million miles on her way, or about halfway to Terra. Three hours later, driving free, the *Ariadne* was passing Terra, having missed the planet by several million miles.

Back in space, at a no longer existent junction between the beams from Venus Equilateral and the *Ariadne*, Arden Channing's latest message was indicating all sorts of minor punishment for her husband when she got him home.

By the time that the *Ariadne* should have been dropping out of the sky at Mojave Spaceport, the ship would be one hundred and ninety million miles beyond Terra and flirting with the imaginary line that marked the orbit of Mars.

That would be in seventeen hours.

Weightless, Channing pursued a crazy course in the salon of the spinning ship. He ached all over from the pressure, but the gravanol had kept his head clear and the adhesive tape had kept his body intact. He squirmed around in the dimness and could see the inert figures of the rest of the people who had occupied the salon at the time of the mishap. He became sick. Violence was not a part of Channing's nature – at least he confined his violence to those against whom he required defense. But he knew that many of those people who pursued aimless orbits in the midair of the salon with him would never set foot on solidness again.

He wondered how many broken bones there were among those who had lived through the ordeal. He wondered if the medical staff of one doctor and two nurses could cope with it.

Then he wondered what difference it made, if they were to go on and on? Channing had a rough idea of what had happened. He knew something about the conditions under which they had been traveling, how long, and in what direction. It staggered him, the figures he calculated in his mind. It behoved him to do something.

He bumped an inert figure and grabbed. One hand took the back of the head and came away wet and sticky. Channing retched, and then threw the inert man from him. He coasted back against a wall, and caught a handrail. Hand-over-hand he went to the door and into the hall. Down the hall he went to the passengers' elevator shaft, and with no thought of what his action would have been on any planet, Channing opened the door and dove down the shaft for several decks. He emerged and headed for the sick ward.

He found the doctor clinging to his operating table with his knees and applying a bandage to one of his nurse's head.

'Hello, Doc,' said Channing. 'Help?'

'Grab Jen's feet and hold her down,' snapped the doctor.

'Bad?' asked Don as he caught the flailing feet.

'Seven stitches, no fracture,' said the doctor.

'How's the other one?'

'Unconscious, but unharmed. Both asleep in bed, thank God. So was I. Where were—? You're Channing; all doped up with gravanol and adhesive. Thank yourself a god for that one, too. I'm going to need both of my nurses, and we'll all need you.'

'Hope I can do some good,' said Don.

'You'd better. Or any good I can do will be wasted. Better start right now. Here,' the doctor produced a set of keys, 'these will unlock anything on the ship but the purser's safe. You'll need 'em. Now get along and do something and leave the body-mending to me. Scram!'

'Can you make out all right?'

'As best I can. But you're needed to get us help. If you can't, no man in the Solar System can. You're in the position of a man who cannot afford to help in succoring the wounded and dying. It'll be tough, but there it is. Get cutting. And for Heaven's sake, get us two things: light and a floor. I couldn't do more than slap on tape whilst floating in air. See you later, Channing, and good luck.'

The nurse squirmed, groaned, and opened her eyes. 'What happened?' she asked, blinking into the doctor's flashlight.

'Tell you later, Jen. Get Fern out of her coma in the ward and then we'll map out a plan. Channing, get out of here!'

Channing got after borrowing a spare flashlight from the doctor.

He found Hadley up in the instrument room with a half dozen of his men. They were a mass of minor and major cuts and injuries, and were working under a single incandescent lamp that had been wired to the battery direct by means of spare cable. The wire went snaking through the air in a foolish, crooked line, suspended on nothing. Hadley's gang were applying first aid to one another and cursing the lack of gravity.

'Help?' asked Channing.

'Need it or offer it?' asked Hadley with a smile.

'Offer it. You'll need it.'

'You can say that again – and then pitch in. You're Channing, of Communications, aren't you? We're going to have a mad scramble on the main circuits of this tub before we can unwind it. I don't think there's an instrument working in the whole ship.'

168

'You can't unravel the whole works, can you?'

'Won't try. About all we can do is replace the lighting system and hang the dead cathodes in again. They'll be all right to take us out of this cock-eyed skew-curve and probably will last long enough to keep a half-G floor under us for tinkering, for maybe forty or fifty hours. Assistant Pilot Darlange will have to learn how to run a ship by the seat of his pants – as far as I can guess there isn't even a splinter of glass left in the pilot room – so he'll have to correct this flight by feel and by using a haywire panel.'

'Darlange is a school pilot,' objected one of Hadley's men.

'I know, Jimmy, but I've seen him work on a bum autopilot, and he can handle haywire all right. It'll be tough without Greenland, but Greenland—' Hadley let the sentence fall; there was no need to mention the fact that Greenland was probably back there with the rest of the wreckage torn from the *Ariadne*.

Jimmy nodded, and the action shook him from his position. He floated. He grabbed at a roll of tape that was floating near him and let it go with a laugh as he realized it was too light to do him any good.

'Too bad that this gyration is not enough to make a decent gravity at the ends, at least,' snorted Hadley. He hooked Jimmy by an arm and hauled the man back to a place beside him. 'Now look,' he said. 'I can't guess how many people are still in working condition after this. Aside from our taped and doped friend here, the only ones I have are we who were snoozing in our beds when the crush came. I'll bet a cookie that the rest of the crowd are all nursing busted ribs, and worse. Lucky that full ten G died slowly as the cathodes went out; otherwise we'd all have been tossed against the ceiling with bad effects.

'Jimmy, you're a committee of one to roam the crate and make a list of everyone who is still in the running and those who can be given minor repairs to make them fit for limited work.

Doc has a pretty good supply of Stader splints; inform him that these are to be used only on men who can be useful with them. The rest will have to take to plaster casts and the old-fashioned kind of fracture support.

'Pete, you get to the executive desk and tell Captain Johann-son that we're on the job and about to make with repairs. As power engineer, I've control of the maintenance gang, too, and we'll collect the whole, hale, and hearty of Michaels' crew on our merry way.

'Tom, take three of your men and begin to unravel the mess with an eye toward getting us lights.

'Tony, you can do this alone since we have no weight. You get the stale cathodes from the supply hold and hang 'em back in the tubes.

'Channing, until we get a stable place, you couldn't do a thing about trying to get help, so I suggest you pitch in with Bennington, there, and help unscramble the wiring. You're a circuit man, and though power-line stuff is not your forte, you'll find that running a lighting circuit is a lot easier than neutraliz-ing a microwave transmitter. Once we get light, you can help us haywire a control panel. Right?'

'Right,' said Channing. 'And as far as contacting the folks back home goes, we couldn't do a darned thing until the time comes when we should be dropping in on Mojave. They won't be looking for anything from us until we're reported missing; then I imagine that Walt Franks will have everything from a spinthariscope to a gold-foil electroscope set up. Right now I'm stumped, but we have seventeen hours before we can start hoping to be detected. Tom, where do we begin?'

Bennington smiled inwardly. To have Don Channing asking him for orders was like having Captain Johannson request the batteryman's permission to change course. 'If you can find and remove the place where the shorted line is, and then splice the lighting circuit again, we'll have a big hunk of our work done.

170

The rest of us will begin to take lines off of the pilot's circuits right here in the instrument room, so that our jury-controls can be hooked in. You'll need a suit, I think, because I'll bet a hat that the shorted circuit is in the well.'

For the next five hours, the instrument room became a bee-hive of activity. Men began coming in driblets, and were put to work as they came. The weightlessness gave quite a bit of trouble; had the instrument panels been electrically hot, it would have been downright dangerous, since it was impossible to do any kind of work without periodically coming into contact with bare connections. Tools floated around the room in profusion, and finally Hadley appointed one man to do nothing but roam the place to retrieve 'dropped' tools. The soldering operations were particularly vicious, since the instinctive act of flinging excess solder from the tip of an iron made droplets of hot solder go zipping around the room to splash against something, after which the splashes would continue to float.

Men who came in seeking to give aid were handed tools and told to do this or that, and the problem of explaining how to free a frozen relay to unskilled help was terrific.

Then at the end of five hours, Channing came floating in to the instrument room. He flipped off the helmet and said to Hadley: 'Make with the main switch. I think I've got it.'

Throughout the ship the lights blinked on.

With the coming of light, there came hope also. Men took a figurative hitch in their belts and went to work with renewed vigor. It seemed as though everything came to a head at about this time, too. Hadley informed Darlange that his jury-control was rigged and ready for action, and about the same time, the galley crew came in with slender-necked bottles of coffee and rolls.

'It was a job, making coffee,' grinned the steward. 'The darned stuff wanted to get out of the can and go roaming all over the place. There isn't a one of us that hasn't got a hot coffee scar on us somewhere. Now if he' – nodding at Darlange – 'can get this thing straightened out, we'll have a real dinner.'

'Hear that, Al? All that stands between us and a dinner is you. Make with the ship-straightening. Then we'll all sit around and wait for Channing to think.'

'Is the ship's communicator in working order?' asked Darlange.

'Sure. That went on with the lights.'

Darlange called for everyone in the ship to hold himself down, and then he tied his belt to the frame in front of the haywired panel. He opened the power on drivers 1 and 2, and the ship's floor surged ever so little.

'How're you going to know?' asked Hadley.

'I've got one eye on the gyrocompass,' said Darlange. 'When it stops turning, we're going straight. Then all we have to do is to set our bottom end along the line of flight and pack on the deccl. Might as well do it that way since every MPS we can lose is to our advantage.'

He snapped switches that added power to driver 3. Gradually the gyrocompass changed from a complex rotation-progress to a simpler pattern, and eventually the simple pattern died, leaving but one freedom of rotation. 'I'm sort of stumped,' grinned Darlange. 'We're now hopping along, but rotating on our long axis. How we stop axial rotation with drivers set parallel to that axis I'll never guess.'

'Is there a lifeship in working order?' asked Hadley.

'Sure.'

'Tom, turn it against the rotation and apply the drivers on that until we tell you to stop.'

An hour later the ship had ceased to turn. Then Darlange jockeyed the big ship around so that the bottom was along the line of flight. Then he set the power for a half-G, and everyone relaxed.

172

Ten minutes later Captain Johannson came in.

'You've done a fine job,' he told Hadley. 'And now I declare an hour off for dinner. Dr. MacLain has got a working medical center with the aid of a few people who understand how such things work, and the percentage of broken bones, though terrific in number, is being take care of. The passengers were pretty restive at first, but the coming of light seemed to work wonders. This first glimmer of power is another. About nine or ten who were able to do so were having severe cases of skysickness.' He smiled ruefully. 'I'm not too sure that I like no-weight myself.'

'Have you been in the observation dome?' asked Don.

'Yes. It's pierced, you know.'

'Did the meteor hit the telescope?'

'No, why?'

'Because I'm going to have to get a sight on Venus Equilateral before we can do anything. We'll have to beam them something, but I don't know what right now.'

'Can we discuss that over a dinner?' asked the captain. 'I'm starved, and I think that the rest of this gang is also.'

'You're a man after my own heart,' laughed Channing. 'The bunch out at the station wouldn't believe me if I claimed to have done anything without drawing it up on a tablecloth.'

'Now,' said Channing over his coffee, 'what have we in the way of electronic equipment?'

'One X-ray machine, a standard set of communicating equipment, one beam receiver with 'type machine for collecting stuff from your station, and so on.'

'You wouldn't have a betatron in the place somewhere?' asked Don hopefully.

'Nope. Could we make one?'

'Sure. Have you got about a hundred pounds of Number 18 wire?'

173

'No.'

'Then we can't.'

'Couldn't you use a driver? Isn't that some kind of a beam?'

'Some kind,' admitted Channing. 'But it emits something that we've never been able to detect except in an atmosphere where it ionizes the air into a dull red glow.'

'You should have been wrecked on the *Sorcerer's Apprentice*,' laughed Hadley. 'They're the guys who have all that kind of stuff.'

'Have they?' asked Johannson.

'The last time I heard, they were using a large hunk of their upper hull for a Van Der Graf generator.'

'That would do it,' said Channing thoughtfully. 'But I don't think I'd know how to modulate a Van Der Graf. A betatron would be the thing. You can modulate that, sort of, by keying the input. She'd give out with hundred-and-fifty-cycle stuff. How much of a trick is it to clear the observation dome from the top?'

'What do you intend to do?'

'Well, we've got a long, hollow tube in this ship. Knock out the faceted dome above, and we can rig us up a huge electron gun. We'll turn the ship to point at the station and beam 'em with a bouquet of electrons.'

'How're you going to do that?'

'Not too tough, I don't think. Down here,' and Channing began to trace on the tablecloth, 'we'll put in a hot cathode. About this level we'll hang the first anode, and at this level we'll put the second anode. Here'll be an acceleration electrode and up near the top we'll put a series of focussing anodes. We'll tap in to the driver-tube supply and take off voltage to suit us. Might use a tube at that, but the conversion to make an honest electron gun out of it would disrupt our power, and then it would be impossible to remake a driver out of it without recourse to a machine shop.'

174

'How are you going to make electrodes?'

'We'll use the annular gratings that run around the central well at each level,' said Channing. 'We'll have a crew of men cut 'em free and insulate the resulting rings with something. Got anything?'

'There is a shipment of methyl-methacrylate rods for the Venus Power Company in hold 17,' said the cargo master.

'Fine,' said Channing. 'What size?'

'Three inches by six feet.'

'It'll be tricky work, and you'll have to wait until your cut edge has cooled before you hook on the rods,' mused Don. 'But that's the ticket.'

'Which floors do you want?'

'Have you got a scale drawing of the *Ariadne*?'

'Sure.'

'Then this is where my tablecloth artistry falls flat. The focussing of an electron beam depends upon the electrode spacing and the voltage. Since our voltage is fixed if we take it from the drivers' electrodes, we'll have to do some mighty fine figuring. I'll need that scale drawing.'

Channing's tablecloth engineering was not completely wasted. By the time the scale drawing was placed before him, Channing had half of the table filled with equations. He studied the drawing, and selected the levels which were to serve as electrodes. He handed the drawings to Hadley, and the power engineer began to issue instructions to his gang.

Then the central well began to swarm with spacesuited men who bore cutting torches. Hot sparks danced from the cut girders that held the floorings, and at the same time, a crew of men were running cables from the various levels to the instrumented room. More hours passed while the circular sections were insulated with the plastic rods.

The big dome above was cut in sections and removed, and then the sky could be seen all the way from the bottom of the ship where the pilot's greenhouse should have been.

Channing looked it over and then remarked: 'All we need now is an electron collector.'

'I thought you wanted to shoot 'em off,' objected Hadley.

'I do. But we've got to have a source of supply. You can't toss baseballs off of the Transplanet Building in Northern Landing all afternoon, you know, without having a few brought to you now and then. Where do you think they come from?'

'Hadn't thought of it that way. What'd happen?'

'We'd get along for the first umpty-gillion electrons, and then all the soup we could pack on would be equalized by the positive charge on the ship and we couldn't shoot out any more until we got bombarded by the sun – and that bombardment is nothing to write home about as regards quantity. We're presenting too small a target. What we need is a selective solar intake plate of goodly proportions.'

'We could use a mental telepathy expert, too. Or one of those new beam tubes that Baler and Carroll dug up out of the Martian desert. I've heard that those things will actually suck power out of any source, and bend beams so as to enter the intake vent, or end.'

'We haven't one of those, either. Fact of the matter is,' grinned Channing, ruefully, 'we haven't much of anything but our wits.'

'Unarmed, practically,' laughed Hadley.

'Half armed, at least. Ah, for something to soak up electrons. I'm now wondering if this electron gun is such a good idea.'

'Might squirt some protons out the other direction,' offered Hadley.

'That would leave us without either,' said Don. 'We'd be like the man who tossed baseballs off of one side and himself off the other – Hey! Of course, we have some to spare. We can cram electrons out of the business end, thus stripping the planetary rings from the atoms in our cathode. From the far

176

side we'll shoot the canal rays, which in effect will be squirting protons, or the nuclei. Since the planetaries have left for the front, it wouldn't be hard to take the protons away, leaving nothing. At our present voltages, we might be able to do it.' Channing began to figure again, and he came up with another set of anodes to be placed beyond the cathode. 'We'll ventilate the cathode and hang these negative electrodes on the far side. They will attract the protons, impelled also by the positive charge on the front end. We'll maintain a balance that way, effectively throwing away the whole atomic structure of the cathode. The latter will fade, just as the cathodes do in the driving tubes, only we'll be using electronic power instead of sub-electronic. Y'know, Hadley, some day someone is going to find a way to detect the – we'll call it radiation for want of anything better – of the driver. And then there will be opened an entirely new field of energy. I don't think that anybody has done more about the so-called sub-electronic field than to make a nice, efficient driving device out of it.'

'Well, let's get our canal-ray electrodes in place. We've got about two hours before they realize that we aren't going to come in at Mojave. Then another two hours of wild messages between Venus Equilateral and Mojave. Then we can expect someone to be on the lookout. I hope to be there when they begin to look for us. At our present velocity, we'll be flirting with the Asteroid Belt in less than nothing flat. That isn't too bad – normally – but we're running without any meteor detector and autopilot coupler. We couldn't duck anything from a robin's egg on up.'

'We'll get your anodes set,' said Hadley.

Walt Franks grinned at Arden Channing. 'That'll burn him,' he assured her.

'It's been on the way for about twenty minutes,' laughed Arden. 'I timed it to arrive at Terra at the same time the

Ariadne does. They'll send out a special messenger with it, just as Don is getting aboard his little scooter. It'll be the last word, for we're not following him from Terra to here.'

'You know what you've started?' asked Franks.

'Nothing more than a little feud between husband and self.'

'That's just the start. Before he gets done, Don will have every ship capable of answering back. I've found that you can catch him off base just once. He's a genius – one of those men who never make the same mistake twice. He'll never again be in a position to be on the listening end only.'

'Don's answer should be on the way back by now,' said Arden. 'Could be you're right. Something should be done.'

'Sure I'm right. Look at all the time that's wasted in waiting for a landing to answer 'grams. In this day and age, time is money, squared. The latter is to differentiate between this time and the first glimmering of speedy living.'

'Was there a first glimmering?' asked Arden sagely. 'I've often thought that the speed-up was a stable acceleration from the dawn of time to the present.'

'All right, go technical on me,' laughed Walt. 'Things do move. That is, all except the message from your loving husband.'

'You don't suppose he's squelched?'

'I doubt it. Squelching Donald Channing is a job for a superbeing. And I'm not too sure that a superbeing could squelch Don and make him stay squelched. Better check on Mojave.'

'Gosh, if Don missed the *Ariadne* and I've been shooting him all kinds of screwy 'types every hour on the hour; Walt, that'll keep him quiet for a long, long time.'

'He'd have let you know.'

'That wouldn't have been so bad. But if the big bum missed and was ashamed of it – that'll be the payoff. Whoa, there goes the 'type!'

Arden drew the tape from the machine:

MESSAGE BEING HELD FOR ARRIVAL OF ARI-
ADNE.

Walt looked at his watch and checked the course constants
of the *Ariadne*. He called the beam-control dome and asked
for the man on the ship's beam.

'Benny,' he said, 'has the *Ariadne* arrived yet?'

'Sure,' answered Benny. 'According to the mechanical mind
here, they've been on Mojave for twenty minutes.'

'Thanks.' To Arden he said: 'Something's strictly fishy.'

Arden sat at the machine and pounded the keys:

ARIADNE DUE TO ARRIVE AT 19:06:41. IT IS
NOW 19:27:00. BEAM CONTROL SAYS TRANS-
MISSIONS ENDED BECAUSE OF COINCIDENCE
BETWEEN TERRA BEAM AND STATION-TO-SHIP
BEAM. PLEASE CHECK.

Arden fretted and Walt stamped up and down the room
during the long minutes necessary for the message to reach
Terra and the answer to return. It came right on the tick of
the clock:

HAVE CHECKED COURSE CONSTANTS. SHIP
OVERDUE NOW FIFTY MINUTES. OBVIOUSLY
SOMETHING WRONG. CAN YOU HELP?

Walt smiled in a grim fashion. 'Help!' he said. 'We go on
and on for years with no trouble – and now we've lost the third
ship in a row.'

'They claim that those things always run in threes,' said
Arden. 'What are we going to do?'

'I don't know. We'll have to do something. Funny, but the one reason we must do something is the same reason why something can be done.'

'I don't get that.'

'With Channing on the *Ariadne*, something can be done. I don't know what. but I'll bet you a new hat that Don will make it possible for us to detect the ship. There is not a doubt in my mind that if the ship is still spaceworthy, we can narrow the possibilities down to a thin cone of space.'

'How?'

'Well,' said Franks taking the fountain pen out the holder on the desk and beginning to sketch on the blotter, 'the course of the *Ariadne* is not a very crooked one, as courses go. It's a very shallow skew curve. Admitting the worst, collision, we can assume only one thing. If the meteor were small enough to leave the ship in a floating but undirigible condition, it would also be small enough to do nothing to the general direction of the ship. Anything else would make it useless to hunt, follow?'

'Yes, go on.'

'Therefore we may assume that the present position of the ship is within the volume of a cone made by the tangents of the outermost elements of the space curve that is the ship's course. We can take an eight-thousand-mile cyinder out of one place – for the origin of their trouble is between Mars and Terra and the "shadow" of Terra in the cone will not contain the *Ariadne*.'

'Might have passed close enough to Terra to throw her right into the "shadow" of Terra by attraction,' objected Arden

'Yeah, you're right. O.K., so we can't take out that cylinder of space. And we add a sort of sidewise cone on to our original cone, a volume through which the ship might have passed after flying close enough to Terra to be deflected. I'll have the slipstick experts give a guess as to the probability of the *Ariadne*'s course, and at the same time we'll suspend all incoming operations. I'm going to set up every kind of detector I can think of, and I don't want anything upsetting them.'

'What kind of stuff do you expect?' asked Arden.

'I dunno. They might have a betatron aboard. In that case we'll eventually get a blast of electrons that'll knock our front teeth out. Don may succeed in tinkering up some sort of electrostatic field. We can check the solar electrostatic field to about seven decimal places right here, and any deviation in the field to the tune of a couple of million electron volts at a distance of a hundred million miles will cause a distortion in the field that we can measure. We'll ply oscillating beams through the area of expectation and hope for an answering reflection, though I do not bank on that. We'll have men on the lookout for everything from smoke signals to helio. Don't worry too much, Arden, your husband is capable of doing something big enough to be heard. He's just the guy to do it.'

'I know,' said Arden soberly. 'But I can't help worrying.'

'Me, too. Well, I'm off to set up detectors. We'll collect something.'

'Have we got anything like a piece of gold leaf?' asked Channing.

'I think so, why?'

'I want to make an electroscope. That's about the only way I'll know whether we are getting out with this cockeyed electron gun.'

'How so?' asked Hadley.

'We can tell from the meter that reads the beam current whether anything is going up the pipe,' explained Channing. 'But if we just build us a nice heavy duty charge – as shown by the electroscope – we'll be sure that the electrons are not going far. This is one case where no sign is good news.'

'I'll have one of the boys set up an electroscope in the instrument room.'

'Good. And now have the bird on the telescope find Venus Equilateral. Have him set the 'scope angles to the figures here and then have him contact Darlange to have the ship slued around so that Venus Equilateral is on the cross hairs. That'll put us on a line with the station. A bundle of electrons of this magnitude will make a reading on any detectors that Walt can set up.'

Hadley called the observation dome. 'Tim,' he said, giving a string of figures, 'set your 'scope for these and then get Darlange to slue the crate around so that your cross hairs are on Venus Equilateral.'

'O.K.,' answered Tim. 'That's going to be a job. This business of looking through a 'scope while dressed in a spacesuit is no fun. Here goes.'

He called Darlange, and the communicator system permitted the men in the instrument room to hear his voice. 'Dar,' he said, 'loop us around about forty-one degrees from driver 3.'

Darlange said: 'Right!' and busied himself at his buttons.

'Three degrees on driver 4.'

'Right!'

'Too far, back her up a degree on 4.'

Darlange laughed. 'What do you think these things are, blocks and tackles? You mean: "Compensate a degree on 2."'

'You're the pilot. That's the ticket – and I don't care if you lift it on one hand. Can you nudge her just a red hair on 3?'

'Best I can do is a hair and a half,' said Darlange. He gave driver 3 just a tiny, instantaneous surge.

'Then take it up two and back one and a half,' laughed Tim. 'Whoa, Nellie, you're on the beam.'

'Fine.'

'Okay, Dar, but you'll have to play monkey on a stick. I'll prime you for any moving so that you can correct immediately.'

'Right. Don, we're on the constants you gave us. What now?'

'At this point I think a short prayer would be of assistance,' said Channing soberly. 'We're shooting our whole wad right now.'

'I hope we make our point.'

'Well, it's all or nothing,' agreed Don as he grasped the switch.

He closed the switch, and the power demand meters jumped up across their scales. The gold leaf electroscope jumped once; the ultra-thin leaves jerked apart by an inch, and then oscillated stiffly until they came to a balance. Channing, who had been looking at them, breathed deeply and smiled.

'We're getting out,' he said.

'Can you key this?' asked Hadley.

'No need,' said Channing. 'They know we're in the grease. We know that if they can collect us, they'll be on their way. I'm going to send out for a half-hour, and then resort to a five-minute transmission every fifteen minutes. They'll get a ship after us with just about everything we're liable to need, and they can use the five-minute transmission for direction finding. The initial shot will serve to give them an idea as to our direction. All we can do now is to wait.'

'And hope,' added Captain Johannson.

Electrically, Venus Equilateral was more silent than it had ever been. Not an electrical appliance was running on the whole station. People were cautioned about walking on deep-pile rugs, or combing their hair with plastic combs, or doing anything that would set up any kind of electronic charge. Only the highly filtered generators in the power rooms were running and these had been shielded and filtered long years before; nothing would emerge from them to interrupt the ether. All incoming signals were stopped.

And the men who listened with straining ears claimed that the sky was absolutely clear save for a faint crackle of cosmic static which they knew came from the corona of the Sun.

One group of men sat about a static-field indicator and cursed the minute wiggling of the meter, caused by the ever moving celestial bodies and their electronic discharges. A sunspot emission passed through the station once, and though it was but a brief passage, it sent the electrostatic field crazy and made the men jump.

The men who were straining their ears to hear became nervous and were jumping at every loud crackle.

And though the man at the telescope knew that his probability of picking up a sight of the *Ariadne* was as slender as a spider's web, he continued to search the starry heavens. He swept the narrow cone of the heavens wherein the *Ariadne* was lost according to the mathematical experts, and he looked at every bit of brightness in the field of his telescope as though it might be the missing ship.

The beam-scanners watched their return-plates closely. It was difficult because the receiver gains were set to maximum and every tick of static caused brief flashes of light upon their plates. They would jump at such a flash and hope for it to reappear on the next swipe, for a continuous spot of light would indicate the ship they sought. Then, as the spot did not reappear, they would go on with their beams to cover another infinitesimal portion of the sky. Moving forward across the cone of expectancy bit by bit, they crossed and recrossed until they were growing restive.

Surely the ship must be there!

At the south end landing stage, a group of men were busy stocking a ship. Supplies and necessities were carried aboard, while another group of men tinkered with the electrical equipment. They cleared a big space in the observation dome, and began to install a replica of the equipment used on the station for detection. No matter what kind of output Channing sent back, they would be able to follow it to the bitter end.

They made their installations in duplicate, with one piece of each equipment on opposite sides of the blunt dome. Balancing the inputs of each kind by turning the entire ship would give them an indication of direction.

Franks did not hope that the entire installation could be completed before the signal came, but he was trying to outguess himself by putting some of everything aboard. When and if it came, he would be either completely ready with everything or he at least would have a good start on any one of the number of detectors. If need be, the detecting equipment in the station itself could be removed and used to complete the mobile installation.

Everything was in a complete state of nervous expectancy. Watchers watched, meter readers squinted for the barest wiggle, audio observers listened, trying to filter any kind of man-made note out of the irregular crackle that came in.

And the station announcing equipment was dead quiet, to be used only in case of emergency or to announce the first glimmer of radiation, whether it be material, electrical, kinetic, potential or wave front.

Long they listened – and then it came.

The station announcing equipment broke forth in a multitude of voices.

'Sound input on radio!'

'Visual indication on scanner plates!'

'Distortion on electrostatic field indicator!'

'Super-electroscopes indicate negative charge!'

'Nothing on the telescope!'

There were mingled cheers and laughter as the speaker system broke away from babel, and each group spoke its piece with no interference. Walt Franks left the ship at the south end and raced to the beam control dome, just as fast as the runway car would take him. He ran into the dome in spacesuit and

185

flipped the helmet back over his shoulder. 'What kind of indication?' he yelled.

Men crowded around him, offering him papers and showing figures.

'Gosh,' he said, 'Don can't have everything going up there.'

'He's hit just about everything but the guy squinting through the 'scope.'

'What's he doing?' asked Franks of nobody in particular.

Charles Thomas, who had been busy with the electrostatic field indicator said: 'I think maybe he's using some sort of electron gun – like the one you tried first off on the meteor destroyer job, remember?'

'Yeah, but that one wouldn't work – unless Don has succeeded in doing something we couldn't do. Look, Chuck, we haven't had time to set up a complete field indicator on the ship – grab yours and give the boys a lift installing it, hey?'

'Sure thing,' said Thomas.

'And look, fellows, any indication of direction, velocity, or distance?'

'Look for yourself,' said the man on the beam scanner. 'The whole plate is shining. We can't get a fix on them this way – they're radiating themselves and that means our scanner-system finder is worthless.'

'We can, but it's rough,' offered one of the radio men. 'It came from an area out beyond Terra – and as for our readings it might have covered a quarter of the sky.'

'The field indicator is a short-base finder,' explained Thomas. 'And no less rough than the radio boys. I'd say it was out beyond Terra by fifty million miles at least.'

'Close enough. We'll have to track 'em down like a radio equipped bloodhound. Chuck, come along and run that mechanico-electro-monstrosity of yours. Gene, you can come along and run the radio finder. Oh, yes, you, Jimmy, may continue to squint through that eyepiece of yours – but on the *Relay Girl*. We need a good, first-class squinter, and you should have an opportunity to help.'

Jimmy laughed shortly. 'The only guy on the station that didn't get an indication was me. Not even a glimmer.'

'Channing didn't know we'd be *looking* for him, or he'd probably light a flare, too. Cheer up, Jimmy, after all this crude, electrical rigmarole is finished, and we gotta get right down to the last millimeter, it's the guy with the eye that polishes up the job. You'll have your turn.'

Twenty minutes after the first glimmer of intelligent signal, the *Relay Girl* lifted from the south end and darted off at an angle, setting her nose roughly in the direction of the signal.

Her holds were filled with spare batteries and a whole dozen replacement cathodes, as well as her own replacements. Her crew was filled to the eyebrows with gravanol, and there must have been a mile of adhesive tape and cotton on their abdomens. At six G she left, and at six G she ran, her crew immobilized but awake because of the gravanol. And though the acceleration was terrific, the tape kept the body from folding of its own weight. When they returned, they would all be in the hospital for a week, but their friends would be with them.

Ten minutes after take-off, the signals ceased.

Walt said: 'Keep her running. Don's saving electricity. Tell me when we pick him up again.'

Franklen, the pilot, nodded. 'We haven't got a good start yet. It'll be touch and go. According to the slipstick boys, they must be clapping it up at between twenty-five hundred and five thousand miles per second to get that far – and coasting free or nearly so. Otherwise they'd have come in. Any suggestions as to course?'

'Sure. Whoop it up at six until we hit about six thousand. Then decelerate to four thousand by using one G. We'll vacil-

187

late in velocity between four and five until we get close.'

Forty-one hours later, the *Relay Girl* made turnover and began to decelerate.

Channing said to Captain Johannson: 'Better cut the decel to about a quarter G. That'll be enough to keep our heads from bumping the ceiling, and it will last longer. This is going to be a long chase, and cutting down a few MPS at a half G isn't going to make much never-mind. I'll hazard a guess that the boys are on their way right now.'

'If you say so,' said Johannson. 'You're the boss from now on. You know that wild bunch on the station better than I do. For myself, I've always felt that an answer was desirable before we do anything.'

'I know Franks and my wife pretty well – about as well as they know me. I've put myself in Walt's place – and I know what Walt would do. So – if Walt didn't think of it, Arden would – I can assume that they are aware of us, have received our signals, and are, therefore, coming along as fast as they can. They'll come zipping out here from five to seven G to what they think is halfway and then decelerate again to a sane velocity. We won't catch sight of them for sixty or seventy hours, and when we do, they'll be going so fast that it will take another twenty hours' worth of manipulation to match their speed with ours. Meanwhile, I've got the gun timed to shoot our signal. When the going gets critical, I'll cut the power and make it continuous.'

'You're pretty sure of your timing?'

'Well, the best they can do as for direction and velocity and distance is a crude guess. They'll place us out here beyond Terra somewhere. They'll calculate the course requirements to get us this far in the time allotted, and come to a crude figure. I'd like to try keying this thing, but I know that keying it won't work worth a hoot at this distance. Each bundle of keyed electrons would act as a separate negative charge that would spread out and close up at this distance. It's tough enough to hope that the electron beam will hold together that far, let alone trying to key intelligence with it. We'll leave well enough alone — and especially if they're trying to get a fix on us; there's nothing worse than trying to fix an intermittent station. Where are we now?'

'We're on the inner fringe of the Asteroid Belt, about thirty million miles north, and heading on a secant course at thirty-four hundred MPS.'

'Too bad Jupiter isn't in the neighborhood,' said Channing. 'We'll be flirting with his orbit by the time they catch us.'

'Easily.' said Johannson. 'In sixty hours, we'll have covered about six hundred and fifty million miles. We'll be nearer the orbit of Saturn, in spite of the secant course.'

'Your secant approaches a radius as you get farther out,' said Don, absently. 'As far as distances go, Titan, here we come!'

Johannson spoke to the doctor. 'How're we doing?'

'Pretty well,' said Doc. 'There's as pretty an assortment of fractured limbs, broken ribs, cracked clavicles, and scars, mars, and abrasions as you ever saw. There are a number dead, worse luck, but we can't do a thing about them. We can hold on for a week as far as food and water goes. Everyone is now interested in the manner of our rescue rather than worrying about it.' He turned to Channing. 'The words Channing and Venus Equilateral have wonderful healing powers,' he said. 'They all think your gang are part magician and part sorcerer.'

'Why, for goodness' sake?'

'I didn't ask. Once I told 'em you had a scheme to contact the relay station, they were all satisfied that things would happen for the better.'

'Anything we can do to help you out?'

'I think not,' answered Doc. 'What I said before still goes. Your job is to bring aid — and that's the sum total of your job.

Every effort must be expended on that and that alone. You've got too many whole people depending on you to spend one second on the hurt. That's my job.'

'O.K.,' said Channing. 'But it's going to be a long wait.'

'We can afford it.'

'I hope we're not complicating the job of finding us by this quartering deceleration,' said Captain Johannson.

'We're not. We're making a sort of vector from our course, but the deviation is very small. As long as the fellows follow our radiation, we'll be found,' Channing said with a smile. 'The thing that is tough is the fact that all the floors seem to lean over.'

'Not much, though.'

'They wouldn't lean at all if we were running with the whole set of equipment,' said Darlange. 'We run a complete turnover without spilling a drop from the swimming pool.'

'Or even making the passengers aware of it unless they're looking at the sky.'

'Stop worrying about it,' said Doc. 'I'm the only guy who has to worry about it and as long as the floor is still a floor, I can stand sliding into the corner once in a while.'

'We might tinker with the turnover drivers,' offered Don. 'We can bring 'em down to a place where the velocity-deceleration vectors are perpendicular to the floor upon which we stand while our ship is sluing. We've got a lot of time on our hands, and I, for one, feel a lot happier when I'm doing something.'

'It's a thought,' said Hadley. 'Wanna try it?'

'Let's go.'

Thirty hours after the *Relay Girl* left the station, Walt and Franklen held a council of war, in which Chuck Thomas was the prime factor.

'We've come about two hundred million miles, and our present velocity is something like four thousand miles per second,' said Walt. 'We're going toward Mars on a slightly-off radial course, to the north of the ecliptic. That means we're a little over a quarter of a billion miles from Sol, or about to hit the Asteroid Belt. Thinking it over a little, I think we should continue our acceleration for another thirty hours. What say?'

'The field has shown no change in intensity that I can detect,' said Thomas. 'If they haven't dropped their radiated intensity, that means that we are no closer to them than we were before. Of course, we'd probably have to cut the distance by at least half before any measurable decrement made itself evident.'

'They must be on the upper limit of that four thousand MPS,' observed Walt. 'There's one thing certain, we'll never catch them by matching their speed.'

'Where will another thirty hours at six G put us and how fast?' asked Franklen.

Silence ensued while they scribbled long figures on scratch paper.

'About eight hundred million miles from Sol,' announced Walt.

'And about eight thousand MPS,' added Chuck.

'That's a little extreme, don't you think?' asked Franklen.

'By about thirty percent,' said Walt, scratching his chin. 'If we hold to our original idea of hitting it for six thousand, where will we be?'

'That would make it about forty-five hours from take-off, and we'd be about four hundred and sixty million miles from Sol.' Chuck grinned widely and said: 'By Jove!'

'What?'

'By Jove!'

' "By Jove!" What?'

'That's where we'd be – By Jove!'

'*Phew!*'

'I agree with you,' said Franklen to Walt. 'Better ignore him.'

'Sure will after that. So then we'll be "By Jove" at six thousand. That would be a swell place to make turnover, I think. At one G decel to about four thousand MPS, that'll put us about – um, that'd take us about ninety hours! We'll make that three G at twenty hours, which will put us about three hundred and fifty million miles along, which plus the original four hundred and sixty million adds up to eight hundred and ten million—'

'When an astronaut begins to talk like that,' interrupted Arden, 'we of the skyways say that he is talking in Congressional figures. The shoe is on the other foot. What on earth are you fellows figuring?'

'Where we'll be and how fast we'll be going at a given instant of particular importance,' offered Walt. 'When did you wake up?'

'About the third hundred million. All of those ciphers going by made a hollow sound, like a bullet whistling in the wind.'

'Well, we're trying to make the theories of probability match with figures. We'll know in about forty-five hours whether we were right or not.'

'It's a good thing we have all space to go around in. Are you sure that we have all eternity?'

'Don't get anxious. They're still coming in like a ton of bricks four times per hour, which means that they're riding easy. I don't want to overrun them at about three thousand MPS and have to spend a week decelerating returning, more decelerating, and then matching velocities.'

'I see. You know best. And where is this Asteroid Belt that I've heard so much about?'

'To the south of us by a few million miles. Those bright specks that you can't tell from stars are asteroids. The common conception of the Asteroid Belt being filled to overflowing with a collection of cosmic rubble like the rings of Saturn is a lot of hooey. We'll be past in a little while and we haven't even come

192

close to one. Space is large enough for all of us, I think.'

'But not when all of us want the same space.'

'I don't care for their area,' said Walt with a smile. 'Let 'em have it, I don't care. I'll stay up here and let them run as they will.'

'You mean the ones that are moving downward?' asked Arden, indicating the sky.

'Those are asteroids, yes. We're up to the north, as you may check by going around the ship to the opposite side. You'll see Polaris almost directly opposite, there. Sol is almost directly below us, and that bright one that you can see if you squint almost straight up is Saturn.'

'I won't bother crossing the ship to see Polaris. I prefer the Southern Cross, anyway. The thing I'm most interested in is: Are we accomplishing anything?'

'I think that we've spent the last thirty hours just catching up,' explained Walt. 'Up to right now, we are going backwards, so to speak; we're on even terms now, and will be doing better from here on in.'

'It's the waiting that gets me down,' said Arden. 'Oh, for something to do.'

'Let's eat,' suggested Walt. 'I'm hungry, and now that I think of it, I haven't eaten since we left the station. Arden, you are hereby elected to the post of galley chief. Get Jimmy from the dome if you need help.'

'Help? What for?'

'He can help you lift it out of the oven. Don must have a cast-iron stomach.'

'That's hearsay. I'll show you! As soon as I find the can opener, breakfast will be served.'

'Make mine dinner,' said Chuck. 'We've been awake all the time.'

'O.K., we will have a combined meal, from grapefruit to ice cream. Those who want any or all parts may choose at will. And fellows, please let me know as soon as you get something tangible.'

'That's a promise,' said Walt. 'Take it easy, and don't worry. We'll be catching up with them one of these days.'

'Hadley, how much coating have we got on those cathodes?' asked Don Channing.

'Not too much. We had about twenty G hours to begin with. We went to a half G for twenty hours, and now we're running on a quarter G, which would let us go for forty hours more.'

'Well, look. If it should come to a choice between floor and signal gun, we'll choose the gun. We've about eight hours left in the cathodes, and since everybody is now used to quarter G we might even slide it down to an eighth G, which would give us about sixteen hours.'

'Your gun is still putting out?'

'So far as I can tell. Six hours from now, we should know, I think, predicating my guess on whatever meager information they must have.'

'We could save some juice by killing most of the lights in the ship.'

'That's a thought. Johannson, have one of your men run around and remove all lights that aren't absolutely necessary. He can kill about three-quarters of them, I'm certain. That'll save us a few kilowatt hours,' said Channing. 'And another thing. I'm about to drop the power of our electron gun and run it continuously. If the boys are anywhere in the neighborhood, they'll be needing continuous disturbance for direction finding. I'd say in another five hours that we should start continuous radiation.'

'You know, Channing, if this thing works out all right, it will be a definite vote for pure, deductive reasoning.'

'I know. But the deductive reasoning is not too pure. It isn't guesswork. There are two factors of known quality. One is that I know Walt Franks and the other is that he knows me. The rest is a simple matter of the boys on the station knowing space to the last inch, and applying the theory of probabilities to it. We'll hear from them soon, or I'll miss my guess. Just you wait.'

'Yeah,' drawled Captain Johannson, 'we'll wait!'

Chuck Thomas made another computation and said: 'Well, Walt, we've been narrowing them down for quite a long time now. We're getting closer and closer to them, according to the field intensity. I've just got a good idea of direction on that last five minute shot. Have Franklen swivel us around on this course; pretty soon we'll be right in the middle of their shots.'

'We're approaching them asymptotically,' observed Walt. 'I wish I knew what our velocity was with respect to theirs. Something tells me that it would be much simpler if I knew.'

'Walt,' asked Arden, 'how close can you see a spaceship?'

'You mean how far? Well, I don't know that it has ever been tried and recorded. But we can figure it out easy enough by analogy. A period is about thirty-thousandths of an inch in diameter, and visible from a distance of thirty inches. I mean visible with no doubt about its being there. That's a thousand to one. Now, the *Ariadne* is about six hundred feet tall and about four hundred feet in its major diameter, so we can assume a little more than the four hundred feet – say five hundred feet average of circular area, say – follow me?'

'Go on, you're vague, but normal.'

'Then at a thousand to one, that becomes five hundred thousand feet, and dividing by five thousand – round figures because it isn't important enough to use that two hundred and eighty feet over the five thousand – gives us one thousand miles. We should be able to see the *Ariadne* from a distance of a thousand miles.'

'Then at four thousand miles per second we'll be in and through and out of visual range in a half second?'

'Oh, no. They're rambling on a quite similar course at an unknown but high velocity. Our velocity with respect to theirs is what will determine how long they're within visual range.'

'Hey, Walt,' came the voice of Chuck Thomas. 'The intensity of Don's beam has been cut to about one-quarter and is now continuous. Does that mean anything?'

'Might mean trouble for them. Either they're running out of soup and mean for us to hurry up, or they assume we're close enough to obviate the need for high power. We'd better assume they want haste and act accordingly. How're the boys on the radio detectors coming along?'

'Fine. They've taken over the direction finding and claim that we are right on their tail.'

'Anything in the sights, Jimmy?'

'Not yet. But the electroscope boys claim that quarter power or not, the input is terrific.'

'Take a rest, Jimmy. We won't be there for a while yet. No use burning your eyes out trying to see 'em. There'll be time enough for you to do your share after we get 'em close enough to see with the naked eye. What do the beam-scanners say?'

'Shucks,' answered the man on the scanners, 'they're still radiating. How are we going to fix 'em on a reflected wave when they're more powerful on their own hook? The whole plate is glaring white. And, incidentally, so is the celestial globe in the meteor spotter. I've had to cut that or we'd never be able to hold this course. Anything like a meteor that comes in our way now will not register, and—'

The *Relay Girl* lurched sickeningly. All over the ship, things rattled and fell to the floors. Men grabbed at the closest solid object, and then the *Relay Girl* straightened out once more.

'*Whoosh!*' said Franks. 'That was a big one!'

'Big one?' called Jimmy. 'That, my friend, was none other than the *Ariadne!*'

'Can you prove that?'

'Sure,' chuckled Jimmy. 'I saw 'em. I can still see 'em!'

'Franklen, hang on about seven G and follow Jimmy's orders. Chuck, see if you can get anything cogent out of your gadget. Holy Green Fire, with a cubic million million million megaparsecs in which to run, we have to be so good that we run right into our quarry. Who says that radio direction finding is not a precise science? Who says that we couldn't catch—'

'Walt, they're losing fast.'

'O.K., Jimmy, can you give me any idea as to their velocity with respect to ours?'

'How long is she?'

'Six hundred feet.'

Jimmy was silent for some seconds. 'They're out of sight again, but I make it about four to seven hundred miles per second.'

'At seven G we should match that seven hundred in about four hours.

'And then go on decelerating so that they'll catch up?'

'No,' said Walt. 'I used the max figures and we can assume they aren't going that fast, quite. At the end of four hours, we'll turnover and wait until they heave in sight again and then we'll do some more oscillating. We can match their velocity inside of ten hours, or Franklen will get fired.'

'If I don't,' promised Franklen, 'I'll quit. You can't fire me!'

'We should be able to contact them by radio,' said Walt.

'We are!' called the radio man. 'It's Channing. He says: "Fancy meeting you here." Any answer?'

'Just say, "Dr. Channing, I presume?"'

Channing's voice came out of the ship's announcer system as the radio man made the necessary connections. It said: 'Right – but what kept you so long?'

'Our boss was away,' replied Walt. 'And we can't do a thing without him.'

'Some boss. Some crew of wild men. Can't go off on a fishing trip without having my bunch chasing all over the Solar System.'

'What's wrong with a little sight-seeing tour? We didn't mean any harm. And speaking of harm, how are you and the rest of that bunch getting along?'

'We're O.K. What do you plan after we finally get close enough together to throw stones across?'

'We've got a whole hold full of spare batteries and a double set of replacement cathodes. There is a shipload of gravanol aboard, too. You'll need that and so will we. By the time we finish this jaunt, we'll have been about as far out as anybody ever gets.'

'Yeah – got any precise figures? We've been running on a guess and a hope. I make it about seven hundred million.'

'Make it eight and a half. At six G you'll cover another hundred and fifty million miles before you stop. Take it twenty-two hours at six G – and then another twenty-two at six. That should put you right back here but going the other way at the same velocity. But wait, you've been coasting. Mark off that last twenty-two hours and make it like this: You'll be one thousand million miles from Sol when you come to a stop at the end of the first twenty-two hours at six G. That hangs you out beyond the orbit of Saturn by a couple of hundred million. Make it back forty-four hours at six G, turnover and continue. By that time we'll all be in so close that we can make any planet at will – preferably you to Terra and we'll head for Venus Equilateral. You'll come aboard us? No need for you to with the rest.'

'I can have the scooter sent out from Terra,' said Channing. 'How's Arden?'

'I'm fine, you big runabout. Wait until I get you!'

'Why, Arden, I thought you might be glad to see me.'

'Glad to see you?'

'But Arden—'

'Don't you "But Arden" me, you big gadabout. Glad to see you! Boy, any man that makes me chase him all over the Solar System! You just wait. As soon as I get ahold of you, Don Channing, I'm going to – to bust out and bawl like a kid! Hurry up, willya?'

'I'll be right over,' said Don soberly.

And, strangely enough, Don did not deviate.

Interlude:

Six thousand years ago, Sargon of Akkad held court on the plains of Assyria by torchlight. Above his head there shone the myriad of stars, placed there to increase his power and glory.

But on one of the stars above called Mars, there were people who knew a mighty civilization and a vast world of science. They flew above the thin air of Mars and they hurled power by energy beam across the face of the planet.

Then they – died. They died, and they left but broken fragments of their once-mighty civilization buried in the shifting, dusty sands of Mars. Long centuries afterwards, man crossed space to find these fragments and wonder.

How or why they died is a matter of conjecture. It is known that iron is the most stable of all known atomic structures besides helium. It is also known that the surface of Mars has its characteristic reddish hue because of the preponderance of iron compounds there. From the few remaining artifacts, it is known that Mars exceeded the present Terran science, which includes atomic power. The inference is that Mars died completely in the horror of atomic war.

This is but reasoning. The facts that are of interest include the finding of a gigantic vacuum tube fastened to a shattered steel tower in the sands between Canalopsis and Lincoln Head, Mars.

The original finders, Martian archeologists Baler and Carroll, were versed enough in electronics to make tests. They discovered many interesting facts about this tube before they sold it to Terran Electric for a monumental sum of money. Their reasons for selling the thing were simple. They preferred digging in the sands of Mars to plunging into the depths of a highly technical manufacturing business, and the money was more than adequate.

Don Channing's main objection was that Carroll and Baler did not consult Venus Equilateral before they disposed of their find.

That made it necessary for Venus Equilateral to acquire a tube for their research by dealing with Terran Electric, which in this case was similar to obtaining a ton of uranium ore from Oak Ridge back in the year 1945. Often, of course, the shortest distance home is . . .

THE LONG WAY

Don Channing stood back and admired his latest acquisition with all of the fervency of a high school girl inspecting her first party dress. It was so apparent, this affection between man and gadget, that the workmen who were now carrying off the remnants of the packing case did so from the far side of the bench so that they would not come between the Director of Communications and the object of his affection. So intent was Channing to the adoration of the object that he did not hear the door open, nor the click of high heels against the plastic flooring. He was completely unaware of his surroundings until Arden said:

'Don, what on earth is that?'

'Ain't she a beaut,' breathed Channing.

'Jilted for a jimcrack,' groaned Arden. 'Tell me, my quondam husband, what is it?'

'Huh?' asked Don, coming to life once more.

'In plain, unvarnished words of one cylinder, what is that . . . that *that?*'

'Oh, you mean the transmission tube?'

'How do you do?' said Arden to the big tube. 'Funny looking thing, not like any transmitting tube I've ever seen before.'

'Not a transmitting tube,' exclaimed Channing. 'It is one of those power transmission tubes that Baler and Carroll found on the Martian Desert.'

'I presume that is why the etch says: 'Made by Terran Electric, Chicago"?'

Channing laughed. 'Not the one found – there was only *one* found. This is a carbon copy. They are going to revolutionize the transmission of power with them.'

'Funny-looking gadget.'

'Not so funny. Just alien.'

'Know anything about it?'

'Not too much. I've got Barney Carroll coming out here and a couple of guys from Terran Electric. I'm going to strain myself to keep from tinkering with the thing until they get here.'

'Can't you go ahead? It's not like you to wait.'

'I know,' said Channing. 'But the Terran Electric boys have sewed up the rights of this dingus so tight that it is squeaking. Seems to be some objection to working on them in the absence of their men.'

'Why?'

'Probably because Terran Electric knows a good thing when they see it. Barney's latest 'gram said that they were very reluctant to lend this tube to us. Legally they couldn't refuse, but they know darned well that we're not going to run power in here from Terra – or anywhere else. They know we want it for experimentation, and they feel that it is their tube and that if any experimentation is going to take place, they're going to do it.'

The workmen returned with two smaller cases; one each they placed on benches to either side of the big tube. They knocked the boxes apart and there emerged two smaller editions of the center tube – and even Arden could see that these two were quite like the forward half and the latter half, respectively, of the larger tube.

'Did you buy 'em out?' she asked.

'No,' said Don simply. 'This merely makes a complete circuit.'

'Explain that one, please.'

'Sure. This one on the left is the input-terminal tube which they call the power-end. The good old D.C. goes in across these big terminals. It emerges from the big end, here, and bats across in a beam of intangible something-or-other until it gets to the relay tube, where it is once more tossed across to the load-end tube. The power is taken from these terminals on the back end of the load-end tube and is then suitable for running motors, refrigerators, and so on. The total line-loss is slightly more than the old-fashioned transmission line. The cathode-dynode requires replacement about once a year. The advantages over high-tension wires are many; in spite of the slightly-higher line-losses, they are replacing long-lines everywhere.

'When they're properly aligned they will arch right over a mountain of solid iron without attenuation. It takes one tower every hundred and seventy miles, and the only restriction on tower height is that the tube must be above ground by ten to one the distance that could be flashed over under high intensity ultraviolet light.'

'That isn't clear to me.'

'Well, high tension juice will flash over better under ultra-violet illumination. The tube must be high enough to exceed this distance by ten to one at the operating voltage of the stuff down the line. The boys in the Palanortis Jungles say they're a godsend, since there are a lot of places where the high tension towers would be impossible since the Palanortis Whitewood grows about a thousand feet tall.'

'You'd cut a lot of wood to ream a path through from Northern Landing to the power station on the Boiling River,' said Arden.

'Yeah,' drawled Don, 'and towers a couple of hundred miles apart are better than two thousand feet. Yeah, these things are the nuts for getting power shipped across country.'

'Couldn't we squirt it out from Terra?' asked Arden. 'That would take the curse off of our operating expenses.'

'It sure would,' agreed Channing heartily. 'But think of the trouble in aligning a beam of that distance. I don't know —

there's this two hundred miles' restriction, you know. They don't transmit worth a hoot over that distance, and it would be utterly impossible to maintain stations in space a couple of hundred miles apart, even from Venus, from which we maintain a fairly close tolerance. We might try a hooting big one, but the trouble is that misalignment of the things result in terrible effects.'

The door opened and Chuck Thomas and Walt Franks entered.

'How's our playthings?' asked Walt.

'Cockeyed looking gadgets,' commented Chuck.

'Take a good look at 'em,' said Channing. 'Might make some working X-ray plates, too. It was a lucky day that these got here before the boys from Terran Electric. I doubt that they'd permit that.'

'O.K.,' said Chuck. 'I'll bring the X-ray up here and make some pix. We'll want working prints; Warren will have to take 'em and hang dimensions on to fit.'

'And we,' said Channing to Walt Franks, 'will go to our respective offices and wait until the Terran Electric representatives get here.'

The ship that came with the tubes took off from the landing stage, and as it passed their observation dome, it caught Don's eye. 'There goes our project for the week,' he said.

'Huh?' asked Walt.

'He's been like that ever since we tracked him down on the *Ariadne*,' said Arden.

'I mean the detection of driver radiation,' said Channing.

'Project for the week?' asked Walt. 'Brother, we've been tinkering with that idea for months, now.'

'Well,' said Don, 'there goes four drivers, all batting out umpty-ump begawatts of something. They can hang a couple of G on a six hundred foot hull for hours and hours. The radiation they emit must be detectable; don't tell me that such power is not.'

'The interplanetary companies have been tinkering with drivers for years and years,' said Walt. 'They have never detected it?'

'Could be, but there are a couple of facts that I'd like to point out. One is that they're not interested in detection. They only want the best in driver efficiency. Another thing is that the radiation from the drivers is sufficient to ionize atmosphere into a dull red glow that persists for several minutes. Next item is the fact that we on Venus Equilateral should be able to invent a detector; we've been tinkering with detectors long enough. Oh, I'll admit that it is secondary-electronics—'

'Huh? That's a new one on me.'

'It isn't electronics,' said Channing. 'It's subetheric or something like that. We'll call it subelectronics for lack of anything else. But we should be able to detect it somehow.'

'Suppose there is nothing to detect?'

'That smacks of one hundred percent efficiency,' laughed Don. 'Impossible.'

'How about an electric heater?' asked Arden.

'O, Lord, Arden, an electric heater is the most ineffic—'

'Is it?' interrupted Arden with a smile. 'What happens to radiation when intercepted?'

'Turns to heat, of course.'

'That takes care of the radiation output,' said Arden. 'Now, how about electrical losses?'

'Also heat.'

'Then everything that goes into an electric heater emerges as heat,' said Arden.

'I get it,' laughed Walt. 'Efficiency depnds on what you hope to get. If what you want is losses, anything that is a total loss is one hundred percent efficient. Set your machine up to waste power and it becomes one hundred percent efficient as long as there is nothing coming from the machine that doesn't count as waste.'

'Fine point for arguing,' smiled Channing. 'But anything that will make atmosphere glow dull red after the passage of a ship will have enough waste to detect. Don't tell me that the red glow enhances the drive.'

The door opened again and Chuck Thomas came in with a crew of men. They ignored the three, and started to hang heavy cloth around the walls and ceiling. Chuck watched the installation of the barrier-cloth, and then said: 'Beat it – if you want any young Channings!'

Arden, at least, had the grace to blush.

The tall, slender man handed Don an envelope full of credentials. 'I'm Wesley Farrell,' he said. 'Glad to have a chance to work out here with you fellows.'

'Glad to have you,' said Don. He looked at the other man.

'This is Mark Kingman.'

'How do you do?' said Channing. Kingman did not impress Channing as being a person whose presence in a gathering would be demanded with gracious shouts of glee.

'Mr. Kingman is an attorney for Terran Electric,' explained Wesley.

Kingman's pedestal was lowered by Channing.

'My purpose,' said Kingman, 'is to represent my company's interest in the transmission tube.'

'In what way?' asked Don.

'Messrs. Baler and Carroll sold their discovery to Terran Electric outright. We have an iron-bound patent on the device and/or any developments of the device. We hold absolute control over the transmission tube, and therefore may dictate all terms on which it is to be used.'

'I understand. You know, of course, that our interest in the transmission tube is purely academic.'

'I have been told that. We're not too certain that we approve. Our laboratories are capable of any investigation you may desire, and we prefer that such investigations be conducted under our supervision.'

'We are not going to encroach on your power rights,' explained Channing.

'Naturally,' said Kingman in a parsimonious manner. 'But should you develop a new use for the device, we shall have to demand that we have complete rights.'

'Isn't that a bit high-handed?' asked Don.

'We think not. It is our right.'

'You're trained technically?' asked Don.

'Not at all. I am a lawyer, not an engineer. Dr. Farrell will take care of the technical aspects of the device.'

'And in looking out for your interests, what will you require?'

'Daily reports from your group. Daily conferences with your legal department. These reports should be prepared prior to the day's work so that I may discuss with the legal department the right of Terran Electric to permit or disapprove the acts.'

'You understand that there may be a lot of times when something discovered at ten o'clock may change the entire program by ten oh six?'

'That may be,' said Kingman, 'but my original statements must be adhered to, otherwise I am authorized to remove the devices from your possession. I will go this far however; if you discover something that will change your program for the day, I will then call an immediate conference which should hurry your program instead of waiting until the following morning for the decision.'

'Thanks,' said Channing dryly. 'First, may we take X-ray prints of the devices?'

'No. Terran Electric will furnish you with blueprints which we consider suitable.' Kingman paused for a moment. 'I shall expect the complete program of tomorrow's experiments by five o'clock this evening.'

Kingman left, and Wes Farrell smiled uncertainly. 'Shall we begin making the list?'

'Might as well,' said Channing. 'But, how do you lay out a complete experimental program for twelve hours ahead?'

'It's a new one on me, too,' said Farrell.

'Well, come on. I'll get Walt Franks, and we'll begin.'

'I wonder if it might not be desirable for Kingman to sit in on these program-settings?' said Channing, after a moment of staring at the page before him.

'I suggested that to him. He said "No." He prefers his information in writing.'

Walt came in on the last words. Channing brought Franks up to date and Walt said: 'But why should he want a written program if he's going to disallow certain ideas?'

'Sounds to me like he's perfectly willing to let us suggest certain lines of endeavor; he may decide that they look good enough to have the Terran Electric labs try themselves,' said Channing.

Wes Farrell looked uncomfortable.

'I have half a notion to toss him out,' Channing told Farrell. 'I also have half a notion to make miniatures of this tube and go ahead and work regardless of Kingman or Terran Electric. O.K., Wes, we won't do anything illegal. We'll begin by making our list.'

'What is your intention?' asked Wes.

'We hope that these tubes will enable us to detect driver radiation, which will ultimately permit us to open ship-to-ship two-way communications.'

'May I ask how you hope to do this?'

'Sure. We're going to cut and try. No one knows a thing

about the level of driver-energy; we've selected a name for it: Subelectronics. The driver tube is akin to this transmission tube, if what I've been able to collect on the subject is authentic. By using the transmission tube—'

'Your belief is interesting. I've failed to see any connection between our tube and the driver tube.'

'Oh, sure,' said Channing expansively. 'I'll admit that the similarity is of the same order as the similarity between an incandescent lamp and a ten dynode electron-multiplier such as we use in our final beam stages. But recall this business of the cathode-dynode. In both, the emitting surface is bombarded by electrons from electron guns. They both require changing.'

'I know that, but the driver cathode disintegrates at a rate of loss that is terrific compared to the loss of emitting surface in the transmission tube.'

'The driver cathode is worth about two hundred G-hours. But remember, there is no input to the driver such as you have in the transmission tube. The power from the driver comes from the disintegration of the cathode surface – there isn't a ten-thousandth of an inch of plating on the inside of the tube to show where it went. But the transmission tube has an input and the tube itself merely transduces this power to some level of radiation for transmission. It is re-transduced again for use. But the thing is this: your tube is the only thing that we know of that will accept subelectronic energy and use it. If the driver and the transmission tubes are similar in operational spectrum, we may be able to detect driver radiation by some modification.'

'That sounds interesting,' said Wes. 'I'll be darned glad to give you a lift.'

'Isn't that beyond your job?' asked Channing.

'Yeah,' drawled Farrell, 'but could you stand by and watch me work on a beam transmitter?'

'No—'

'Then don't expect me to watch without getting my fingers dirty,' said Farrell cheerfully. 'Sitting around in a place like this would drive me nuts without something to do.'

'O.K., then,' smiled Don. 'We'll start off by building about a dozen miniatures. We'll make 'em about six inches long – we're not going to handle much power, you know. That's first.'

Kingman viewed the list with distaste. 'There are a number of items here which I may not allow,' he said.

'For instance?' asked Channing with lifted eyebrows.

'One, the manufacture or fabrication of power transmission tubes by anyone except Terran Electric is forbidden. Two, your purpose in wanting to make tubes is not clearly set forth. Three, the circuit in which you intend to use these tubes is unorthodox, and must be clearly and fully drawn and listed.'

'Oh, spinach! How can we list and draw a circuit that is still in the embryonic stage?'

'Then clarify it. Until then I shall withhold permission.'

'But look, Mr. Kingman, we're going to develop this circuit as we go along.'

'You mean that you're going to fumble your way through this investigation?'

'We do not consider a cut-and-try program as fumbling,' said Walt Franks.

'I am beginning to believe that your research department has not the ability to reduce your problems to a precise science,' said Kingman coldly.

'Name me a precise science,' snapped Channing, 'or even a precise art!'

'The legal trade is as precise as any. Everything we do is done according to legal precedent.'

'I see. And when there is no precedent?'

'Then we all decide upon the proper course, and establish a precedent.'

'But I've got to show you a complete circuit before you'll permit me to go ahead?'

'That's not all. Your program must not include reproducing these tubes either in miniature or in full size – or larger. Give me your requirements and I shall request Terran Electric to perform the fabrication.'

'Look, Kingman, Venus Equilateral has facilities to build as good a tube as Terran Electric. I might even say better, since our business includes the use, maintenance, and development of radio tubes; your tubes are not too different from ours. Plus the fact that we can whack out six in one day, whilst it will take seventy-three hours to get 'em here after they're built on Terra.'

'I'm sorry, but the legal meaning of the patent is clear. Where is your legal department?'

'We have three. One on each of the Inner Planets.'

'I'll request you to have a legal representative come to the station so that I may confer with him. One with power of attorney to act for you.'

'Sorry,' said Channing coldly. 'I wouldn't permit any attorney to act without my supervision.'

'That's rather a backward attitude,' said Kingman. 'I shall still insist on conducting my business with one of the legal mind.'

'O.K. We'll have Peterman come out from Terra. But he'll still be under my supervision.'

'As you wish. I may still exert my prerogative and remove the tubes from your possession.'

'You may find that hard to do,' said Channing.

'That's illegal!'

'Oh, no, it won't be. You may enter the laboratory at any time and remove the tubes. Of course, if you are without technical training you may find it most difficult to disconnect the tubes without getting across a few thousand volts. That might be uncomfortable.'

'Are you threatening me?' said Kingman, bristling. His stocky frame didn't take to bristling very well, and he lost considerable prestige in the act.

'Not at all. I'm just issuing a fair warning that the signs that say: "DANGER! HIGH-VOLTAGE!" are not there for appearance.'

'Sounds like a threat to me.'

'Have I threatened you? It sounds to me as though I were more than anxious for your welfare. Any threat of which you speak is utterly without grounds, and is a figment of your imagination; based upon distrust of Venus Equilateral, and the personnel of Venus Equilateral Relay Station.'

Kingman shut up. He went down the list, marking off items here and there. While he was marking, Channing scribbled a circuit and listed the parts. He handed it over as Kingman finished.

'This is your circuit?' asked the lawyer skeptically.

'Yes.'

'I shall have to ask for an explanation of the symbols involved.'

'I shall be happy to present you with a book on essential radio technique,' offered Channing. 'A perusal of which will place you in possession of considerable knowledge. Will that suffice?'

'I believe so. I cannot understand how; being uncertain of your steps a few minutes ago, you are now presenting me with a circuit of your intended experiment.'

'The circuit is, of course, merely symbolic. We shall change many of the constants before the day is over – in fact, we may even change the circuit.'

'I shall require a notice before each change so that I may pass upon the legal aspects.'

'Walt,' said Don, 'will you accompany me to a transparency experiment on the Ninth Level?'

'Be more than glad to,' said Walt. 'Let's go!'

They left the office quickly, and started for Joe's. They had not reached the combined liquor vending and restaurant establishment when the communicator called for Channing. It was announcing the arrival of Barney Carroll, so instead of heading for Joe's they went to the landing stage at the south end of the station to greet the visitor.

'Barney,' said Don, 'Of all the companies, why did you pick on Terran Electric?'

'Gave us the best deal,' said the huge, grinning man.

'Yeah, and they're getting the best of my goat right now.'

'Well, Jim and I couldn't handle anything as big as the power transmission set-up. They paid out a large slice of jack for the complete rights. All of us are well paid now. After all, I'm primarily interested in Martian artifacts, you know.'

'I wonder if they had lawyers,' smiled Walt dryly.

'Probably. And, no doubt, the legals had a lot to do with the fall of the Martian civilization.'

'As it will probably get this one so wound up with red tape that progress will be impossible – or impractical.'

'Well, Barney, let's take a run up to the lab. We can make paper-talk even if Brother Kingman won't let us set it to soldering iron. There are a lot of things I want to ask you about the tube.'

They sat around a drawing table and Channing began to sketch. 'What I'd hoped to do is this,' he said, drawing a schematic design. 'We're not interested in power transmission, but your gadget will do a bit of voltage amplification because of its utter indifference to the power-line problem of impedance matching. We can take a relay tube and put in ten watts, say, across ten thousand ohms. That means the input will be somewhat above three hundred volts. Now, if our output is across a hundred thousand ohms, ten watts will give us one thousand volts. So we can get voltage amplification at the expense of current – which we will not need. Unfortunately, the relay tube as well as the rest of the system will give out with the same kind of power that it is impressed with – so we'll have amplification of driver radiation. Then we'll need a detector. We haven't been able to get one either yet, but this is a start, providing that Terran Electric will permit us to take a deep breath without wanting to pass on it.'

'I think you may be able to get amplification,' said Barney. 'But to do it, you'll have to detect it first.'

'Huh?'

'Sure. Before these darned things will work, this inphase anode must be right on the beam. That means that you'll require a feed-back circuit from the final stage to feed the inphase anodes. Could be done without detection, I suppose.'

'Well, for one thing, we're going to get some amplification if we change the primary anode – so. That won't permit the thing to handle any power, but it will isolate the output from the input and permit more amplifications. Follow?'

'Can we try it?'

'As soon as I get Terran Electric's permission.'

'Here we go again!' groaned Walt.

'Yeah,' said Don to Barney, 'now you'll see the kind of birds you sold your gadget to.'

They found Kingman and Farrell in conference. Channing offered his suggestion immediately, and Kingman looked it over, shaking his head.

'It is not permitted to alter, change, rework, or repair tubes owned by Terran Electric,' he said.

'What are we permitted to do?' asked Channing.

'Give me your recommendation and I shall have the shop at Terran Electric perform the operation.'

'At cost?'

'Cost plus a slight profit. Terran Electric, just as Venus Equilateral, is not in business from an altruistic standpoint.'

'I see.'

'Also,' said Kingman severely, 'I noticed one of your men changing the circuit slightly without permission. Why?'

'Who was it?'

'The man known as Thomas.'

'Charles Thomas is in charge of development work,' said Channing. 'He probably noted some slight effect that he wanted to check.'

'He should have notified me first – I don't care how minute the change. I must pass on changes first.'

'But you wouldn't know their worth,' objected Barney.

'No, but Mr. Farrell does, and will so advise me.'

Wes looked at Channing. 'Have you been to the Ninth Level yet?'

'Nope,' said Channing.

'May I accompany you?'

Channing looked at Farrell critically. The Terran Electric engineer seemed sincere, and the pained expression on his face looked like frustrated sympathy to Don. 'Come along,' he said.

Barney smiled cheerfully at the sign on Joe's door. 'That's a good one, "Best Bar in Twenty-seven Million Miles, Minimum!" What's the qualification for?'

'That's as close as Terra ever gets. Most of the time the nearest bar is at Northern Landing, Venus; sixty-seven million miles from here. Come on in and we'll get plastered.'

Farrell said, 'Look, fellows, I know how you feel. They didn't tell me that you weren't going to be given permission to work. I understood that I was to sort of walk along, offer suggestions and sort of prepare myself to take over some research myself. This is sickening.'

'I think you mean that.'

'May I use your telephone? I want to resign.'

'Wait a minute. If you're that sincere, why don't we out-guess 'em?'

'Could do,' said Wes. 'How?'

'Is there any reason why we couldn't take a poke to Sol himself?'

'You mean haul power out of the sun?'

'That's the general idea. Barney, what do you think?'

'Could do – but it would take a redesign.'

'Fine. And may we pray that the redesign is good enough to make a difference to the Interplanetary Patent Office.' Channing called Joe. 'The same. Three Moons all around. Scotch,' he explained to the others, 'synthesized in the Palanortis Country.'

'Our favorite import,' said Walt.

Joe grinned. 'Another tablecloth session in progress?'

'Could be. As soon as we oil the think-tank, we'll know for sure.'

'What does he mean?' asked Barney.

Joe smiled. 'They all have laboratories and draftsmen and textbooks,' he said. 'But for real engineering, they use my tablecloths. Three more problems and I'll have a complete tablecloth course in astrophysics, with a sideline in cartooning and a minor degree in mechanical engineering.'

'Oh?'

'Sure. Give 'em a free hand, and a couple of your tubes and a tablecloth and they'll have 'em frying eggs by morning. When I came out here, they demanded a commercial bond and I thought they were nuts. Who ever heard of making a restaurateur post a bond? I discovered that all of their inventions are initially tinkered out right here in the dining room – I could steal 'em blind if I were dishonest!' Joe smiled hugely. 'This is the only place in the System where the tablecloths have been through blueprint machines. That,' he said confidentially to Barney, 'is why some of the stuff is slightly garbled. Scotch mixed with the drawings. They have the cloths inspected by the engineering department before they're laundered; I lose a lot of tablecloths that way.'

Joe left cheerfully amid laughter.

The Three Moons came next, and then Don began to sketch. 'Suppose we make a driver tube like this,' he said. 'And we couple the top end, where the cathode is, to the input side of the relay tube. Only the input side will require a variable-impedance anode, coupled back from the cathode to limit the input to the required value. Then the coupling anodes must be served with an automatic-coupling circuit so that the limiting power is passed without wastage.'

Barney pulled out a pencil. 'If you make that automatic-coupling circuit dependent upon the output from the terminal ends,' he said, 'it will accept only the amount of input that is required by the power being used from the output. Overcooling these two anodes will inhibit the power-intake.'

'Right,' said Wes. 'And I am of the opinion that the power available from Sol is of a magnitude that will permit operation over and above the limit.'

'Four million tons of energy per second!' exploded Walt. 'That's playing with fire!'

'You bet. We'll fix 'em with that!'

'Our experience with relay tubes,' said Farrell slowly, 'indicates that some increase in range is possible with additional anode-focussing. Build your tube-top with an extra set of anodes, and that'll give us better control of the beam.'

'We're getting farther and farther from the subject of communications,' said Channing with a smile. 'But I think that we'll get more of this.'

'How so?'

'Until we get a chance to tinker with those tubes, we won't

get ship-to-ship two ways. So we'll gadgeteer up something that will make Terran Electric foam at the mouth, and swap a hunk of it for full freedom in our investigations. Or should we bust Terran Electric whole-heartedly?'

'Let's slug 'em,' said Walt.

'Go ahead,' said Wes. 'I'm utterly disgusted, though I think our trouble is due to the management of Terran Electric. They like legal tangles too much.'

'We'll give 'em a legal tangle,' said Barney. He was adding circuits to the tablecloth sketch.

Channing, on his side, was sketching in some equations, and Walt was working out some mechanical details. Joe came over, looked at the tablecloth, and forthright went to the telephone and called Warren. The mechanical designer came, and Channing looked up in surprise. 'Hi,' he said, 'I was just about to call you.'

'Joe did.'

'O.K. Look, Warren, can you fake up a gadget like this?'

Warren looked the thing over. 'Give me about ten hours,' he said. 'We've got a spare turnover driver from the *Relay Girl* that we can hand-carve. There are a couple of water-boilers that we can strip, cut open, and make to serve as the top end. How're you hoping to maintain the vacuum?'

'Yes,' said Wes Farrell, 'that's going to be the problem. If there's any adjusting of electrodes to do, this'll take months.'

'That's why we, on Venus Equilateral, are ahead of the whole dingbusted Solar System in tube development,' said Don. 'We'll run the thing out in the open – and I *do* mean open! Instead of the tube having the insides exhausted, the operators will have their envelopes served with fresh, canned air.'

'Like a cartoon I saw somewhere,' grinned Walt. 'Had a bird in full armor tinkering with a radio set. The caption was: "Why shield the set?"'

'Phooey,' said Warren. 'Look, Tom Swift, is this another of Franks' brainchildren?'

'Tom Swift?' asked Wes.

'Yeah. That's the nom de plume he invents under. The other guy we call Captain Lightning.'

'Oh?' asked Farrell. 'Do you read him, too?'

'Sure,' grinned Warren. 'And say, speaking of comics, I came upon an old, old volume of Webster's International Dictionary in a rare-edition library in Chicago a couple of months ago, and they define "Comic" as amusing, funny, and ludicrous; not imaginative fiction. How things change.'

'They do.'

'But to get back to this Goldberg, what is it?'

'Warren,' said Channing soberly, 'sit down!' Warren did. 'Now,' grinned Channing, 'this screwball gadget is an idea whereby we hope to draw power out of the sun.'

Warren swallowed once, and then waved for Joe. 'Double,' he told the restaurateur. Then to the others he said, 'Thanks for seating me. I'm ill, I think. Hearing things. I could swear I heard someone say that this thing is to take power from Sol.'

'That's it.'

'Um-m-m. Remind me to quit Saturday. This is no job for a man beset by hallucinations.'

'You grinning idiot, we're not fooling!'

'Then you'd better quit,' Warren told Don. 'This is no job for a bird with delusions of grandeur, either. Look, Don, you'll want this in the experimental blister at south end? On a coupler to the beam-turret so that it'll maintain direction at Sol?'

'Right. Couple it to the rotating stage if you can. Remember, that's three miles from south end.'

'We've still got a few high-power selsyns,' said Warren, making some notations of his own on the tablecloth. 'And thanks to the guys who laid out this station some years ago, we've plenty of unused circuits from one end to the other.

We'll couple it, all right. Oh, Mother. Seems to me like you got a long way off of your intended subject. Didn't you start out to make a detector for driver radiation?'

'Yup.'

'And you end up tapping the sun. D'ye think it'll ever replace the horse?'

'Could be. Might even replace the coal mine. That's to be seen. Have you any idea of how long you'll be?'

'Make it ten hours. I'll get the whole crew on it at once.'

'Fine.'

'But look. What's the reason for this change in program?'

'That's easy,' said Don. 'First, we had a jam session. Second, we've come to the conclusion that the longest way 'round is the shortest way home. We're now in the throes of building something with which to dazzle the bright-minded management of Terran Electric and thus make them susceptible to our charm. We want a free hand at the transmission tubes, and this looks like a fair bit of bait.'

'I get it. Quote: "Why buy power from Terran Electric? Hang a Channing Power Beam on your chimney pot and tap the sun!" Whoa, Mazie. Bring on the needle, Watson. Hang out the flags, fire the cannon, ring the bells; for Venus Equilateral is about to hang a pipeline right into four million tons of energy per second! Don, that's a right, smart bit of power to doodle with. Can you handle it?'

'Sure,' said Channing with a wave of his hand, 'we'll hang a fuse in the line!'

'O.K.,' said Warren sweeping the tablecloth off the table like Mysto, the Magician, right out from under the glasses. 'I'll be back – wearing my asbestos pants!'

Wes Farrell looked dreamily at the ceiling. 'This *is* a screwy joint,' he said idly. 'What do we do for the next ten hours?'

'Red Herring stuff,' said Channing with what he hoped was a Machiavellian leer.

'Such as?'

'Making wise moves with the transmission tubes. Glomming the barrister's desk with proposed ideas for his approval; as many as we can think of so that he'll be kept busy. We might even think of something that may work, meanwhile. Come, fellow conspirators, to horse!' Channing picked up his glass and drained it, making a wry face. 'Rotten stuff – I wish I had a barrel of it!'

Channing surveyed the set-up in the blister. He inspected it carefully, as did the others. When he spoke, his voice came through the helmet receivers with a slightly tinny sound: 'Anything wrong? Looks O.K. to me.'

'O.K. by me, too,' said Farrell.

'Working in suit is not the best,' said Don. 'Barney, you're the bright-eyed lad, can you align the plates?'

'I think so,' came the muffled booming of Barney's powerful voice. 'Gimme a screwdriver!'

Barney fiddled with the plate-controls for several minutes. 'She's running on dead center alignment, now,' he announced.

'Question,' put in Wes, 'do we get power immediately, or must we wait whilst the beam gets there and returns?'

'You must run your power line before you get power,' said Walt. 'My money is on the wait.'

'Don't crack your anode-coupling circuit till then,' warned Wes. 'We don't know a thing about this; I'd prefer to let it in easy-like instead of opening the gate and letting the whole four million tons per second come tearing in through this ammeter!'

'Might be a little warm having Sol in here with us,' laughed Channing. 'This is once in my life when we don't need a milli-ameter, but a million-ammeter!'

'Shall we assign a pseudonym for it?' chuckled Walt.

'Let's wait until we see how it works.'

The minutes passed slowly, and then Wes announced: 'She

should be here. Check your anode-coupler, Barney.'

Barney advanced the dial, gingerly. The air that could have grown tense was, of course, not present in the blister. But the term is just a figure of speech, and therefore it may be proper to say that the air grew tense. Fact is, it was the nerves of the men that grew tense. Higher and higher went the dial, and still the meter stayed inert against the zero-end pin.

'Not a wiggle,' said Barney in disgust. He twisted the dial all the way 'round and snorted. The meter left the zero pin ever so slightly.

Channing turned the switch that increased the sensitivity of the meter until the needle stood halfway up the scale.

'Solar power, here we come,' he said in a dry voice. 'One-half ampere at seven volts! Three and one-half watts. Bring on your atom-smashers. Bring on your power-consuming factory districts. Hang the whole load of Central United States on the wires, for we have three and one-half watts! Just enough to run an electric clock!'

'But would it keep time?' asked Barney. 'Is the frequency right?'

'Nope – but we'd run it. Look, fellows, when anyone tells you about this, insist that we got thirty-five hundred milliwatts on our first try. It sounds bigger.'

'O.K., so we're getting from Sol just about three-tenths of the soup we need to make the set-up self sustaining,' said Walt. 'Wes, this in-phase anode of yours – what can we do with it?'

'If this thing worked, I was going to suggest that there is enough power out there to spare. We could possibly modulate the in-phase anode with anything we wanted, and there would be enough junk floating round in the photosphere to slam on through.'

'Maybe it is that lack of selectivity that licks us now,' said Don. 'Run the voltage up and down a bit. There should be D.C. running around in Sol, too.'

224

'Whatever this power-level is running at,' said Barney, 'we may get in-phase voltage – or in-phase power by running a line from the power terminal back. More over, boys, I'm going to hang a test clip in here.'

Barney's gloved hands fumbled a bit, but the clip was attached. He opened the anode-counter once again, and the meter slammed against the full-scale peg.

'See?' he said triumphantly.

'Yup,' said Channing cryptically. 'You, Bernard, have doubled our input.'

'Mind if I take a whack at aligning it?' asked Wes.

'Go ahead. What we need is a guy with eyes in his finger-tips. Have you?'

'No, but I'd like to try.'

Farrell worked with the deflection plate alignment, and then said, ruefully: 'No dice. Barney had it right on the beam.

'Is she aligned with Sol?' asked Channing.

Walt squinted down the tube. 'Couldn't be better,' he said, blinking.

'Could it be that we're actually missing Sol?' asked Don. 'I mean, could it be that line-of-sight and line-of-power aren't one and the same thing?'

'Could be,' acknowledged Wes. Walt stepped to the verniers and swung the big intake tube over a minute arc. The meter jumped once more, and Channing stepped the sensitivity down again. Walt fiddled until the meter read maximum and then he left the tube that way.

'Coming up,' said Channing. 'We've now four times our original try. We now have enough juice to run an electric train – toy size! Someone think of something else, please. I've had my idea for the day.'

'Let's juggle electrode-spacing,' suggested Wes.

'Can't do,' said Walt, brandishing a huge spanner wrench in one gloved hand.

Four solid, futile hours later, the power output of the solar beam was still standing at a terrifying fourteen watts. Channing was scratching furiously on a pad of paper with a large pencil; Walt was trying voltage-variations on the supply-anodes in a desultory manner; Barney was measuring the electrode spacing with a huge vernier rule, and Wes was staring at the sun, dimmed to seeable brightness by a set of dark glasses.

Wes was muttering to himself. 'Electrode-voltages, O.K. . . . alignment perfect . . . solar power output . . . not like power-line electricity . . . solar composition . . . Russell's Mixture—'

'Whoooo said that!' roared Channing.

'Who said what?' asked Barney.

'Why bust our eardrums?' objected Walt.

'What do you mean?' asked Wes, coming to life for the moment.

'Something about Russell's Mixture. Who said that?'

'I did. Why?'

'Look, Wes, what are your cathodes made of?'

'Thorium, C.P. metal. That's why they're shipped in metal containers in a vacuum.'

'What happens if you try to use something else?'

'Don't work very well. In fact, if the output cathode and the input dynode are not the same metal, they won't pass power at all.'

'You're on the trail right now!' shouted Channing. 'Russell's Mixture!'

'Sounds like a brand of smoking tobacco to me. Mind making a noise like an encyclopedia and telling me what is Russell's Mixture?'

'Russell's Mixture is a conglomeration of elements which go into the making of Sol – and all the other stars,' explained Don. 'Hydrogen, Oxygen, Sodium, and Magnesium, Iron, Silicon, Potassium, and Calcium. They, when mixed according to the formula for Russell's Mixture, which can be found in any book on the composition of the stars, become the most probable mixture of metals. They – Russell's Mixture – go into the composition of all stars, what isn't mentioned in the mix isn't important.'

'And what has this Russell got that we haven't got?' asked Walt.

'H, O, Na, Mg, Fe, Si, K, and Ca. And we, dear people, have Th, which Russell has not. Walt, call up the metallurgical lab and have 'em whip up a batch.'

'Cook to a fine edge and serve with a spray of parsley? Or do we cut it into cubes—'

'Go ahead,' said Channing. 'Be funny. You just heard the man say that dissimilar dyno-cathodes do not work. What we need for our solar beam is a dynode of Russell's Mixture so that it will be similar to our cathode – which in this case is Sol. Follow me?'

'Yeah,' said Walt, 'I follow, but, brother, I'm a long way behind. But I'll catch up,' he promised as he made connection between his suit-radio and the station communicator system. 'Riley,' he said, 'here we go again. Can you whip us up a batch of Russell's Mixture?'

Riley's laugh was audible to the others, since it was broadcast by Walt's set. 'Yeah, man, we can – if it's got metal in it? What, pray tell, is Russell's Mixture?'

Walt explained the relation between Russell's Mixture and the composition of Sol.

'Sun makers, hey?' asked Riley. 'Is the chief screwball up there?'

'Yup,' said Walt, grinning at Don.

'Sounds like him. Yeah, we can make you an alloy consisting of Russell's Mixture. Tony's got it here, now, and it doesn't look hard. How big a dynode do you want?'

Walt gave him the dimensions of the dynode in the solar tube.

'Cinch,' said Riley. 'You can have it in two hours.'

'Swell.'

'But it'll be hotter than hell. Better make that six or seven hours. We may run into trouble making it jell.'

'I'll have Arden slip you some pectin,' said Walt. 'Tomorrow morning, then?'

'Better. That's a promise.'

Walt turned to the rest. 'If any of us can sleep,' he said, 'I suggest it. Something tells me that tomorrow is going to be one of those days that mother told me about. I'll buy a drink.'

Walt opened the anode-coupler circuit, and the needle of the output ammeter slammed across the scale and wound the needle halfway around the stop pin. The shunt, which was an external, high-dissipation job, turned red, burned the paint off of its radiator fins, and then proceeded to melt. It sputtered in flying droplets of molten metal. Smoke spewed from the case of the ammeter, dissipating in the vacuum of the blister.

Walt closed the coupler circuit.

'Whammo!' he said. 'Mind blowing a hundred-amp meter?'

'No,' grinned Don. 'I have a thousand-amp job that I'll sacrifice in the same happy-hearted fashion. Get an idea of the power?'

'Voltmeter was hanging up around ten thousand volts just before the amp-meter went by.'

'Um-m-m. Ten thousand volts at a hundred amps. That is one million watts, my friends, and no small potatoes. To run the station's communicating equipment we need seven times that much. Can we do it?'

'We can. I'll have Warren start running the main power bus down here and we'll try it. Meanwhile, we've got a healthy cable from the generator room; we can run the non-communicating drain of the station from our plaything here. That should give us an idea. We can use a couple of million watts right there. If this gadget will handle it, we can make one that will take the whole load without groaning. I'm calling Warren right now. He can start taking the load over from the generators as we increase our intake. We'll fade, but not without a flicker.'

Walt hooked the output terminals of the tube to the huge cable blocks, using sections of the same heavy cable.

Warren called: 'Are you ready?'

'Fade her in,' said Walt. He kept one eye on the line voltmeter and opened the anode-coupler slightly. The meter dipped as Warren shunted the station load over to the tube circuit. Walt brought the line voltage up to above normal, and it immediately dropped as Warren took more load from the solar intake. This jockeying went on for several minutes until Warren called: 'You've got it all. Now what?'

'Start running the bus down here to take the communications load,' said Don. 'We're running off of an eight hundred thousand mile cathode now, and his power output is terrific. Or better, run us a high-tension line down here and we'll save silver. We can ram ten thousand volts up there for transformation. Get me?'

'What frequency?'

'Yeah,' drawled Channing, 'have Chuck Thomas run us a control line from the primary frequency standard. We'll control our frequency with that. O.K.?'

'Right-o.'

Channing looked at the set-up once more. It was singularly unprepossessing, this conglomeration of iron and steel and plastic. There was absolutely nothing to indicate that two and one-third million watts of power coursed from Sol, through its maze of anodes, and into the electric lines of Venus Equilateral. The cathodes and dynode glowed with their usual dull red glow, but there was no coruscating aura of power around the elements of the system. The gimbals that held the big tube slid easily, permitting the tube to rotate freely as the selsyn motor kept the tube pointing at Sol. The supply cables remained cool and operative, and to all appearances the set-up was inert.

'O.K., fellows,' said Channing, 'this is it—'

He was interrupted by the frantic waving of Kingman, from the other side of the air lock.

'I feel slightly conscious-stricken,' he said with a smile that showed that he didn't mean it at all. 'But let us go and prepare the goat for shearing.'

Kingman's trouble was terrific, according to him. 'Mr. Channing,' he complained, 'you are not following our wishes. And you, Mr. Farrell, have been decidedly amiss in your hobnobbing with the engineers here. You were sent out as my consultant, not to assist them in their endeavors.'

'What's your grief?' asked Channing.

'I find that your laboratory has been changing the circuits without having previously informed me of the proposed change,' complained Kingman. 'I feel that I am within my rights in removing the tubes here. Your investigations have not been sanctioned—' He looked out through the air lock. 'What are you doing out there?'

'We have just succeeded in taking power from the sun,' said Don. He tried to keep his voice even, but the exultation was too high in him, and his voice sounded like sheer joy.

'You have been—' Kingman did a double-take. 'You *what*?' he yelled.

'Have succeeded in tapping Sol for power.'

'Why, that's wonderful!'

'Thank you,' said Don. 'You will no doubt be glad to hear that Wes Farrell was instrumental in this program.'

'Then a certain part of the idea is rightfully the property of Terran Electric,' said Kingman.

'I'm afraid not,' said Don. 'Dr. Farrell's assistance was not requested. Though his contribution was of great value, it was given freely. He was not solicited. Therefore, since Terran Electric was not consulted formally, Dr. Farrell's contribution to our solar power beam can not be considered as offering a hold on our discovery.'

'This is true, Dr. Farrell?'

'I'm afraid so. You see, I saw what was going on and became interested, academically. I naturally offered a few minor suggestions in somewhat the same manner as a motorist will stop and offer another motorist assistance in changing a tire. The problem was interesting to me and as a problem it did not seem to me—'

'Your actions in discussing this with members of the Venus Equilateral technical staff without authorization will cost us plenty,' snapped Kingman. 'However, we shall deal with you later.'

'You know,' said Farrell with a cheerfully malicious grin, 'if you had been less stuffy about our tubes, they might be less stuffy about my contribution.'

'Ah, these non-legal agreements are never satisfactory. But that is to be discussed later. What do you intend to do with your invention, Dr. Channing?'

Channing smiled in a superior manner. 'As you see, the device is small. Yet it handles a couple of million watts. An even smaller unit might be made that would suffice to supply a home, or even a community. As for the other end, I see no reason why the size might not be increased to a point where it may obsolete all existing power-generating stations.'

Kingman's complexion turned slightly green. He swallowed hard. 'You, of course, would not attempt to put this on the market yourself.'

'No?' asked Channing. 'I think you'll find that Venus Equilateral is as large, if not larger, than Terran Electric, and we have an enviable reputation for delivering the goods. We could sell refrigerators to the Titan colony, if we had the V-E label on them and claimed they were indispensable. Our escutcheon is not without its adherents.'

'I see,' said Kingman. His present volubility would not have jogged a jury into freeing the armless wonder from a pick-pocketing charge. 'Is your invention patentable?'

'I think so. While certain phases of it are like the driver tube, which, of course, is public domain, the applications are quite patentable. I must admit that certain parts are of the power transmission tube, but not enough for you to claim a hold. At any rate, I shall be busy for the next hour, transmitting the details to Washington, so that the Interplanetary Patent Office may rule on it. Our Terran legal department has a direct line there, you know, and they have been directed to maintain that contact at all costs.'

'May I use your lines?'

'Certainly. They are public carriers. You will not be re-stricted any more than any other man. I am certain that our right to transmit company business without waiting for the usual turn will not be contested.'

'That sounds like a veiled threat.'

'That sounds like slander!'

'Oh, no. Believe me. But wait, Dr. Channing. Is there no way in which we can meet on a common ground?'

'I think so. We want a free hand in this tube proposition.'

'For which rights you will turn over a nominal interest in solar power?'

'Forty percent,' said Channing.

'But we—'

'I know, you want control.'

'We'd like it.'

'Sorry. Those are our terms. Take 'em or leave 'em.'

'Supposing that we offer you full and unrestricted rights to any or all developments you or we make on the Martian transmission tubes?'

'That might be better to our liking.'

'We might buck you,' said Kingman, but there was doubt in his voice.

'Yes? You know, Kingman, I'm not too sure that Venus Equilateral wants to play around with power except as a maintenance angle. What if we toss the solar beam to the public domain? That is within our right, too.'

Kingman's green color returned, this time accompanied with beads of sweat. He turned to Farrell. 'Is there nothing we can do? Is this patentable?'

'No – Yes,' grinned Farrell.

Kingman excused himself. He went to the office provided for him and began to send messages to the Terran Electric Company offices at Chicago. The forty-minute wait between message and answer was torture to him, but it was explained to him that light and radio crossed space at one hundred and eight-six thousand miles per second and that even an Act of Congress could do nothing to help him hurry it. Meanwhile, Channing's description tied up the Terran Beam for almost an hour at the standard rate of twelve hundred words per minute. Their answers came within a few minutes of one another.

Channing tossed the 'gram before Kingman. 'Idea definitely patentable,' said the wire.

Kingman stood up. Apparently the lawyer believed that his pronouncement would carry more weight by looming over the smiling, easy-going faces of his parties-of-the-second-part. 'I am prepared to negotiate with your legal department; offering them, and you, the full rights to the transmission tube. This will include full access to any and all discoveries, improvements, and/or changes made at any time from its discovery to the termination of this contract, which shall be terminated only by absolute mutual agreement between Terran Electric and Venus Equilateral.

'In return for this, Venus Equilateral will permit Terran Electric to exploit the solar beam tube fully and freely, and exclusively—'

'Make that slightly different,' said Channing. 'Terran Electric's rights shall prevail exclusively – *except* within the realm of space, upon man-made celestial objects, and upon the satellites and minor natural celestial bodies where sub-relay stations of the Interplanetary Communications Company are established.'

Kingman thought that one over. 'In other words, if the transport companies desire to use the solar beam, you will hold domain from the time they leave an atmosphere until they again touch—'

'Let's not complicate things,' smiled Don cheerfully. 'I like uncomplicated things.'

Kingman smiled wryly. 'I'm sure,' he agreed with fine sarcasm. 'But I see your point. You intend to power the communications system with the solar beam. That is natural. Also, you feel that a certain amount of revenue should be coming your way. Yes, I believe that our legal departments can agree.'

'So let's not make the transport companies change masters in mid-space,' smiled Don.

'You are taking a lot on your shoulders,' said Kingman. 'We wouldn't permit our technicians to dictate the terms of an agreement.'

'You are not going to like Venus Equilateral at all,' laughed Don. 'We wouldn't permit our legal department to dabble in things of which they know nothing. Years ago, when the first concentric beam was invented, which we now use to punch a hole in the Heaviside Layer, communications was built about a group of engineers. We held the three inner planets together by the seat of our pants, so to speak, and nurtured communications from a slipshod, hope-to-God-it-gets-through proposition to a sure thing. Funny thing, but when people were taking their messages catch as catch can, there was no reason for legal lights. Now that we can and do insure messages against their loss, we find that we are often tied up with legal red tape.

'Otherwise, we wouldn't have a lawyer on the premises. They serve their purpose, no doubt, but in this gang, the engineers tell the attorneys how to run things. We shall continue to do so. Therefore you are speaking with the proper parties, and once the contract is prepared by you, we shall have an attorney run through the whereases, wherefores, and parties of the first, second, and third parts to see that there is no sleight of hand in the microscopic type.'

'You're taking a chance,' warned Kingman. 'All men are not as fundamentally honest as Terran Electric.'

'Kingman,' smiled Channing, 'I hate to remind you of this, but who got what just now? We wanted the transmission tube.'

'I see your point. But we have a means of getting power out of the sun.'

'We have a hunk of that, too. It would probably have been a mere matter of time before some bright bird at Terran found the thing as it was.'

'I shall see that the contract gives you domain over man-made objects in space – including those that occasionally touch upon the natural celestial objects. Also the necessary equipment operating under the charter of Venus Equilateral, wherever or whenever it may be, including any future installations.'

'Fine.'

'You may have trouble understanding our feelings. We are essentially a space-born company, and as such we can have no one at the helm who is not equipped to handle the technical details of operations in space.' Channing smiled reminiscently. 'We had a so-called efficiency expert running Venus Equilateral a couple of years ago, and the fool nearly wrecked us because he didn't know that the airplant was not a mass of highly complicated, chemical reaction machinery instead of what it really is. Kingman, do you know what an airplant is?'

'Frankly, no. I should imagine it is some sort of air-purifying device.'

'You'll sit down hard when I tell you that the airplant is just what it is. Martian sawgrass! Brother Burbank tossed it out because he thought it was just weeds, cluttering up the place. He was allergic to good engineering, anyway.'

'That may be good enough in space,' said Kingman, 'but on Terra, we feel that our engineers are not equipped to dabble in the legal tangles that follow when they force us to establish precedent by inventing something that has never been covered by a previous decision.'

'O.K.,' said Don. 'Every man to his own scope. Write up your contract, Kingman, and we'll all climb on the band wagon with our illiterary X's.'

In Evanston, north of Chicago, the leaves changed from their riotous green to a somber brown, and fell to lay a blanket over the earth. Snow covered the dead leaves, and Christmas, with its holly, went into the past, followed closely by New Year's Eve with its hangover.

And on a roof by the shore of Lake Michigan, a group of men stood in overcoats beside a huge machine that towered above the great letters of the Terran Electric Company sign that could be seen all the way from Gary, Indiana.

It was a beautiful thing, this tube; a far cry from the haywire thing that had brought solar power to Venus Equilateral. It was mounted on gimbals, and the metal was bright-plated and perfectly machined. Purring motors caused the tube to rotate to follow the sun.

'Is she aligned?' asked the project engineer.

'Right on the button.'

'Good. We can't miss with this one. There may have been something sour with the rest, but this one ran Venus Equilateral – the whole relay station – for ten days without interruption.'

He faced the anxious men in overcoats. 'Here we go,' he said, and his hand closed upon the switch that transferred the big tube from test power to operating power.

The engineer closed the switch, and stepped over to the great, vaned, air-cooled ammeter shunt. On a panel just beyond the shunt the meter hung—

At Zero!

'Um,' said the project engineer. 'Something wrong, no doubt.'

They checked every connection, every possible item in the circuit.

'Nothing wrong!'

'Oh, now look,' said the project engineer. 'This isn't hell, where the equipment is always perfect except that it doesn't work.'

'This is hell,' announced his assistant. 'The thing is perfect – except that it doesn't work.'

'It worked on Venus Equilateral.'

'We've changed nothing, and we handled that gadget like it was made of cello-gel. We're running the same kind of voltage, checked on standard voltmeters. We're within one-tenth of one percent of the original operating conditions. But – no power.'

'Call Channing.'

The beams between Terra and Venus Equilateral carried furious messages for several hours. Channing's answer said: 'I'm curious. Am bringing the experimental ship to Terra to investigate.'

The project engineer asked: 'Isn't that the job they hooked up to use the solar power for their drive?'

His assistant said: 'That's it. And it worked.'

'I know. I took a run on it!'

Channing was taking a chance, running the *Relay Girl* to Terra, but he knew his ship, and he was no man to be over-cautious. He drove it to Terra at three G, and by dead reckoning, started down into Terra's blanket of air, heading for the Terran Electric plant which was situated on the lake shore.

Then down out of the cloudless sky came the *Relay Girl* in a free fall. It screamed with the whistle of tortured air as it fell, and it caught the attention of every man that was working at Terran Electric.

Only those on the roof saw the egg-shaped hull fall out of the sky unchecked; landing fifteen hundred yards offshore in Lake Michigan.

The splash was terrific.

'Channing—!' said the project engineer, aghast.

'No, look there – a lifeship!'

Cautiously sliding down, a minute lifeship less than the size of a freight car came to a landing in the Terran Electric constructioin yard. Channing emerged, his face white. He bent down and kissed the steel grille of the construction yard fervently.

Someone ran out and gave Channing a brown bottle. Don nodded, and took a draw of monstrous proportions. He gagged, made a face, and smiled in a very wan manner.

'Thanks,' he said shakily. He took another drink, of more gentlemanly size.

'What happened?'

'Dunno: Was coming in at three G. About four hundred miles up, the deceleration just quit. Like that! I made it to the skeeter, here, in just about enough time to get her away with about two miles to go. *Woosh!*'

Don dug into his pocket and found cigarettes. He lit up and drew deeply. 'Something cockeyed, here. That stoppage might make me think that my tube failed; but—'

'You suspect that our tube isn't working for the same reason? finished the project engineer.

'Yes. I'm thinking of the thick, ultra-high powered, concentric beams we have to use to ram a hole through the Heaviside Layer. We start out with three million watts of sheer radio frequency and end up with just enough to make our receivers worth listening to. Suppose this had some sort of Heaviside Layer?'

'In which case, Terran Electric hasn't got solar power,' said the project engineer. 'Tim, load this bottle into the *Electric Lady*, and we'll see if we can find this barrier.' To Channing, he said: 'You look as though you could stand a rest. Check into a hotel in Chicago and we'll call you when we're ready to try it out.'

Channing agreed. A shave, a bath, and a good night's sleep did wonders for his nerves, as did a large amount of Scotch. He was at Terran Electric in the morning, once more in command of himself.

Up into the sky went the ship that carried the solar tube. It remained inert until the ship passed above three hundred and forty miles. Then the ammeter needle swung over, and the huge shunt grew warm. The tenuous atmosphere outside of the ship was unchanged, yet the beam drew power of gigantic proportions.

They dropped again. The power ceased.

They spent hours rising and falling, charting this unknown barrier that stopped the unknown radiation from bringing solar power right down to earth. It was there, all right, and impervious. Above, megawatts raced through the giant shunt. Below, not even a microammeter could detect a trace of current.

'O.K., Don,' said the project engineer. 'We'll have to do some more work on it. It's nothing of your doing.'

Mark Kingman's face was green again, but he nodded in

agreement. 'We seem to have a useless job here, but we'll think of something.'

They studied the barrier and established its height as a constant three hundred and thirty-nine, point seven six miles above Terra's mythical sea level. It was almost a perfect sphere, that did not change with the night and day, as did the Heaviside Layer. There was no way to find out how thick it was, but thickness was of no importance, since it effectively stopped the beam.

Then as Don Channing stepped aboard the *Princess of the Sky* to get home again, the project engineer said: 'If you don't mind, I think we'll call that one the Channing Layer!'

'Yeah,' grinned Don, pleased at the thought, 'and forever afterward it will stand as a cinder in the eye of Terran Electric.'

'Oh,' said the project engineer, 'we'll beat the Channing Layer.'

But the project engineer was a bum prophet—